APo 35.95/21.57

D0758904

Reasonable Death

Also by Pauline Bell:

The Dead Do Not Praise
Feast Into Mourning
No Pleasure in Death
The Way of a Serpent
Downhill to Death
Sleeping Partners
A Multitude of Sins
Blood Ties
Stalker

REASONABLE DEATH

Pauline Bell

Constable · London

First published in Great Britain 2001
by Constable, an imprint of Constable & Robinson Ltd
3 The Lanchesters, 162 Fulham Palace Road,
London W6 9ER
www.constablerobinson.com

ISBN 1-84119-333-X

Printed and bound in Great Britain

A CIP catalogue record for this book is available from the
British Library

For
Nicholas and Graeme
Craig and Martin
Ella and Jack

I acknowledge, with thanks, help and advice
received from:
Drs David and Lesley Lord
Sergeant David Browning
Dr S N Chater, Consultant Anaesthetist, Calderdale
NHS Trust
Mr Robbie McSkimming, Psychiatric Nurse

And thanks to John for the original idea

1

The area referred to as 'the Love Nest' by the staff of the Colin Hewitt Comprehensive was a patch of concrete that broke the monotony of the surrounding asphalt covering the rest of the playground. Half of it was roofed over with tarred sheets, below which the ground had ridged hollows to accommodate the cycles of the more energetic pupils and of such members of staff as had 'green' inclinations. At the other side, the concrete was bounded by a row of tall wheelie-bins whose contents often spilled over on to the space between. It was rather a far cry from moonlight and roses but it suited the purposes of the pupils who retired there not so much to declare their passionate love as, energetically, to demonstrate their lust.

The Nest's current occupants scorned the shelter of the bins, preferring to misbehave openly. By this method they had been able to divide their teachers usefully into two categories, the confrontational ('What do you mean by . . .?') and the non-confrontational (look the other way and you needn't deal with it). Adele had, on one occasion, explained exactly what she meant by it, after which that particular mistress had had to be recategorised.

Adele and Shaun each had both hands busy, one with a cigarette, one with an exploration of the other's anatomy. Adele's explorations, as she kept an eye open for duty staff to taunt, were perfunctory. So much so that Shaun felt slighted. 'Haven't you read any of those sloppy love books? You're supposed to be showing me that you'll love me to your dying day.'

Adele dug him in his ribs and blew smoke in his face. 'I might be able to manage to the end of next week.' She was happily unaware that Shaun's requirement would have proved the less demanding.

Yorkshire hospitality, so Martin Crossley had been told, was rough and ready but warm-hearted and generous. So far, he had not found it so. Now, in his poky room, examining his distorted reflection in a pitted mirror that faced the narrow window, he found that his shadow blocked most of the light. Tutting frustratedly, he switched on both lamps. He was, after all, paying more than enough for the basic amenities. He inspected his marginally brighter image, and found it satisfactory.

When he had come to Cloughton for his interview, he had concentrated on appearing smart and efficient, on presenting an image that would gain the approval of a headmaster and his board of governors. To this end, during the previous few weeks he had grown his hair from its usual eighth of an inch stubble to a one inch length that he had brushed and gelled into neatness.

Today he would be on view for the first time to his pupils and he tried to see himself in their eyes. He had been tempted to impress them with a return to his barber's Number 1, achievable only with clippers. Then he had decided that it was still too early to risk alienating his senior colleagues. The kids should be impressed by his black suit and shirt and they would have to excuse the obligatory tan and black shot-silk tie.

It was still early. Crossley wandered over to the window and saw that the newsagent's shop across the road was open. He would go and get the local paper. It would do him no harm to show an interest in Cloughton affairs.

He tiptoed quietly down thinly carpeted stairs, found the front door unlocked and braced himself before emerging into the wild weather. The wind flung icy flurries of wetness at him. The trailing ivy in his landlady's window box was flying up into the air, threatening to carry off its flimsy plastic container. Outside the house next door the wind was systematically emptying a skip of the lighter items it had contained and tossing them around in the gutter. Was this really the place, he asked himself, where he and Cherry could make their fresh start?

Crossley wished he had put on a raincoat, even for this short journey. Coming out of the shop, he tucked his copy of the *Clarion* inside his jacket and hurried, head down, back to his bleak accommodation. Seeing the light was on in the dining-room he peered round the door hopefully. The only other guest returned his greeting with a stony nod before returning his gaze to his own copy of the paper. Crossley persevered, explaining, as he dispatched his 'Full English' and lukewarm coffee, that he was about to move into Cloughton and teach in a local school.

He was rewarded by an increased warmth in his fellow guest's manner as he was cast in the role of instructor. His firm, the man offered, in return, had branches in Cloughton and Preston where he lived. 'Humdrum sort o' place is Cloughton. Certainly nowt much happening at present.'

Both men surveyed the front page. Five items merited a place on it, the leading one devoted to a gynaecological mishap – 'WOMAN AWAKE DURING OP'. The woman pictured below the head-line appeared particularly pleased with life, a toddler comfort-ably supported on her massive bosom.

'Stupid cow's just attention-seeking. Doesn't look much wrong with her there.'

Crossley grinned. 'Well, I don't suppose there's a snap avail-able of her prone on the operating table in the throes of her suffering.'

The substance of her complaint was that succinylcholine, a drug routinely administered with an anaesthetic before an operation, had rendered her paralysed and therefore unable to indicate to the surgeon that she was still conscious.

A hospital representative had offered a terse 'No comment', pending an investigation of the allegation, and an unnamed 'hospital source' listed all the various drugs purported to have been used. To Crossley, whose teaching subject was history, the medical terms meant little.

He refilled his cup from the thermos jug on a small table by the door, then turned his attention to the long thin column down the right-hand side of the page. It contained an account of the progress made so far in the refurbishing of Cloughton's Town Park. Currently, workmen were removing, section by section, the Victorian statue which had been the centrepiece of a lily pond. The pond had been drained and the statue was to be reas-sembled in Heath Royd Park.

Crossley looked across at his informant. 'I gather that this park at Heath Royd is in a more salubrious area than the Cloughton Town one. Maybe it's frequented by a better class of person who deserves to have an indigenous piece of sculpture to admire.'

'What?'

'The nobs up there will look after the statue better.'

The man nodded and Crossley wondered whether any of his new pupils shared responsibility for the vandalism that was being made good. He decided not to ask.

'What about him, then?'

Crossley examined the picture that was amusing his companion. It was in colour, and showed a lean moustached man with immaculate teeth and thinning, receding dark hair. He wore a black shirt and white neckerchief under a startling jacket with what appeared to be a sequinned star on each shoulder. The heading here was in modest type: *'Rick Robson to wed'*. Crossley remembered that his mother had been fond of this American singer.

Some comment seemed expected and Crossley asked what Robson's connection was with Cloughton.

'He gave a concert here, in the Civic Centre, couple o' year back. That was because some old biddy in the town runs his fan club here in England.'

Crossley's companion sniffed derisively as he read down the column. 'Silly sod's got himself engaged to some teenage tart.'

'I wonder which'll run out first, his energy or his money.' They laughed.

Both men read the sentimental account of the singer's past life, '. . . growing up in a close and loving family, enjoying the outdoor life that the Florida climate encouraged.' Crossley smiled at the final accolade. 'Rick's faith has always been important to him and he has never bowed to pressure to sing what he calls "cheatin' bar room songs". He says, "One of the things I insist on is that every song I sing could be performed in church."' How many tickets, Crossley wondered, had been sold in this little Yorkshire town for the aforementioned concert? And now, by this unwise attachment, he would probably have alienated even the oldies who remembered him.

The rest of the page reported the latest in a series of drug thefts from cars belonging to local GPs and a confirmation of the appointment of a new detective superintendent for the Cloughton police force. The latter item appeared under the tantalising but unexplained headline, 'REPLACEMENT FOR SHAMED EX-POLICE CHIEF'. Crossley glanced at his watch. He'd have to postpone those pleasures until later. It was high time he set off for his day's visit to the school where he would take up his new post after Christmas. It would be interesting to have another look at his future colleagues, though daunting to think that it was their chance to make a second judgement on him.

The two men left the room together, feeling sufficiently acquainted now to part with a handshake, though they omitted to exchange names. Their copies of the *Clarion* had been left on the breakfast table. As Crossley's companion remarked, 'Nowt so important there as we'll want to read again.'

Detective Constable Adrian Clement locked his door behind him. He had finished his stretches and he continued his warm-up with a brisk jog along the road. When he felt he was moving easily, he began to stride out and had soon completed a couple of six minute miles. He was sweating gently and beginning to enjoy himself.

This was a good time of day to be out. Villains preferred the very early hours just after midnight. People moving about around six o'clock – and there weren't many of them – were generally going about their lawful business. There were hardly any passing cars to fill his lungs with petrol or diesel fumes, or to hold him up and break his rhythm when his route crossed a main road.

This wild November morning, the sky was a gory battle-ground, the buildings standing black and solid against it. Clement exulted in his solitary struggle against the wind. In another half-hour there would be almost full daylight and the rest of the world would be out and about. A big black bird squawked at him and he could just make out its shape, cowering against the grey slates behind it. The magic was disappearing.

The bird received an answering call from its mate. Clement wished he knew more about birds. It amazed him that a creature less than a foot long could produce a noise that vied with the wailing of the present weather. Its harsh voice went on but became lost in the chugging and rattling of a bus. It held only a handful of passengers who gaped at Clement as they passed, but they told him that the day was well begun for at least some of the population of Cloughton.

He was running now alongside the low wall and high steel-mesh fencing of the Colin Hewitt Comprehensive, 'Col's Castle' to the town, 'the school from hell' in the unoriginal and unsympathetic reporting of the local television channel. Trees edged the pavement outside but the school's pupils played on an arid stretch of pitted asphalt. The building was huge, Victorian, not unattractive in its way. At not much after seven in the morning the premises were deserted and dignified. Clement suspected that the day would not finish without some incident concerning the school's pupils, staff or parents causing work for his uniformed colleagues.

He turned a corner, saw the lights shining out from the police station and prepared himself for his own working day. He glanced at his watch before slowing down to the fast walk that began his warm-down. Sixty-five minutes for the eleven and a bit miles. 'London Marathon, here I come!' he muttered to himself, and ran up the steps into the station foyer.

The desk sergeant showed no surprise at being confronted by a scarlet-faced, heavy-breathing officer clad in violet tracksters, a thermal vest and reflective bib. He remarked, merely, 'The DI's asking for you. I can't think why. You're not a pretty sight and you probably don't smell very sweet.' He saw that Clement had no breath for a reply. 'It's probably because you can run his errands faster than the rest of us. Anyway, you'd better make yourself respectable, and sharpish.'

Clement wiped his face with his vest sleeve. 'Right, thanks. Know what it's about?'

The sergeant's shoulders signalled his imperfect knowledge. 'Kid missing, Asian girl – sort of.'

'Sort of kid? Sort of Asian? Sort of missing?'

'School thinks she could be out of the country for one of those arranged marriages, or she might have scarpered to avoid it.'

Clement whistled. 'Hell's teeth! That's going to need handling with kid gloves.'

The desk sergeant sniffed. 'Don't know about gloves but you'd better at least improve on your present get-up.'

Clement retired hastily to the shower room, abandoning, for once, the remainder of his warm-down.

Just eight minutes later, cool and sweet-smelling again, in working gear, but ravenous, Clement recrossed the foyer on his way to DI Mitchell's office. He was irritated when the desk sergeant hailed him again, at least until he had taken in the message. 'The DI's been sent for himself.'

'To see the new super?'

The sergeant nodded. 'So, now he'll see you at his eight thirty briefing.'

Thankfully, Clement retreated downstairs again. There would be time for breakfast after all. His spirits rose further as DC Caroline Webster followed him into the canteen. He asked over his shoulder, 'What can I get you?'

'Just coffee. I'll get it.' Her tone was cool. However, carrying her large mug, she at least joined him at his table and regarded his laden plate with mock disapproval. 'Presumably that's your second breakfast.'

'Well, if you count two cups of tea and a slice of toast.'

'I hope you've done the full distance to justify it.'

He nodded smugly. 'You don't fancy trying it?'

'I do, actually – or, at least, doing something energetic – but not taking it as seriously as you do. That wouldn't leave me time for things I enjoy more.'

'Like your piano?'

She nodded. 'Is this new fitness kick to make you sharper on the job or is it just for its own sake?'

'I just love running. It's not new, though. I've always done it except for the year that Joanne died. That's where I met her, at the Bingley Harriers when I lived up there. Most clubs have a good social side too. It gets you away from the job for a while, reminds you there are other things to talk about. It's the Cloughton club's annual dinner next week. You wouldn't . . .' He watched her trying to frame a refusal that would not offend. 'The food should be good and they get the speeches and presentations over quickly.' She shook her head and he relieved her from the necessity to reply in words. 'It's not much notice, is it? Another time then.'

She ignored the half-invitation, drained her mug and pushed back her chair. 'It's fifteen minutes to the briefing and I've a report to finish. See you there.'

DI Mitchell knocked on Superintendent Carroll's door. He had his suspicions about the reason for his summons but held his

13

annoyance in check. When bidden, he went in, accepted the seat he was offered and looked across a vast area of tidy desk-top to the man on the opposite side of it.

Mitchell liked the new super, so far as he could judge on less than two weeks' acquaintance. The man had been pleasant and straightforward in their few dealings but this morning his expression bordered on embarrassment. His opening remark Mitchell interpreted as a ploy to gain time. Perhaps, even now, he had not decided what to do about the situation.

'I use my men's first names unless they object – but you don't look like a man who'll answer to Benedict.'

'Benny.'

The superintendent acknowledged the curt reply with a nod and suddenly seemed to make up his mind. 'I need to have a word with you about Chief Inspector Browne.'

So, it was what he'd thought. Mitchell's expression darkened. 'Not again!'

'I beg your pardon?'

'This is the third time I've been called to account for . . .' Mitchell paused, trying to control his irritation.

'For what, for goodness' sake?'

'For doing a perfectly good job on the same shift as my father-in-law.' Mitchell could hear that his tone was unwisely aggressive.

The superintendent was obviously startled. 'Tom Browne is your father-in-law?'

Mitchell was slightly appeased that no one had thought it necessary to apprise Carroll of the fact. 'He wasn't when I first went on his shift. I married Ginny when I'd been under him for three years.'

'And people have objected?'

'Superintendent Petty questioned it but let it go so long as it caused no problems . . .'

'If it works, don't mend it.'

'And Superintendent Kleever . . .' Mitchell sought vainly for tactful phrases.

'Yes, I know about Kleever.'

Mitchell's tone became more conciliatory. 'So, if you didn't know about us, what was it you wanted to say?'

'About Tom? That there's a problem with his wife that you

probably know more about than I do. He won't be in this morning. Apparently there's a new development and in the circumstances, I'd rather he told you about it himself. What I wanted to ask was whether you can head the shift in his place for a short while.'

Mitchell absorbed the news anxiously. He was aware that his mother-in-law had been vaguely unwell for some months. She had made light of her various symptoms even when they were directly enquired after. However, they had obliged her to curtail her babysitting services. The Mitchells had been dismayed, not because of the inconvenience to themselves but because the surrendering of this regular and much-enjoyed time spent with her grandchildren confirmed the seriousness of Hannah's illness. Now his alarm grew. It was unheard of for his father-in-law to absent himself from work.

He looked up and found the superintendent still waiting for an answer. 'No problem.' He added, repentant, 'I'm sorry I jumped down your throat.'

Carroll almost smiled. 'I've been warned that you're volatile and outspoken. I've also been told that your work compensates. Make sure it does.'

At about the time that DI Mitchell, in his CI's stead, began his daily meeting with his shift, the senior staff of the Colin Hewitt Comprehensive were gathering in their headmaster's office for a rather similar meeting. Martin Crossley, comfortably seated in the head's visitors' chair, scrutinised each new arrival, then smiled round at these future colleagues as he was introduced to them.

'Most of you have at least seen Mr Crossley, Martin, when he was shown round with the other interviewees. He, on the other hand, met so many of us that he probably remembers none.' Crossley nodded to each of the two deputies and the heads of upper and lower school as their various names and particular responsibilities were enumerated.

His social duties completed, Colin Greenwood glanced down at the playground where a considerable number of children were already gathered, then began his remarks. 'Two down and three still to go, I'm afraid. Never mind, it rushes by once Wednesday is over . . .'

With half his mind on the head's neat tabulation of today's particular arrangements, Crossley let the other half register his first impressions of his new school. It stood on a short stretch of road that linked an affluent-looking district to the rougher northern end of the town proper. He had felt the sharp contrast – at one end lush gardens and at the other this sterile building in its vast yard. He had felt his first misgivings about this new challenge he had taken on. Then, the sun had flickered out and flashed momentarily on the glass and delicate white wrought ironwork that so often lightened the sombre aspect of heavy Victorian piles. He had cheered up and entered the building to look for Mr Greenwood.

Now, he had this one day's visit to observe and acclimatise himself to this new environment. He had better concentrate fully on what was being said.

Colin Greenwood was reporting a parent's allegation that, on the previous afternoon, a junior member of staff had struck his son. 'He's threatening to involve the police.'

None of his listeners was noticeably upset. The second deputy asked calmly, 'What did you say to him?' Crossley transferred his attention to her. She was very smartly dressed, as they all were.

The head smiled. 'The fact that he's threatening to tell the police before doing it probably indicates that he wants the matter dealt with in school – though he's reserving the right to go to law if we don't satisfy him.'

'Parents want us to be tough, but only with other people's children.' This came from the head of lower school, a vision in blonde curls and yellow corduroy.

'I've told him,' Greenwood continued, 'that I'll only deal with the matter if he leaves it entirely to me, at least until I've reported back to him. I've promised him a thorough investigation and a prompt report on my conclusions and the action I intend to take. Can I leave it with you?' Greenwood turned to his first deputy.

She had been introduced as somebody Barron. Crossley had not caught the first name but was not concerned. The lady did not appear the sort who would allow newcomers to make free with it. He was surprised that a woman had been left to deal with a dispute involving a boy, a master and a father and he studied Mrs Barron with interest. She had strange light eyes and hair of a bright, unnatural red, though, if she had dyed it, she had managed a good match with her brows. She was a dominant figure, rather overweight, though clever dressing did sterling service in flattery. He wondered if her winter suntan was courtesy of a sunbed or a half-term holiday spent in the tropics. She nodded in acceptance of the task assigned to her and made a note in her diary, observing, 'Thank God it isn't a girl he's supposed to have clobbered.'

Keith Gordon, whose headship of upper school Crossley was about to inherit, now asked, 'What about Nazreen? Any news?' Crossley felt sorry that this man, slow-spoken and frankly fat, would have left the school when he joined it after Christmas. In cabled sweater and slacks, he was the least formally dressed of the group. The expression on his chubby face was benevolent but his mouth was firm.

In the brief time he had had to observe him, Crossley had noted his pupils' respect for him and his concern for them. He would have welcomed more time to learn from him before having to take his place.

The yellow-suited Kay Nelson spoke up. 'I had a quiet word with PC Nazir as I promised. She thought she could make some low-key enquiries but she hasn't got back to me yet. You'll know as soon as I do, Keith.'

The head glanced at his watch. 'Time we got moving. Anyone off?'

Mrs Barron beamed. 'No, a full turn-out. Is this a record?'

The telephone rang and the mock cheer turned to a groan. They all listened as Greenwood offered an ailing member of staff heartfelt good wishes for a speedy recovery, for their own sakes as much as his.

Mrs Barron sighed. 'Shall I see if Derek can come in? Or Cynthia?' Her expression indicated that the former was marginally the better of a bad choice.

Greenwood shrugged. 'Whoever you can get.'

A bell rang and the meeting broke up quickly. Crossley watched his future colleagues file out and felt disappointed that they had shown so little interest in him.

17

Wakened by a branch that chattered against his window pane, in a house at the other end of town, Clifford Summers opened his eyes. This was one of the few movements that had, as yet, not become painful for him. Next, he tried to raise his left arm high enough to see the dial of his wrist-watch, and, after a struggle, succeeded.

Six minutes past six. His bladder was uncomfortably full but the situation was not yet urgent. Cynthia would be up before long. He made an effort to relieve his cramped limbs by turning over. He was almost there when an agonising stab in his hip and knee caught him off guard and caused him to roll back to the position in which he had woken.

He waited for the torment in his back and limbs to subside to the usual miserable ache, then set about reminding himself of his many blessings. Severe osteo-arthritis exacerbated by a stroke could hardly be counted good fortune but his mental faculties were as acute as ever and, even in the worst of his pain, he would never trade them for increased mobility or physical ease. Things could be infinitely worse. He had a caring and attentive daughter which made him a very fortunate old man.

The branch smacked against his window with renewed force, but Clifford's bed was warm and he was a little more comfortable now. He would let Cynthia sleep until seven if he could possibly manage it.

Cynthia's alarm had actually been set for five thirty. She had put it under her pillow and silenced it immediately it began to ring as an extra precaution, though she was not much worried that her father would be disturbed. Her room was on the floor above his and on the other side of the house.

She filled her small kettle at the washbasin in the corner and spooned Lapsang Souchong into the little china pot. Waiting for the water to boil, she sat on the side of the bed and reached for her fiancé's photograph in its expensive frame. He smiled up at her. His hair was receding and he had more sense than to try to disguise it. What was left of it was thick and dark, as were the mobile brows and thick moustache. His features were strong and regular, the cheeks lean, the eyes crinkled up although you could tell they were dark brown.

Cynthia replaced the photograph and filled her china mug

18

with the fragrant brew. After one sip, she reached into her bedside cabinet for writing paper, plumped up her pillows, climbed back under the duvet and began her daily letter, 'My very dearest Fred . . .'

After several paragraphs, she paused to finish her tea, wondering, yet again, whether she shouldn't give in to Fred's urging, marry him now and face all the problems that would lead to. For herself, she would have no hesitation but they would all have to travel such a lot and Father tired so easily these days. He would never be able to stand it. She was grateful that Fred had agreed to hold their plans for another year and she willingly delayed her own pleasure for Father's sake.

Meanwhile she could continue her preparations, make her decisions, so that when the wedding happened, everything would go smoothly. She reasoned with herself this way every day, but this morning her reasoning failed to comfort her. Some things, of course, were already decided. For example, the wedding dress Fred had picked out for her hung in the wardrobe under its two protective coverings, first of muslin and then of polythene. Should she try it on again, just to cheer herself up?

She quickly ruled against this self-indulgence. If Father woke early he might ring for her. It would be such a shock for him to see her dressed in it without being prepared. But then, if he lingered on beyond the end of the summer, their plans would have to be broken to him, very gently.

Cynthia had taken up her pen again when the bell on the landing rang, just once. He would not ring again, tried never to ring at all. He was always considerate, sometimes embarrassed at needing her help. She tied her thick woollen dressing-gown round her and hurried to Father's room.

Half an hour later, she was in the kitchen, busy making toast and listening to her father read snippets from the paper, when the telephone rang. From her own side of the conversation, Cynthia could see that Father understood she was being summoned into school. She glanced at him, eyebrows raised, and he nodded. By this method they agreed that, with the usual help, he could survive the length of a school day without her.

Cynthia's tone was bright. 'Of course I can help you out, Mrs

Barron. I'll be with you just as soon as I've arranged with Mrs Aiken to keep an eye on Father and give him his lunch.' As she collected the briefcase that was always kept ready, Cynthia wondered when she would find a few minutes to finish today's letter to Fred.

2

Detective Sergeant Jennifer Taylor arrived early for the shift's usual eight thirty briefing. She felt exhilarated. She loved the wind and she had risen cheerfully that morning, having been woken before her alarm by the irregular beat of her neighbour's dustbin lid bouncing down the back street.

Another tap at the door preceded the entry of DC Caroline Webster who shivered. 'I hate the wind. It's so destructive and it sends my cat wild.'

Jennifer grinned. 'And my daughters.' They both turned to look out of the window behind them and watched two young civilian employees run, shrieking, towards the station's main entrance. Their skirts ballooned to reveal, in one case at least, what would have been better hidden. 'They're defending their hairstyles rather than their modesty.' When her remark was received in silence, Jennifer scrutinised the young DC. 'It isn't just the weather, is it? What's up?'

Caroline shrugged. 'Nothing much. I've just had to give Adrian the brush-off again.'

'Don't tell me you've no technique for keeping him in line.'

Caroline shook her head. 'No, but I've no technique for not feeling rotten afterwards, especially when he thinks I was leading him on last year.'

'Last year you helped keep him sane. It's quite different now that . . .' The door opened again, with no knocking, this time to admit Mitchell. 'Later,' she muttered to Caroline before she raised her voice and faced him to ask, 'Where's the CI?'

Mitchell was succinct. 'The super told me he's not in this morning. You'll have to manage with me. And where's Adrian?'

DC Clement appeared appropriately to explain himself but his lateness was ignored as attention passed to the girl who had followed him in. She was a PC newly appointed to the Cloughton station, a lively-looking Pakistani, known to the shift only by sight. Mitchell introduced her as PC Shakila Nazir.

He interrupted the murmurs of greeting. 'Let's get on.' His manner was short and they sensed his distracted mood. 'There's been another doctor's car broken into. Late last night. Usual method. A small explosive device to beggar up the boot lock and the windows broken just for devilment. Same surgery as last time, Heath Lees, but Dr Ahmed this time. A briefcase was taken and a medical bag with drugs. There's a list in the file for anyone who might understand it. Ahmed thinks there are precious few items of any street value and that we'll probably find his case and bag in a skip somewhere. On the other hand, he's worried that the stuff could do plenty of harm to small kids who might find it.'

'It's probably the Sainted City lot.'

Mitchell was pretty sure Jennifer was right. 'That's why I sent for you, Adrian, to go and dig friends Grant and Stepney out of their pits before they had a chance to sort out the loot and dump it. I knew you'd arrive before this lot were even out of bed.'

Jennifer noticed the new PC looking bewildered. 'Sorry, Shakila. Sainted City is a set of four tower blocks. Grant and Stepney who live there are our friendly local joyriders cum petty thieves. First port of call when something like this turns up but we haven't managed to pin this series on to them yet.'

'The super scuppered plan A,' Mitchell cut in. 'They've had a bit more time to move the stuff out. Still, I suggest Adrian convinces the doting mothers that a search of their rooms will prove their innocence. Both boys are at Col's Castle, or, at least, they're on roll and should be there. Probably what they're actually doing is finding another vehicle to break into.'

Caroline shifted slightly so as to share the radiator with Shakila. 'Aren't we looking any further than those two?' she asked.

Mitchell sniffed. 'If it isn't them, I'd go bail for them knowing who else it is. I want them both questioned, separately. If you can do it with Keith Gordon as chaperone rather than the parents, so much the better.' He glanced at his watch. 'We'd better move on. You'll all have heard, I expect, that we have an unofficial report of a missing girl. That's why Shakila is with us.'

He gestured to her an invitation to take his place and address the gathering and observed that she did so with aplomb. 'I have a friend, Kay Nelson, who teaches at the Colin Hewitt. Yesterday she spoke to me about a sixth-form pupil, Nazreen Akram.' The voice was low-pitched, the accent local, though the sentences were careful, deliberately phrased, and the substance of her report well prepared. Born and bred in Bradford, Mitchell decided, and gave his full attention to what the girl was saying.

'She's a clever girl, taking four science A levels and planning to be a doctor. She was absent from school on Friday. On Saturday evening she failed to turn up for a junior disco at which she'd volunteered to help. She's hardly ever away from school and she's a reliable and well-mannered girl. Kay thought that she wouldn't have willingly let them down and if she had to she would certainly have warned them and sent an explanation.'

She looked up at Jennifer's interruption. 'Maybe her parents disapproved of such antics. Are they strict Muslims?'

Shakila shrugged. 'I don't know. She still wasn't at school yesterday so her form master rang her home. He spoke to a Dr Akram who said the school would be getting a letter. Kay spoke to the girl's friends but they'd heard nothing. At Kay's request, I went to see the family last night and asked to see Nazreen. Only her younger brother was in. I was in civvies and he assumed I was a teacher. I let him go on thinking. He was wearing a Bradford Grammar School blazer. They obviously concentrate on educating boys.'

'You'd better not say that at Col's Castle,' Mitchell warned her.

She nodded. 'The lad said he thought she was visiting relatives, he didn't know which or where. When I asked if she wasn't afraid she would fall behind with her school work, he said she was clever enough to catch up and that Miss Summers would help her if she'd missed something important.'

'Cocky!'

'I don't think so. He just stated it as a fact. Anyway, if the visit had been planned even as late as the day before, Nazreen would have let the school know – unless the family planned it and didn't tell her. So, the school wonders whether she's going under duress and whether her visit is back to Pakistan.'

Shakila indicated that she had told all she knew by dropping back into her chair. There was a thoughtful silence, broken after some moments by Mitchell. 'So, how seriously are we going to take this business?' He was not sure, in his own mind, whether he was inviting the opinions of his shift or warning them that they would have to wait for his decision.

He was not surprised when Jennifer made the former interpretation and offered, 'The remit of the 1989 Children's Act is to move if she might "suffer significant harm".'

'But is she a child?' They all looked at Caroline. 'She's a sixth-former. How old is she?'

Now they looked back at Shakila who screwed up her forehead in thought. 'I don't think her precise age was mentioned but I got the impression she was at the beginning of her courses.'

'So, she's probably still sixteen.'

'Have you checked that she hasn't turned up at school this morning?'

'They don't register till nine, sir.'

'Right. You'd better check now.'

The girl slipped out with a satisfied expression, hardly believing her luck. On her shift the previous afternoon, the most exciting events had been stopping two truanting schoolboys from spraying a shop front with aerosol paint and earning the undying gratitude of an elderly lady by allowing the woman's missing white mongrel to bound up and follow her back to the station. Today, she was reporting in before starting out on her beat when she had been picked up and whirled into her first CID investigation.

Clement, who had been standing, appropriated her chair, which happened to be next to Caroline's. Mitchell favoured him with another glare and came to a decision. 'The school's done all it can. She's past the leaving age and they can't force her to attend. If Nazreen is being smuggled out to Pakistan we may already have missed her. As the Bradford unit is always telling us, if she's already left the country there's nothing we can do. If she's still on her way, it's their pigeon anyway. They're all set up for the fastest checking of ports, airports and vehicles likely to be used and ours would be just a monitoring job.' He looked up as Shakila returned and answered his unspoken question with a shake of her head.

'But what,' Jennifer demanded, 'if something quite different has happened to her?'

24

'We start digging now, just in case.' Mitchell took a handful of action sheets from Browne's desk and began writing rapidly. 'Adrian to Col's Castle to see Grant and Stepney. Caroline, take Shakila and track down the Akram parents. Get the names and addresses of these supposed relatives and be more up-front than last time. Tell them their daughter will officially be a missing person if we haven't contacted her by the end of the day. Jennifer, see what the school can tell you about her friends, anyone she might have confided in.' He handed a small pile of sheets each to its respective recipient. 'Any questions?'

Jennifer had one. 'When will the CI be back?'

Mitchell shrugged. 'Wish I knew. As soon as I do, I'll tell you.' He had rung his wife immediately on leaving Superintendent Carroll's office but she had not answered. Now he tried again, letting the ringing continue for almost a minute, with no result. Hesitating to disturb the Browne household, he decided to go home for a brief lunch. Virginia would have picked up Caitlin from nursery school by then and would almost certainly be at home.

Meanwhile, he tried to suppress his reprehensible glee at this second chance in his short career as a DI to be in charge of the shift at the beginning of an intriguing enquiry.

As the Colin Hewitt staff departed to begin another routine school day, Crossley saw that he was expected to remain where he was and gratefully accepted the coffee that the secretary produced. He was pleased when the head offered, 'Any questions arise out of all that?'

He considered. 'Is there a feeder junior school sharing this vast building?'

'No. Why do you ask?'

'I looked out of the window when the meeting broke up and saw children who scarcely looked old enough to be at school at all.'

'Yes, you would.' Greenwood's tone contained a mixture of acceptance and exasperation. 'Their parents leave them for their older siblings to mind and then take to their various infant schools and nurseries when they open. Then, of course, our own pupils are late.' He grinned suddenly. 'They're not without initiative, though. Some of them have organised their own version of the school run.'

'Can't you forbid it?'

'Only with the knowledge that the infants would then be left completely unsupervised. And, of course, should one of the little ones be knocked down whilst in the care of an older child, the mother would have little trouble convincing herself that the responsibility was mine.'

'But –'

'But we have to deal with our own pupils as they are, with the parents they have. We can't do much about the parents – at least, not in the mass. Occasionally we can get through to the odd one.' He grinned ruefully. 'Only last week a mother arrived at school with her daughter. The girl had been taken home by friends after being assaulted on the bus by another girl. The friends had volunteered the aggressor's name and the school she attended, so the mother thought that, perhaps, we could link up with them and sort it out.'

'Did you?'

Greenwood smiled. 'The girl wasn't badly hurt. I asked her mother whether, if the attack had happened in August, she'd have rung me at home to deal with it.' Crossley waited for the punchline. 'She said, "Oh, can you do that?"'

He noted his new staff member's expression and spoke reprovingly. 'We talked about feckless parents before, at your interview. You don't have to pander to them but you have to accept how they are and do what you feel is in their children's best interests.'

Crossley nodded. 'What will Mrs Barron do about the assault allegation?'

'You'll have to ask her. I imagine she'll interview the boy and the probationer master separately, look for evidence of a physical assault – I may have to do that for her if it means removing any of the lad's clothing. We may decide to let a doctor examine him. Mavis will advise the master to consult his union. Then she'll look for any other witnesses and interview them today before they have much opportunity for collusion. Then it will come back to a heads' meeting again.'

'Right. Have you time to tell me who Nazreen is?'

'Yes, briefly. She's very bright, just embarking on A levels and hoping to read medicine. Obviously, she's an Asian girl. Her family's well off compared with the rest of our pupils. Her brothers have been given an expensive education but she's just expected to marry. In the summer, we had trouble persuading her father to allow her to enter the sixth form. She's been absent for three days now without a letter from home and with our Asian adolescents we're instantly on our guard. We're afraid –'

'That she's being shipped off to Pakistan to marry and provide her husband with legal entry into the country. We watch for that in Leicester too. At least, they did in the school where I had my first job. It's not exactly a problem at St Mark's. Do I gather you have trouble getting people on supply?'

'What do you think?' Greenwood's tone was philosophical rather than bitter. 'We're about fifty per cent Asian and most of those children speak Urdu or Hindi whenever they're not at school. The white parents in our vicinity who're concerned for their children's education don't send them to us. It's not really racism. They just don't want them spending all day with teachers whose main preoccupation is basic English tuition, so our white children are mainly the offspring of the parents who don't care. Jobs here are not sought after by ambitious teachers, though we have a generous number of competent and dedicated ones.

'Supply staff prefer easier schools so we get the ones no one else wants, hence Cynthia and Derek, our regulars. She makes it painfully obvious that she's scared of the children and pleads for their co-operation. He bawls and shouts and threatens. They shout back at him and laugh at her. The classes might be better left to their own devices with no one there to be baited, but I have to comply with the law. We're hoping for rather a lot from you.'

Crossley contemplated his new head, well-groomed but weary-looking even at this early hour, and vowed to give everything that was expected.

'Who are you spending the first period with?'

Taking this as his dismissal, Crossley made for the door, but stopped at the sound of a shrill altercation from outside. Both men moved to the window and saw that a quarrel between two mothers of late-coming pupils had an avid audience. The women seemed equally matched in invective and in their ability to inflict injury.

Greenwood sighed. 'It would be an easy matter to separate them but . . .'

'Then they'd unite gleefully in accusing us of assault.'

Greenwood raised an eyebrow. 'I think you're going to be our man.' His hand was reaching towards the phone when the caretaker appeared from the nether regions of the boiler room. Crossing the yard, he grabbed an arm of each woman in his huge hands and shook them both before yelling at them, 'Go an' mek that racket in yer own backyard!'

The women went off meekly and their children, seeing the show was over, dawdled towards the cloakrooms. Crossley could not make out the words that the now reconciled mothers shouted to the caretaker through the railings. Their demeanour suggested that they were good-natured.

Greenwood laughed. 'Occasionally,' he remarked, 'the gods are on our side.'

Cynthia Summers stood in the corridor outside the human biology room. Shrieks and bangs came from within. The teachers of the classes in the rooms on either side had not yet appeared but one class sat waiting reasonably quietly and the other, keeping even more strictly to the rule, was lined up in pairs on the far side of its classroom door, waiting for permission to go in.

The human biology room door suddenly opened, and the girl who was pushed out lurched across the width of the corridor. The door slammed shut again and Frankie Leonard rubbed her shoulder where it had hit the tiled wall and stopped her staggering progress.

A one-to-one confrontation was not so bad. Tight-lipped, Cynthia regarded the child. 'You stand there till I tell you you can come in.'

Deprived of Adele Batty, her mentor, Frankie had as little stomach for defiance as Cynthia herself. She stood meekly, a little distance from the door where her obedience to authority would not be observed by her derisive classmates when it should open again. Bereft of further excuses for delay, Cynthia pushed it and went into the room.

There was a momentary quiet whilst the class checked that it was only Miss Summers. She used it in a desperate and hopeless attempt to assert herself. 'Stop this noise at once! We'll begin all over again. File out quietly and line up as you should have done in the first place.' There was another silence, this time marking their surprise. In it her nervous and high-pitched tones echoed.

A few timid and biddable souls in front of her took a half-hearted step or two towards the door until the lazy tones of the Batty girl halted them. 'I don't think so, do you, Miss Summers? You're four minutes late and it would be a shame to miss even more of the lesson.' The girl sat down and began to arrange her books and pens as though eager to begin work.

Trying to get a grip on herself, Cynthia walked to the table in the front corner. The class ignored her, their eyes on Adele, trying to read their orders from her body language. Since she continued to set out her possessions with exaggerated care, they followed suit. Frankie's face appeared at the only patch of the glass wall giving on to the corridor that was not covered with posters and displays of work.

Cynthia thought she was probably curious to know why all was quiet. Cynthia wanted to know too. Or did she? She wasn't sure she would like the answer. She ought to bring the child in before a senior member of staff saw her and made polite enquiries. Going back into the corridor, her face crimsoned with embarrassment as she realised that her 'Do you think you can behave yourself now?' had been heard by Mr Greenwood and the new head of upper school as they passed on a tour of the building.

Frankie entered the classroom and went quietly to her place, following the example of the rest of the class in fixing her eyes on Adele. Satisfied, Adele raised her hand. 'We're on page 129 in the textbook, Miss Summers.' Adele's politeness and the class's docility and contained amusement told Cynthia what was afoot. She turned with foreboding to the suggested page in the book hastily passed to her by the harassed head of biology. As she'd guessed, it was the chapter on human reproduction. What a farce to explain the sexual act and its repercussions to this streetwise collection of adolescents whose experience was now neatly summarised in a hackneyed mutter from the front row. 'Seen it, done it, got the T-shirt and the video.' She met the lad's stare but dropped her own eyes first.

Most of the class had now found the page and a tide of nudging and sniggering arose, to be immediately turned back by a single glance round the room from Adele. Cynthia closed her eyes, trying to shut it all out. What an irony to call these children deprived and herself cultured, educated. Educated for what? They were the ones who were educated to survive.

She opened her eyes to find a hand was raised. 'Yes?' Cynthia knew from the angelic expression that this would be Adele at her most insolent. 'Do you know a lot of science, Miss Summers?'

'I studied at one time for a degree, at the university.'

'Mr Jackman says, miss, that all scientific knowledge comes from experiment.'

'I suppose you could say that, experiment, trial and error, testing out ideas . . .'

'So how can you teach us sex, miss, when you haven't done it?'

What a perfect example of Morton's fork! There was no right answer – for herself, anyway. Anything she could possibly say would serve Adele's purpose. 'I – I don't believe that this is the place you have reached in your books.'

Adele handed over her exercise book. Cynthia saw that her last piece of work was neatly ruled off and a new heading 'Reproduction' had been made, with a double underlining. 'We got as far as the heading last time.'

Cynthia saw that the ink was very nearly dry and was surprised to see that Adele didn't scrawl in smudgy biro like her classmates. 'Shut your books.' She tried to keep her voice low, relaxed, in control. She was successful in patches, so that it broke, mid-sentence, like an adolescent boy's. 'Since I can't prove you right or wrong, we'll do something quite different.' She took file paper from her briefcase and placed an appropriate number of sheets at the front of each row of desks. 'Pass those back and head them with your names and the date.'

'What's the title?' came from the back row.

'You'll have to find your own. I want an essay from each of you. And since any topic you're given you describe as boring before you've even considered it, you can choose your own. I won't accept less than three hundred words.'

'You mean we can write what we like?' This from Adele.

Cynthia had misgivings but there was no going back. 'That's what I said.'

Adele nodded to the class to begin writing and they set to work quietly, at least for them. Cynthia sat down thankfully. Whatever they were up to, she'd accept it if it kept them quiet enough to be sure the staff in the rooms on either side would not come in to offer humiliating assistance . . . The industrious near-silence and concentrated effort lasted longer than Cynthia had dared hope.

Then her anxiety became dread as Adele, her face wearing its usual smirk, enquired with mock civility, 'Could you tell us how much time we have left, Miss Summers?' Cynthia glanced at her watch. Less than five minutes, thank goodness. Adele began counting aloud the number of words she had written. The class followed suit, in canon, so that the bell, when it rang at last, could hardly be heard over the clamour. She took her pupil's papers from them at the door and carried the pile back to her table.

She could not face the staff room and decided to spend break time where she was. She shuffled the class's attempts at an essay into a tidy stack. As she glanced at the top sheet a tide of crimson washed over her face and neck. She waited as the heat of it rose, then died away. It occurred to her that no one had asked whether what they had written would be shown to the head of year, or to the headmaster. They were safe in the knowledge that, if she revealed the obscenities they had handed in to her, she would suffer a worse punishment than their own.

Since she had been there before, Caroline elected Shakila to drive the marked car to the Akrams' house. It stood on the boundary where 'Little Pakistan' bordered on one of Cloughton's affluent areas. Pressing a brass bell push to the side of the front door brought forth a handsome Pakistani woman in a sari of sump-tuous, rose-coloured silk. She had opened the door sufficiently to reveal only herself and an area of entrance hall wall. Its hangings were deep crimson below and dark orange above, with discreet gilded patterning on each. Caroline wondered why the effect was rich rather than garish. She decided that part of the reason was that in Asian houses she had come to expect this use of colour so that it did not startle.

The woman surveyed her visitors without speaking. Caroline reciprocated, interpreting Mitchell's instruction to be 'up-front' by silently producing her warrant. The woman shrugged and uttered an unintelligible sentence. Shakila at once stepped forward and spoke at greater length, apparently in the same tongue. Turning back to Caroline, she grinned. 'What Mrs Akram said to you was not polite. I've told her she can be interviewed by you in English or me in Urdu, just as she pleases.'

The officers' unobtrusive steps forward had driven Mrs Akram back through her own hall, until, on reaching an internal door, she grudgingly invited them into a glowing turquoise and gold sitting-room. Once there, however, she kept them on their feet by remaining standing herself.

The interview proceeded in accented English with Shakila's occasional services as interpreter. At every possible opportunity, the woman diverted the conversation from her daughter to one or other of her sons, her husband or her retired hospital consultant father-in-law. Faisal, five years older than Nazreen, was 'good businessman', manager of the biggest estate agency in Cloughton. She specified the firm and Caroline remembered that its staff was exclusively Asian in spite of its local title, Heptinstall & Hudson. Her husband, *very* good businessman', ran a fleet of taxis and Shahid, at Bradford Grammar School, was studying for no fewer than eleven GCSEs.

Slyly, Shakila asked if the relatives Nazreen was visiting were equally prosperous. Mrs Akram shrugged, seemingly torn between the pleasure of further boasting and the possibility of having her immediate family outshone. She settled for a smug assertion that the rest of the family in Leicester was 'doing extremely well'.

'So, Nazreen is in Leicester. Perhaps you'll supply us with a telephone number and an address so that we can assure ourselves that she arrived safely.'

Mrs Akram appeared annoyed with herself. On being pressed, she assented grudgingly. 'I write the address. I believe no telephone number.'

Neither officer believed this assertion and each wondered

whether the address they were eventually given would turn out not to exist. 'You ask my husband, not me,' was all they could get out of the woman by further questioning.

Caroline delivered Mitchell's warning, making the implications of Nazreen's being officially missing quite explicit. 'By this evening, every port and airport will be looking for her, every vehicle she might be travelling in will be stopped and searched. All her details will be on the police national computer.' At Caroline's suggestion, Shakila repeated the warning in Urdu.

Mrs Akram shook her head angrily. 'How is Nazreen missing,' she demanded, 'when she has gone to see Asif?'

'Asif?' the two officers asked, in chorus.

They listened in some embarrassment to Mrs Akram's stilted account of the illustrious career at Leicester University of the distant cousin who was Nazreen's intended husband. So, the young man was not, after all, in need of a passport to the United Kingdom.

3

Sue and Derek Swindell were taking their mid-morning coffee at the kitchen table. His wife having monopolised the *Clarion* at breakfast, Derek was skimming its main items now whilst trying to ignore her derogatory commentary. 'It beats me, what some folk will do to grab attention and be the focus of everyone's sympathy.'

Derek continued to read. She was making statements. No questions to find the right answers for yet.

'It was quite clever of her in a way. No one could prove she couldn't feel what the surgeon was doing, even though no one with any common sense would believe her.' Relieved that no more was required of him, Derek grunted.

Sue snatched his cup away to wash it up, even though there was at least another half-cup left in the pot. She found a new complaint. 'I'll bet there are vandals wrecking that park faster than those council slouches can patch it up. I expect most of the little devils are from Colin Hewitt.'

Derek actually agreed with most of what his wife said to him. It was depressing, though, to have these opinions constantly put into words. What he minded was the impression she gave him that the greater part of what she deplored was his fault.

Sue clashed crockery irritably and Derek knew that, by association of ideas, she would get round to her dissatisfaction with his erratic teaching career. She fulfilled his expectation as she dried cups and saucers. 'I don't know why you can't get a proper job instead of traipsing up there at everyone's beck and call. A bit of discipline and those children could be organised into mending things themselves – putting something into community life instead of taking out. They're brought up to expect, and not to earn. I wouldn't be surprised if they think their O-levels will come from the government, free, like family allowance and clinic orange juice.' Derek knew she was quoting her mother and didn't trouble to update her remark.

Derek wished she would go to the Colin Hewitt in his place

and perform these transforming wonders. He didn't doubt that she could. Provoked out of his usual tacit endurance, he poured the dregs of the coffee in the pot into one of her newly washed cups. 'Perhaps I'd have a chance of a permanent job if you would consider a move to wherever I can find one.' It was a mild enough rejoinder, but he knew he was calling down her wrath. He retired behind his paper and tried to shut his mind to the rasping voice. '. . . at least one of us earning a crust . . . fine mess we'd be in if I left my job . . . we'd find we'd wrecked my career only to find you're no more use wherever you'd dragged us than you are in this god-forsaken place.'

In spite of himself, Derek smiled at 'my career'. He was thankful for Sue's three days a week 'housekeeping' for the owner and manager of Cloughton's small theatre. If he had shared her ill nature, he would have called her a glorified charwoman, but he respected such work and was sure she did it efficiently.

He felt suddenly dizzy with dislike of her. He made a mental list of what he hated about her – the instant judgements on everyone she encountered or heard about, the military precision with which she ran the household, the nicotine stains on the first and second fingers of her right hand, the hard, blue eyeshadow she wore, even at the breakfast table and, worse than everything else, the avid sex, for which she chose the time and took the lead and during which she had the knack of producing in him that physical excitement which, eight years ago, had caused him to fancy himself in love with her.

His sister found her amusing. She had suggested he should make a tape recording of Sue's jaundiced commentary on life and turn it into a television script. She had advised him to take a less serious view of it all. It was just Sue's way of dealing with life's frustrations. Mary, though, didn't have to live with Sue. Derek knew that his television script would come back, labelled, 'Woman's ill nature hopelessly overwritten.'

Now, Sue had gone upstairs. After coffee on Tuesdays was her time for an hour and a half's cleaning in their bedroom. This included emptying and relining drawers in rotation. Today, thank goodness, was the turn of her own small chest containing underwear and blouses. He remained at the kitchen table, the vestige of a smile lighting his eyes as his lips soundlessly recited the little parody he had composed, just for his own amusement, of the well-known Elizabeth Barrett Browning poem. His version began, 'How can I kill thee? Let me count the ways.'

He had a book upstairs, the only object he had ever stolen. It was a textbook, written for forensic pathologists. He had found it in a sale at the library of books that people no longer borrowed. The other books he wanted, he had queued and paid for, but this one he would use in secret and it had seemed important to smuggle it out. He had learned from it enough to write several verses in mockery of Mrs Browning's poem and, in his fantasies, he had killed his wife many times and by many methods.

Today, he would use carbon monoxide. Inside his head, he persuaded Sue into the garage to advise him about the exact place to put up another shelf. He had left a spanner ready on a ledge behind the door and had studied the book to find just how much force would be needed for the tap behind the ear that would stun her. He carried her into the front of the car, closed the door and fixed the hose to the end of the exhaust. He dragged its other end carefully round to the front passenger window, where he trapped it, not too tightly, into the crack where the window was not quite closed. It remained only to close the gap at the bottom of the garage door with old rolled towels, retrieved from under his work bench. He added another roll of wadding on the house side of the door leading from the integral garage into the hall. All he had to do now was wait.

Before the fantasy could reach its cathartic conclusion, the telephone rang. Sue came scuttling down the stairs to listen as he picked up the receiver. The conversation was brief, then Derek turned to his wife. 'They want me this afternoon and again tomorrow.' She knew he meant the school. Did they really want him? He doubted it. Still, the summons at least rescued him from more of his wife's dispiriting opinions. Bleakly, he faced the prospect of many more years spent lurching from the hell of home to the hell of the classroom, each change promising relief only until he had made it.

Sue was stomping upstairs again. Her words floated down to him. 'I knew you'd find some excuse not to mend the back gate this afternoon.'

*   *   *

When Mitchell reached the police house that was his family's temporary home, he found three of his four children already seated round the kitchen table. Virginia, struggling with the cooker's temperamental grill, spoke over her shoulder to him. 'Did you realise when you offered to take pot luck that it would amount to three and a half fish fingers?'

Mitchell was thankful. Nursery lunch would reach the Tesco standard of edibility, unless, of course, Ginny burnt it. He'd hoped for sandwiches, a safe and filling option, but had feared it might be one of his wife's 'stews' which were usually more imaginative than palatable.

He reflected that his offspring seemed to thrive on their mother's culinary challenges, though the two older children had recently begun to receive invitations to eat with the families of their classmates and make less than tactful comparisons.

The police house's cooker seemed reluctant today to heat up the food at all and the hungry twins were becoming impatient. Caitlin, with her two years' experience as a big sister, distracted Sinead from unfastening the safety strap of her booster seat by biting a piece of bread and butter into the shape of a face. Mitchell improved on this work of art with blobs of tomato ketchup until he felt his wife's glare and desisted.

The grill became more co-operative. Virginia supplied filled plates and the family munched lukewarm fish fillets philo-sophically.

'We've . . .' Caitlin caught her mother's eye and swallowed the food she was chewing before beginning again. 'We've been doing wind pictures at nursery this morning.'

'You can't see the wind. How can you draw it?'

Caitlin favoured her father with a replica of the glance of reproof she had just received. 'You know exactly what I mean.' Then, relenting, 'There's a torn-up umbrella stuck in the back hedge. I drew that. The real one's boring black but I did mine red and purple, with a green hedge and a blue sky and . . .'

Mitchell, who had come in through the front door, went to the window and surveyed with annoyance the debris that the wild weather had deposited on the lawn. Virginia, knowing how much untidiness annoyed him in any sector of his life, sym-pathised. 'Still, there's not much point in getting it all how you want it. We'll be moving again before long.' Her mouth tightened. 'Anyway, there isn't going to be much time for gardening, nor house-hunting either.'

Mitchell turned back into the room. 'So I gather.' He glanced at his watch. 'I've called the shift together for two o'clock. If you deal with these folk, I'll make coffee and then you can tell me what's going on.' Virginia let him take the kettle from her and scooped up the twins. Michael was almost asleep already, his head lolling on a tablemat. She propped him on her shoulder and led Sinead by the hand towards the stairs and their bedroom. She admonished her elder daughter, 'Come on, Kat.'

Caitlin had hoped for an extension of this untoward midday conversation with her father and trailed after Virginia with some reluctance. Mitchell busied himself with grinding coffee beans and preheating the stoneware coffee jug he always insisted on using. His hands busy, he speculated on the seriousness of his mother-in-law's indisposition and its implications within the family.

Virginia reappeared as he set the pot to stand, wrinkling her nose in appreciation of the coffee smell. 'Mmm. Michael was asleep before I put him down. Sinead's yelling but she knows better than to come downstairs. I've promised Kat a chocolate biscuit if she can finish her new jigsaw in half an hour.'

Mitchell lifted a restraining hand as she reached for the coffee jug. 'Don't touch it for another two minutes – and I've got to go in twenty.'

Virginia nodded, settled herself at the table and gave him a terse summary of her mother's medical history over the last couple of years. A little they had already known; most of the details and the end of the story had been communicated to her by her father, only that morning. When Hannah had had difficulty in raising her right arm, her GP had diagnosed a frozen shoulder that would gradually cure itself over eighteen months. When, instead, it became worse, he had sent Hannah for X-rays that had revealed some arthritis. Hannah had the sense not to expect, in her mid-fifties, the agility of an adolescent and had been undismayed.

Recently, she had concealed from her daughter that she was unable to climb out of her bath or put on her own jacket. Her left arm was affected too. Her doctors had talked of trapped nerves, even a minor stroke. Finally, Hannah had been referred to a neurologist in Leeds. This august physician had summoned her parents the previous afternoon and given them a final diagnosis of motor neurone disease.

Mitchell was saddened. The name of the disease meant nothing specific to him but it sounded ominous and Ginny's tone confirmed this impression. He tried to think of an adequate response, and, after a moment, produced, 'What does that mean in practical terms? What's going to happen?'

Virginia stared at him bleakly. 'I think the short answer is wait and see but nothing good.'

Half an hour later, in his father-in-law's office, it was a sober Mitchell who awaited his team. He was used to feeling angry and impatient in this room. Throughout his terms as detective constable and sergeant, this had been his stock response to reproof. And reproof had often been earned by his lack of subtlety and disregard of ordained procedure in seeking out his villains.

His resentment had always been short-lived, soon replaced by renewed enthusiasm for the job. His present misery, though, was not so easily controlled. He had known that Hannah was ill, had suspected recently that the illness was serious. Only now did he and Virginia understand that it would follow an inexorable course to an early death.

He knew men who would be secretly pleased to lose a mother-in-law, though not, of course, in this cruel way. He had laughed at his colleagues' mother-in-law jokes without connecting them in any way with Hannah. When he had first joined the CID she had been his DI's lively and kindly wife. When he had seduced the Brownes' daughter, she had been his ally, once she was certain that he loved Virginia, in reconciling her husband to the situation and facilitating the marriage.

Now, it seemed, there was nothing to be done for her. Mitchell knew himself to be a doer, not well equipped to stand by and endure the suffering of someone he respected, even loved.

His musing was disturbed by the arrival of DS Taylor. Paying no attention to Mitchell, she claimed her usual chair by the window and looked out at the weather. 'It's calming down a bit. Is the DI ill?'

'He's got a migraine.'

Jennifer turned back sharply. 'He used to get them all the time but he hasn't had one for years. What's upset him?' She looked harder at Mitchell. 'And you?'

Mitchell was unsure how much of the situation the Brownes would want to reveal at this point and risked only, 'Hannah's ill.'

The door opened again and the rest of the team, led by Clement, trailed in at intervals, settling themselves round him, fishing for their notebooks and chatting quietly. Glad of the reprieve, Mitchell invited Caroline Webster to report on her visit to the Akrams.

Ruefully, the DC described her conversation with Nazreen's mother and the news that her daughter's chosen husband was already resident in Britain. 'Have the Bradford folk made a move yet? I suppose we'll have to cancel our request.'

Mitchell shook his head. 'Let's at least check that the girl's in Leicester first.'

'Surely she will be.'

DS Taylor, as always, was quick to disagree with Clement. 'She might have run off to avoid the marriage anyway. We don't know how she feels about this Asif.'

Mitchell intervened before a wrangle could begin. 'We don't need to argue about it. We've rung Charles Street in Leicester to ask. Someone's going out to the family this afternoon. At least they've assured us that the address Mrs Akram gave us is a real place.'

'The Cloughton Akrams will have telephoned. If the girl's not there, they'll have had time to think of an excuse.'

'Of course she will be.' Clement glared at Jennifer who ignored him.

'All right!' Mitchell's raised voice brought the discussion to an end. Jennifer observed that, whatever had been troubling him, he was now concentrating wholly on matters in hand. 'We'll reopen this particular discussion when Leicester reports back. We'll have the fruits of your labours, Adrian.'

Clement grinned. His search of Shaun Grant's bedroom in St Oswald's House had certainly borne fruit. The haul amounted to a fair number of Ecstasy tablets, three car radios, two already identified by their owners, a pile of compact discs, their titles from a list of those stolen from a nearby branch of WHS. At this point of his account, Clement's face fell. 'We couldn't find anything that Dr Ahmed reported missing. The other stuff was all in the Grants' flat. The Stepneys' was clean. Mrs Stepney was all injured innocence and Shaun Grant's mother claimed Stepney had planted them. When I went up to the school to find the lads, Stepney was virtuously attending his games lesson. Grant was missing.'

Mitchell smiled. 'You'll be pleased to hear, then, that Shaun's little dabs have turned up – not on the car. He was careful not to touch that. They were on the wallet that he dropped down the side of the driver's seat.'

Clement was pleased but not surprised. 'He isn't a very quick learner.'

'Was the wallet nicked?'

Mitchell turned to answer Jennifer. 'We shall see. It was empty and not quite young Shaun's style. What did you pick up from the school?'

Jennifer shook her head. 'Not a lot. They're grateful we're taking the girl's absence seriously and anxious to co-operate, but, with school in session, no one's free. The head was called away to a playground fight. Mrs Barron had taken a girl to hospital because she'd fallen from a rope, fooling around in the gym that someone had forgotten to lock. Unless Nazreen has turned up in Leicester in the meantime, I'm seeing Greenwood and Mrs Barron after school. They said Nazreen doesn't have a boyfriend in school.'

'That might suggest she isn't opposed to marrying this Asif.'

'Or that she's just keeping a low profile, being careful not to antagonise her parents whilst she makes her own plans.'

'Well, that's your day filled in. Has Jane got the girls?' Jennifer's nod assured Mitchell that, if overtime were required, her daughters would be cared for. 'Adrian . . .'

'I know. Find Shaun Grant and follow up the wallet and the cache of goodies in his room.'

'I see I'm redundant. This team needs no one to organise it. I suppose you two have plans.' He eyed the two remaining girls.

Caroline hurried away, pleading a court appearance. Shakila regarded Mitchell, hopeful of another task that would allow her to remain with the team. He grinned at her. 'You'd better brush up your Urdu. You might need it again before we're done.'

She was indignant. 'I brush it up every day. It's all we speak at home.'

Mitchell was startled. Shakila's dress, though she always wore trousers, was conventionally English. Her speech was careful but fluent and idiomatic. He wondered what her family thought of her choice of career.

When the rest of the shift had trooped out, Mitchell found that Jennifer had remained behind. As if their conversation had not been interrupted by a twenty-minute briefing, she asked, 'What's wrong with her?'

Mitchell considered briefly, tempted to confide. He and Jennifer had been appointed as detective constables in the Cloughton force together. For most of the time since then, they had worked on the same team and on the same cases. During that time, Jennifer had become a close friend of Ginny and Ginny was going to need her friends. Nodding to Jennifer to sit down again, he told her as much as the Mitchells knew themselves.

On Tuesday afternoon, Derek Swindell collected the list Mrs Barron had left for him of the classes he was to supervise that afternoon. Trepidation gave way to relief as he studied it. Two double periods, the first a Year 7 group that was expecting a geography lesson and, after break, a Year 10 group of only ten pupils who had opted for his own subject, French.

The geography class was waiting quietly in double file outside its scheduled room. These pupils had been in the school for just two months, were not, so far, acquainted with Derek and knew that Mrs Barron would be teaching next door. Determined not to let them get the upper hand, he inspected them testily, ordering a couple of lads to straighten their ties and a girl to fasten her shoelaces.

He glared as they obeyed. Since he had heard the headmaster warning a student teacher that too much smiling at a class would be taken as a sign that she was anxious to ingratiate herself with them, he had not smiled in the classroom or corridor. Now, he picked on a boy at the back of the line, whose bulging duffel sack of books was weighing down one shoulder.

Embarrassed, the child tried not to giggle at the lecture on good deportment and the even distribution of loads.

By now, the erstwhile well-behaved class had become restive. Irritated, Derek ordered them to walk into the room smartly, heads up. The fourth boy to enter was a chancer. As he reached the door, he halted, saluted with a 'Sir!' and clicked his heels. When no retribution fell on him, the rest of the class followed suit, their gestures becoming increasingly exaggerated and insolent.

Next door, Mavis Barron heard Derek begin to shout. Sighing, she set her own class a short written exercise before tapping on Derek's door. 'I'm sorry to interrupt you, Mr Swindell, but I believe I may have left my mark book on your table.'

The two teachers looked around for the book that each knew would not be found. Then Mrs Barron apologised again and departed, having reminded the class that she was within ear-shot.

When she returned to the staff room at afternoon break, she found the headmaster pinning a card to the noticeboard. 'Agenda for tomorrow's staff meeting?'

He nodded, then looked harder at her. 'Something wrong?'

'Nothing unusual.' She described the fracas as Derek had battled with these youngest and, as yet, most docile of the school's charges. 'That lot had hardly begun to test their muscles yet.'

Greenwood sighed. 'I'll have a word with him. I need to see him this afternoon about another matter. You couldn't find anybody better?'

She grimaced. 'Anybody better recognises my voice when I ring them and immediately invents a prior commitment. I don't know what we can do.'

The head grinned. 'You could try persuading Keith Gordon that retirement won't suit him and that he needs to keep his hand in here. Joke!' he added, as her face lit up.

She shook her head as she went to pour herself coffee. 'Not to me it isn't.'

Mitchell knocked on Superintendent Carroll's door for the second time that day, this time to report, as required, on the shift's progress without its CI. He was determined, on this occasion, to be more conciliatory. Mitchell considered that, so far, the new super had struck a nice balance between authority and adaptability. He had not once quoted 'the way we did it in Birmingham', from where he had been transferred. Station rumour had it that a fellow officer in Birmingham, of equal rank, had taken the job in Newcastle that Carroll had coveted. If this were the case, he did not seem to be treating his appointment in Cloughton as a consolation prize.

Now, Mitchell sat in the chair his superintendent indicated and described the day's achievements, making as much as he dared of his dissatisfaction with the explanation offered for the absence of Nazreen Akram. He was not surprised to find that Carroll was unwilling to give him his head. Choosing his words with care, he was unable to control their angry tone, so that he argued his case in his usual aggressive manner. 'Even if the girl isn't abroad, she probably doesn't want to marry the chap her parents have picked. If she wants to get into medical school, she wouldn't go on holiday in term time. The school thinks she's being coerced.'

'If she's as clever as they say, she won't fail her exams because she's spent a week or so on a family visit.' Carroll's tone was still patient.

'But it might be just an excuse.'

'I understand.' The superintendent's tone was firmer. 'I'm not suggesting we cancel our request to Bradford, but I won't sanction any more hassling of the Akram family in the meantime. Our brief is to combat crime. If a clever girl from another culture is being denied what we consider a suitable education, and Cloughton produces one less doctor, no crime has been committed –'

'That's a matter of opinion.'

'It's a matter of rules and regulations. It's also a matter of common sense. From what I've heard there's very good integration between the native and Pakistani communities in Cloughton. We don't have any serious racial problems. We have Asians on the town council in reasonable proportion to their numbers in the town population. In pursuing a romantic crusade on behalf of one individual about which the public and the local press will love to spread rumours and take sides, we might well

44

lose more than we gain. At the moment we're managing to enjoy the best of both cultures in the life of the town and I'm very conscious of how rare that achievement is.'

The ringing of the telephone on the superintendent's desk forestalled Mitchell's objections. After a moment, he was glad that he had been given time to modify the voicing of his opposition. After a series of monosyllables and an expression of thanks, Carroll's lips curled into a half-smile. 'That was an apposite interruption for both of us. When is this girl supposed to have left for Leicester?'

'On Friday. Four days ago.'

'She must be walking then.'

Mitchell beamed. 'She isn't there. I thought as much.' He stopped, bit his tongue very hard, then asked, silkily, 'How do you want us to proceed now then, sir?'

4

Colin Greenwood shepherded an over-anxious mother out of his office and sank into the chair behind his desk, wondering whether the woman had listened to anything he had said. The people she really needed were Relate counsellors, or, possibly, the police, to help her deal with an ill-tempered, often violent husband. Their offspring was a surprisingly well-balanced girl who felt more concern for her parents than her father did for her.

Now, he awaited another inadequate. Resting his head in his hands, the soft skin of his palms soothing the tense facial muscles, he tried to summon up sufficient energy to find something suitable to say to Derek Swindell. The only useful message to give him was that he should get out of a profession for which he was totally unsuited. There was little to be gained from the coming interview. The man's whole approach to children was wrong. He had no ability to see the classroom situation from their point of view, or give them what they needed. Nor did he see that this was usually something quite different from what they wanted.

If the man was concerned about any aspect of the children in his charge, it was about their view of himself. Of course, their view of him was a problem. Most classes quickly and shrewdly assessed him and realised his anger was pretended. It fooled him and not them.

When Derek's peremptory rapping on his door disturbed his depressing analysis, Greenwood had found nothing to offer but the usual advice, relevant, helpful and resented. 'Keep them busy, Derek. Get them in with the minimum of fuss. Have worksheets ready for them, or go in before the lesson and put any necessary information on the board. Prepare clear instructions that they can't pretend to misunderstand – and don't threaten what you can't or are unwilling to do to discipline them.'

'But you know I do all that.'

Greenwood punished the lie with silence before proceeding to his next concern. 'I've had another complaint about your language on playground duty.'

'*Me* bloody swearing? You should hear . . .' Greenwood's glare caused the counter-accusation to peter out.

'It's interesting that pupils of all ages become very upset when teachers use what they consider to be bad language – even when they use far worse themselves five minutes later, and when their parents do too. They expect professional standards from school, maybe even get a sense of security from them. I've already given you an informal word of advice about this. Now, I'm giving you an official oral warning. Repetition will lead to further measures, possibly to our offering you no more work.'

Derek pushed his chair back angrily and made for the door, intending to slam it. He found that Greenwood had somehow got there before him and opened it for him, wishing him goodnight and watching his progress down the corridor.

Returning to his room Greenwood saw that his secretary had put a coffee tray on his desk and was disappearing through the door that communicated with her office. 'What . . .?' He put a hand to his head. 'Oh God, the police about Nazreen. Are they coming in here?'

The secretary's head reappeared. 'They're in Mavis's room. I've told them you won't be free for fifteen minutes. Mavis and Keith have plenty to tell them. Drink your coffee.'

Greenwood took ten of the fifteen minutes' respite this invaluable assistant had gained for him, then he joined the little conference in his deputy's room, feeling a refreshment out of proportion to the brief break. He knew he was solaced partly by her concern.

Mavis Barron, standing by a filing cabinet from which she had produced Nazreen's file, turned to greet him. At the end of this exhausting day, she was still immaculate. Her clothes were uncreased. The unlikely red hair lay as though sculpted to her well-shaped head. Her make-up had cracked, though, and lines of fatigue were scored into her cheeks and chin.

Sergeant Taylor had been given Mavis's visitors' chair and had the file open on her knee. Keith Gordon, spilling over the seating capacity of an upright chair, looked comfortably dishevelled, but no more so now than early in the day. He was looking over the sergeant's shoulder, pointing out the details of Nazreen's excellent academic record, the originals of letters exchanged between the school and her parents on the subject of her sixth-form studies and the conflict with her destiny as arranged by the family.

Jennifer picked up the most recent school photograph in the file and compared it with some snapshots she had been given from a scrapbook of school activities. Nazreen was not a pretty girl but she had an interesting face. The jaw was broad and the nose large but they were compensated for by gracefully arching brows. Jennifer thought it was a face that would win trust and confidence from her future patients.

Thick black hair was pulled tightly and unflatteringly back from her face and fastened at the nape of her neck in a heavy, untidy bunch that hung over one shoulder. The girl was slim but heavy-breasted. In the school photograph she wore the trousered version of the school uniform and none of the gold studs and chains favoured by the other Asian girls Jennifer had seen departing on the school buses a short while ago.

She enquired, as tactfully as possible, about the level of teaching available at the Colin Hewitt for a girl hoping to enter medical school. Keith Gordon answered her, good-naturedly. 'When we interview teaching candidates, I imagine the governors' chief concerns are good discipline and an empathy with our type of pupil, but we aren't idiots. Many of us are well qualified and delighted to have a chance to exercise our mental muscles – and there's Cynthia.'

'Cynthia?'

Mavis Barron wrinkled her nose. 'As a supply teacher she's bad news but she's well qualified. There isn't a specialist biologist on the regular staff and Cynthia's a good communicator so long as her pupil is anxious to learn. As far as we can, we find her some time with Nazreen when she's called in. I've heard that she's coaching her at home out of the goodness of her heart. The family would never pay for it just for a daughter. Cynthia admires Nazreen and is sorry for her.'

Colin Greenwood took up the account. 'The grandfather was a consultant neurologist, yet her grandmother speaks no English and rarely leaves the house. Both parents have come to all our parents' evenings so far, though the mother just smiles and never speaks.'

Jennifer looked up from her notebook. 'Does anyone here know much about these relatives in Leicester? Or the intended husband, Asif?'

They all looked at Keith Gordon who shrugged. 'Only that they exist.'

'Would her friends know more?'

Mrs Barron smiled. 'Nazreen isn't exactly gregarious. There was another Pakistani girl, Amara Mahmood, who was her friend until Amara left us in the summer. She's working now at the supermarket on Blake Street. If you want to talk to her, I'm afraid you'll have to start from there because she's moved from the address in our records.'

'So, who does Nazreen spend her time with now?'

They all spoke at once, then left the explanation to Mrs Barron. 'We've talked about this before. Nazreen seems to spend lunchtimes with a girl who . . . well, to quote Keith, is not a proper sixth-former.'

Gordon grinned. 'I don't mean it as a reflection on the girl's morals. She's taking extra GCSEs rather than As and her parents are probably just keeping her at school as a way of keeping her off the streets. She'll probably fail all of them, but with capitation controlling income, you don't refuse to take in sixth-formers. Anyhow, none of us can understand what the two of them see in each other.'

'What's this girl's name?'

'Rebecca Sparks.' Mrs Barron had gone back to her filing cabinet. 'We do have a current address for her, of course. We've already asked her if she knows where Nazreen is but she says not. She's a bit lightweight academically but she's a very straightforward, truthful girl.'

Keith Gordon eased himself gently off his protesting chair. 'She wouldn't have the nous to lie convincingly. And one thing we can promise you. If there's any gossip the rest of us have failed to pick up, Miss Sparks is your woman.'

Rebecca Sparks was obviously disappointed when she opened the door and found only Jennifer waiting outside. She seemed to be preparing herself for a night on the town and peered at the warrant offered for her inspection through spiky lashes. She took her visitor into the kitchen and proved to be very willing to gossip and speculate on any matter put before her.

Throughout their conversation, she showed a casual sympathy for Nazreen and cheerfully paraded her prejudices against and misjudgements of the Pakistani culture without the slightest intention to wound.

The friendship that puzzled her teachers she explained without being asked. 'We have this arrangement, see? I'm older than Naz, had to stay in Year 11 and repeat my GCSEs. I'm eighteen. My birthday was two weeks ago . . .' Jennifer's niggling doubts about interviewing a minor without her parents present were gratefully relinquished. '. . . So, I've passed my driving test. My dad's promised me a little car of my own if I pass my exams. I often get stuck with my work, though, because I'm thick and she gets stuck with hers because the school hasn't got the right teachers.'

Rebecca sniffed and walked over to a fridge that was masquerading as one of the limed oak kitchen units. Pulling out a can, she offered it to Jennifer. 'Want a Coke?' Jennifer refused politely. The hope of coffee as an alternative receded as Rebecca pulled the ring and drank. '. . . So, she comes here and helps me with my coursework for a bit and then I drive her to Miss Summers' house and she helps Naz. Afterwards, I pick her up and take her back home.

'I thought she was a bit of a wimp when I first got to know her, not having the gorm to stand up to her dad, even to let her do her schoolwork. When she explained the family set-up, though, I saw what she meant. They have a sort of Asian mafia, and when she doesn't do just what they've worked out for her, all the family gang up. That includes dozens of men from Birmingham and Leicester, cousins and other relations.

'I don't know if they actually beat her up. I've not noticed anything, but you can't see marks on her skin like you could on mine. Anyway, they have all these rules about having themselves all covered up. P'raps all these Paki families bully the women and that's why they make them wear saris and things – so they don't get into trouble for knocking them about.

'Shahid gets by at his posh school because Naz does his

homework and helps him learn for tests and things. They don't mind her being clever enough for that but her dad's dead narked that she's got all the brains and his precious sons are dead thick. He's thick himself. He's only a taxi driver. Naz is the one who's got the grandad's brains.'

'What do you know about Asif?'

'The boyfriend? I saw him once when he came over for a family do. He's quite dishy and Naz . . . well, as my mum says, she's no oil painting. She's not exactly a barrel of laughs to make up for it either. I'd snap him up if I was her. Still, if he didn't turn her on . . .' Rebecca shrugged and confided in Jennifer, pityingly, 'She isn't really into boys. She's still at the stage of having crushes. She follows Miss Pearson about as if they were in love. Still, she's only sixteen and they don't grow up as quick as we do.'

'Depends on your criteria.'

'What?'

'Asian girls, as a rule, are very mature at sixteen. They prepare themselves very seriously for marriage. You just mean Nazreen isn't streetwise, hasn't played the field, doesn't rebel against her parents.'

'That's right.'

'So, it depends what standards you judge by.'

Rebecca struggled to be fair. 'S'pose so. And Naz has rebelled a bit. She won't marry Asif and she's dead set on getting into medical school.'

'Does she have no support from her grandfather?'

'Not really. She shows him her homework sometimes and starts talking about it. He gets dead keen and starts telling her stuff, then remembers she's only a girl and stamps off. She says it's a game she plays. Boring sort of game!'

'I know you've told the people at school that you don't know where Nazreen is, but what would your guess be?'

'Haven't a clue. Last time I saw her, apart from school, we were just doing my essay. Then she was telling me about a book old Summers was going to lend her. That was more than a week since.' She anticipated Jennifer's question. 'She said what it was but I can't remember. She borrowed a lot of them and they were all boring, all science, not proper reading books.'

'Which night was it?'

'Monday last week. The lessons are Mondays and Fridays, but Naz can't get away always. She has to help at home. She didn't go last Friday, didn't come to school either. Then, this Monday, she missed again and old Summers rang me. We decided she must be ill and I said I'd find out.'

'And?'

'They said she'd gone off to see her relations.'

The front doorbell rang. Without pausing to excuse herself, Rebecca rushed to answer the summons and admit the visitor. Jennifer, peering unobtrusively into the hall, saw a greasy-haired youth. The two youngsters were involved in enthusiastic and very physical greetings. Knowing when to cut her losses, Jennifer took her leave. She might seek out Rebecca again when there was a chance of engaging her full attention.

Scribbling her report on what Rebecca Sparks had told her, Jennifer wondered whether she should visit Cynthia Summers before clocking off for the day. Then her interest in the fate of the missing girl lost its fight against her greater desire to spend more than a few fleeting moments with her two young daughters before they went to bed. If Benny wanted her to interview the woman he would send her later.

Mitchell called into his office to scoop up the day's pile of reports from his desk. Stuffing them into his case, he made for his car and home. He had arranged for his own mother to sit with the sleeping twins whilst the rest of the family visited the Brownes.

In his imagination the delivery of a suspended death sentence had given Hannah a corpse-like appearance and a lethargic, defeated manner. It was a shock to him to find her looking and behaving very much as she had the last time he had seen her. It was Virginia's father, recovered somewhat from his migraine attack, who looked ghastly. They enquired first how he was feeling. It was easier.

Once the preliminary greetings were over, Mitchell sent his children to play upstairs. Declan was not pleased and regarded his father solemnly. 'Are you going to talk about something you don't want us to hear?'

'Yes, we are.'

'Will you tell us about it later?'

Mitchell glanced at Virginia who answered, 'Some of it.'

Declan nodded, satisfied that the promise would be kept. When Caitlin remained immobile, staring huge-eyed at the adults, he came back from the doorway and led her by the hand from the room.

Watching them, Mitchell realised that his children represented a further dimension of the horrific situation in which the family found itself. Blearily, Browne regarded his son-in-law. 'We thought it was a social call. You seem to have an agenda.'

Virginia had tried to prepare herself for any and every reaction she could imagine her parents might show. Now she spoke with some asperity. 'Of course we wanted to see you. But we also wanted to begin to work out what we're going to do.'

Hannah had spent the first eighteen years of Virginia's life, those she had lived in the family home, cooling heated arguments between her husband and her daughter. It was not a function she was going to relinquish yet. 'We're going to do nothing. A new aspect of my life, our lives, has opened up and all of us are going to experience it.'

They regarded her in silence. Virginia broke it. 'You can't just dismiss it like that! You must feel –'

Hannah reached for Virginia's hand. 'I feel a whole spectrum of things, fear, anger, a strange sort of curiosity, even an odd sort of exhilaration at the challenge – oh, and hope, that won't be quashed even though it's been relentlessly explained to us that there isn't any.'

Virginia pulled her hand away. 'I don't believe I'm hearing this.'

Hannah smiled. 'The news wasn't such a shock to me as to you. I've been speculating about something similar for quite a time.' She looked across at her husband, who had sat since the children's departure with his head in his hands. 'I know you feel quite differently, Tom. For you, it's simply a tragedy because, for you, it's not an experience. You're a spectator. You have to cope with all the frustration of not being actively involved.'

Browne remained immobile and Hannah turned back to her daughter and son-in-law. She smiled. 'Don't worry, I'm not promising not to become angry as things progress. I know all the theory that's just been explained to us will amount to lots more infuriating curbs on all the activities we've always taken for granted . . .'

Virginia turned to Mitchell and spoke in an undertone. 'She sounds as if she's delivering a speech.'

Her mother laughed aloud. 'That's because I am. I wanted to be able to explain to you just how I felt and I've spent most of the day working out how to do it.'

'Have you . . . Did the consultant say . . .?' Virginia fell silent as she realised that her question might well dissipate her mother's fragile optimism.

'For goodness' sake, Ginny, stop going all round the houses. You've never done it before. Ask what you want to know. We probably won't know either, but if we do, we'll tell you.'

The sharp tone restored Virginia's presence of mind. So far, she still had the mother she knew. 'OK, but it's not easy to ask your mother when she's going to die.' Virginia's tone was more aggressive than she had intended.

Browne raised his head and spoke thickly. 'The answer's a load of damned statistics. X per cent die in three years, Y per cent in two, the lucky few in five or more. Hannah's age is against her. It's probably between two and three.'

'Very occasionally the disease can appear to stop progressing and become stable for a long period.' Virginia tried to assess the degree of desperation in her mother's voice.

Mitchell thought the silence that followed felt disbelieving and filled it. 'Why has it taken the doctors so long to decide?'

Hannah answered smoothly. 'I asked that. The answer was a string of smug phrases that included "diagnosis by exclusion", "sophisticated tests" and, most poetic, "the investigation of time".' Her giggle verged on hysteria.

Suddenly, Browne leapt up. 'God, Hannah! Why can't you just cry like a normal woman?' He left the room, then the house, slamming all the doors. Mitchell slipped out after him. Virginia put her arms round Hannah who, as she was bidden, began to cry.

Early on Wednesday, Shaun Grant woke to find himself not as stiff and uncomfortable as he had expected to be after a night spent on the Crossley Park allotments. It was where he always went when he knew he had driven his mother to the point where she might rat on him to the fuzz 'for his own good'.

He'd noticed that this end plot had been taken over by a chap who arrived most afternoons in psychedelic waterproofs. He must be the one who had done up the old shed – almost made a Cloughton version of the Ritz out of it. The armchair was shabby but a sight more comfortable than the black plastic jobs his mother had bought on the never for the flat. There were all the mod cons here, a Primus stove, a little Calor gas heater, even matches left ready.

Shaun was pretty sure this wasn't the place where the bloke had his five-minute tea break to rest from his digging. No, it was a place to escape to, probably out of the way of his nagging wife. He hoped their rows wouldn't get too serious or the bloke would be coming here one night and finding his emergency lodgings had been double booked.

He began tidying up after himself, leaving the door ajar. The wind was blowing in and nearly freezing the knobs off him but he had to get rid of the pong of fish and chips and cool the place down. If the old codger realised he was sharing his hideaway he'd put a better lock on it. He had a critical look at the old one. He'd managed to force it without breaking it. Better be on the safe side, though. He rubbed soil into a couple of shiny new scratches as he considered his position.

For now, he'd well reached the end of the rope his mother allowed him. What she could do with was another bloke. She had too much time on her hands to keep an eye on him. She was easier to fix when she had a distraction, didn't keep getting delusions about making a good citizen out of him. For a few moments he considered going into school. It would get him a few Brownie points both there and at home.

A glance at his watch told him he'd be late, even if a bus came straight away. He was meeting Adele at lunchtime. He wasn't going to traipse all the way there just to trail back again. Besides, no point in swanning round the bus station while that rozzer was still looking for him. Not that he had anything to do with the job Clement was working on. Soft sort of name for a cop.

It made Shaun bloody annoyed to be suspected of doing doctors' cars. He had the common sense to know you had to go for chemists to get enough stuff to be worth selling. You'd only find enough in a doc's bag for your own use and Shaun was having none of that game. He was going to be rich and powerful, not mess up his life, in debt to the dealers himself.

He helped himself to two custard creams from the opened packet on the heater, then carefully folded the top of the packet under the rest as he'd found it. Then he filled last night's Coke can from the tap two plots away and drank the odd-tasting water, all the time keeping a lookout over the houses whose back gardens faced him. He didn't want some fat cow reporting she'd seen him whilst she was pegging her knickers on the line.

He wondered where Jonno would be. His mother should be at work by now. He took his own mother's mobile phone from his anorak pocket, chuckling as he thought about the twenty well-spent minutes 'helping' in her pointless search for it. He punched the numbers hopefully but Ma Stepney's voice answered him, rough and hoarse, and he hastily cancelled the call. Oh well, no cosy morning there. He'd have to trawl round the shops instead. See if he could nick something to give Adele and put her in a good mood.

'It looks as though the *Clarion* can only get hold of the one photo of this Rick Robson. It's the same picture as yesterday.' Browne moved the double page spread from which he was reading so that Hannah could examine it.

The man's face had been enlarged, leaving less space for the garish neckerchief and none for the sequin. 'RICK ROBSON RETURNS TO CLOUGHTON' was the banner headline. The editor had paid his readers the compliment of expecting them to have remembered the biographical details with which they had been regaled the previous day. Below the picture, therefore, a small paragraph sufficed to tell the further news.

Browne pulled the paper back to a position where he could read it without the aid of his spectacles. Neither he nor Hannah acknowledged that the reading aloud was necessitated by her no longer being able to hold the broadsheet pages up for long enough to read a whole article.

'"Veteran rock star Rick Robson has announced his intention of making a whistle-stop tour of Great Britain with his intended bride. His agent told our reporter, "The fact that Cloughton is included in a list of such prestigious venues as Manchester, Glasgow and London is all down to the Cloughton lady who first organised and still runs the Rick Robson Appreciation Society of Great Britain." Negotiations are in progress which it is hoped will lead to a concert being arranged in Cloughton. Details of the date and venue will be published as soon as they are available."'

'Riveting!' Hannah's tone was deadpan.

'We've got our little mention, I see. "Concern is growing for the safety of a sixteen-year-old Cloughton girl. Nazreen Akram left Cloughton on Friday to spend a few days with relatives in Leicester." Ah, but did she? "She is the granddaughter of Mr Ibrahim Akram, a consultant physician at the Cloughton Royal Infirmary until his retirement in 1992. Nazreen's headmaster, Mr Colin Greenwood of the Colin Hewitt Comprehensive School, told our reporter that Nazreen is a clever girl with every prospect of eventually becoming a doctor. 'She is not a streetwise girl at all,' he said last night. 'She is not the type to cause her family or her teachers any worry by running away.' Nazreen was about to be married to Mr Asif Patel of Leicester. He is a distant cousin. A reporter from the *Leicester Mercury* told our reporter, 'Mr Patel is out of his mind with worry.'"'

'What a perfect piece of tabloid journalism.'

'It's a pernicious bit of scandal-mongering, full of sloppy slang.' Browne stretched his aching arms. 'Anyway, the *Clarion* isn't a tabloid.'

'I agree, on all counts. It gets better as it goes on. The fact that the girl is missing is a valid piece of news. The mention of her age suggests that she's vulnerable, which is fair and relevant. Then it gets tastier. Her grandfather is rich and well respected so the snobs are interested. The quotation – probably misquotation – of her headmaster suggests both that she's run away and that she won't be able to cope.'

'He says he thinks she hasn't run off.'

'That's right. Then, to stir up some racial controversy, an arranged marriage is mentioned with the suggestion that the girl's desperate to avoid it. It's tucked in right next to the "excellent scholar" bit to remind us that the Asians are reputed not to educate girls and that Nazreen's brains will be wasted. And all without the word Pakistani being mentioned. Brilliant!'

Hannah spilled some coffee and they both averted their eyes from the spreading stain. 'Find something a bit more cheerful.'

Browne put the paper down and got up. 'That's your job. Ginny will have something cheerful to say when she arrives. If I don't get a move on, I'll find Benny's taken over my office again.'

Some half-hour later, whistling tunelessly, Mitchell made his way along the corridor to Browne's office. Mentally rehearsing the items to be dealt with at this morning's briefing, he flung open the door, then stopped short. Browne sat behind his own desk, pale-faced still, but otherwise looking much as usual. Mitchell's first reaction was a shaming anger at the idea of his CI's reassertion of control of the current cases.

Browne waved away his son-in-law's apology for not knocking. 'I should have rung you.'

'It doesn't matter.' Mitchell dropped the small sheaf of reports of the previous day's activities on the desk. 'I took these home last night. I wanted to get straight over to your place and read them later.' Refusing to analyse his motive, he asked, 'Are you sure this is where you want to be?'

'It's where Hannah wants me to be. Apparently everything has to remain normal.'

'Well, she can't just sit around for however long it is, just waiting for things to get worse. Normality sounds the best plan to me, so long as we can keep it up.'

Browne rewarded this with a definite smile. 'Thanks for the "we".' He pulled the reports towards him. 'Find someone to rustle up some coffee while I glance at these.'

Mitchell's face and spirits fell. This was relegation and, in the circumstances, he had better accept it gracefully. 'Quicker to do it myself.' He left the CI to acquaint himself with the details of the drugs thefts and the search for Nazreen Akram and went to spread the news of his return.

Five minutes later, Mitchell returned with a huge tray bearing two jugs of coffee, a white snake of paper cups and a mini-mountain of sugar sachets. As he'd expected, the office was now full, the shift sitting and standing where it could. Browne had placed himself beside Jennifer, leaving his own chair empty. He waved Mitchell to the position behind his desk. 'You'd better carry on running the show, at least until I've caught up with the flow of it. You can pour everyone's coffee first, just to keep you humble.'

Mitchell had filled two of the flimsy cups before the task was taken from him by Shakila. He did not regret the fifteen minutes spent in procuring and drinking the coffee. In some way it seemed to represent their solidarity with their CI and did away with the need for embarrassing words of sympathy. Now, he quickly called the meeting to order. Picking up on his change of tone, the shift pulled out notebooks and prepared to offer their reports.

Clement was thankful that he had run into Shaun in the amusement arcade that morning and reported the conversation they had had. 'He genuinely seems to know nothing about the job done on Dr Ahmed's car. He's admitted to buying the Es in a pub, intending to sell them on. He says he found Ahmed's car after it had been done and took the radio from it.'

'And the wallet?'

'Picked it up, found it empty and dropped it again. He came out with that before I asked him about it.'

'Sounds like covering his tracks.' Mitchell turned next to Jennifer who condensed her interview with Rebecca Sparks to a few sentences.

'Right. Caroline and Shakila's set-to with Mrs Akram seems to be common knowledge so we'll have a general airing of views on how to proceed with the rather delicate Akram situation.'

'Delicate isn't a word that often falls from your lips.'

Mitchell ignored Jennifer's taunt and turned to his CI. 'What do you make of it all, coming fresh to the facts?'

'Her relatives say they were expecting her?'

'Yes, but they would.'

Browne frowned. 'Depends what they'd been told by both the family and the police.'

'And which came first.' Browne let Clement elaborate his point. 'If the Leicester people said the Akrams claimed the girl was visiting, they'd have wanted to back them up, but they wouldn't know the best thing to say. On the other hand, if the family in Cloughton alerted them before the Leicester police called, they might be trying to make us think something happened to her on the way . . .' Observing the shift's bewildered expressions, Clement wished he had allowed the CI to complete his observations.

Caroline, at least, seemed to have understood him. 'Maybe they're all telling the truth and Nazreen did set off for Leicester but never arrived.'

'Would the Akrams have let her go on her own?'

They all looked at Shakila to answer Mitchell's question. She considered for a moment. 'Probably, so long as they thought she was being co-operative about the marriage.'

'Or the family in Cloughton have spirited her away when she objected.'

'Or the family in Cloughton have sent her for the Leicester lot to sort out and they've dealt with her in some way for being uncooperative.'

Suggestions continued but now no one was listening to anyone else. Mitchell called for order and reached for his action sheets. 'Adrian, I want you to keep digging at Shaun Grant.'

'I don't think I'm going to get much more out of him.'

'Then try his little friend Stepney.' Ignoring Clement's glum expression, Mitchell dispatched the rest of his officers. Caroline was to see Miss Summers. Shakila he would take with him to Leicester. He grinned at his sergeant. 'I hope you've got some shopping to do. Make sure you take your basket of bargains to Amara Mahmood's checkout.' The two remaining DCs regarded him hopefully.

Mitchell glanced at Browne. 'Is it too early to go on the knocker round the Akrams' neighbourhood?' He decided without waiting for a reply. 'No. We'll do it. We can't carry on pussy-footing round a clash of cultures. For all we know, somebody might have done away with the girl.'

5

Derek Swindell thankfully dismissed his Year 10 class of a dozen boys who had been timetabled to do woodwork. In fact, they had been filling in – or, in most cases, failing to fill in – a worksheet left by their absent teacher. The boys had made no attempt to hide their displeasure.

'This is supposed to be a practical lesson.'

'Why can't we get on with our tables?'

'We've got to get them finished for our assessment!' Everyone in the room knew the reason was that Derek could not be trusted to ensure that potentially lethal tools would be used only on the pieces of wood the boys were shaping.

'Why do we have to do this rubbish?' Derek tried to remember exactly when his pupils had begun to omit from their questions and comments the at least respectful-sounding 'sir'. He knew it had been very early in his acquaintance with them.

'This is the work Mr Wardley has left for you.' Derek was shouting already. 'If you don't like it, then save your objections for him.'

There had been a momentary silence as they contemplated this idea, then a bellow of laughter at the idea of addressing Mr Wardley in this way. Derek collected the sheets that the boys had left randomly scattered about the room and put them in his own briefcase. He baulked at letting Ben Wardley see the standard of work they had offered him. He would say he had marked it himself. Ben wouldn't follow it up. He'd know what happened.

Derek wondered if his problem was simply a lack of experience with older children. After all, his training was for juniors. He knew this was not the reason. It was living with Sue that undermined him. As he got into the car to drive home for lunch, he knew he would have to find another way to get rid of her.

Hannah's consultant having advised that she should begin her physiotherapy immediately, Virginia had spent the morning at the Cloughton Royal Infirmary, getting up early, taking her two eldest children to school, delivering the twins to Benny's mother and collecting her own. She made every effort to behave as usual but conversation in the car was stilted. Hannah desperately wanted to feel that she was the same wife, mother and grand-mother she had been before her diagnosis. Virginia felt, however, that she was dealing with an invalid, a stranger who wanted to push herself into the family. Hating herself, she prattled about the amusing things the twins had done and that Declan and Caitlin had said. Hannah valiantly described, in mind-numbing detail, her plans for next summer's flowerbeds.

Suddenly, Virginia knew it must stop. 'Shut up! You hate gardening. Tell me you're scared. Tell me you're furious.'

Hannah smiled. 'I'm not scared yet. I still don't believe that I can't beat it. I can't even get really angry, though I'm beginning to be pretty annoyed about what it's doing to your father.'

Virginia thought for a moment. 'That's because he does believe it. Give him a few days. He'll pick himself up.' She parked neatly, climbed out of the car and opened the passenger door. Seeing that the weakness in Hannah's arms prevented her from obtaining the leverage necessary to transfer her weight to her feet, she hauled on the nearest arm till her mother stood upright. Then she stood back and watched. Hannah seemed to be walk-ing normally as she made for the hospital entrance. Virginia followed.

'Stop staring at me!'

Virginia was beginning to learn the rules and offered no apology. 'I'll have to. You don't want us to keep asking how you are, what you can do. You can tolerate an objective discussion of your prospects but not having to give a detailed commentary on your physical feelings. Fine, but that means I have to watch you, to see what I need to do for you. You'll have to choose one or the other.'

Hannah nodded without speaking, accepting the choice, con-firming that Virginia had discerned what, for her mother, was the lesser evil. A nurse bore her into the nether regions of the building whilst Virginia waited in the visitors' cafeteria. To her surprise, her mother reappeared in less than half an hour, look-ing genuinely cheerful. She enquired for the good news.

'He asked me what my chief immediate worry was.'

'He being the consultant? And?'

'I told him how your father's taking things, about the return of his migraine. He summoned a physician who gave me a couple of prescriptions for him.' Virginia grinned. 'One tries to stop the attacks, the other treats them if they still happen. They should keep him at work. I don't want to leave him out of a job.'

Virginia laughed aloud. 'Did you get around to what you had actually come for?'

Hannah smugly displayed a card that listed a string of appointments. 'I like the physiotherapist, though I did think it was a bit early for the not particularly comforting reassurance that, when hospital visits become impossible, she'll come to me. Now you can buy me a large coffee.'

'At these prices, you can have the whole urnful.' Virginia went back to the counter, wondering how brittle was Hannah's good humour. Choosing to go along with it for the moment, she allowed herself to be swept along to the hospital pharmacy to collect her father's pills. The place was very crowded but eventually they were attended to by a middle-aged woman wearing an inappropriately lacy cardigan. Hannah spoke to her daughter out of the side of her mouth. 'Just one too many buttons left undone. Necklaces of incipient wrinkles aren't what she intended to reveal.'

Delighted to find her elegant, fashion-conscious mother in such good form, Virginia chuckled. She watched the woman, wondering idly why she was not wearing the regulation starched white overall that more suitably covered the other three women who moved busily between counter and shelves, filing prescriptions on simple wire spikes and fetching the medicines that the patients required. Then she wondered for how much longer her mother would be able to do up her own buttons.

Colin Greenwood was snatching a quiet cup of tea in his office before going, as he made a point of going every day, to eat with his pupils and many of his staff in the school dining hall. Through his window he saw Miss Summers' Escort arrive at the entrance to the staff car park. He had not realised that she had been called in today and he mildly berated himself. He took a pride in keeping his finger on the school's pulse.

When Mavis Barron tapped on the door and came in, Greenwood nodded at the scene through his window. She grinned and they watched the small car come to a halt, then back slowly away.

'She seems in two minds about staying.'

Greenwood laughed. 'The car park's fairly full and the playground's pretty crowded. She's probably unwilling to provide the entertainment they're expecting. She usually needs a thirteen-point turn to get that vehicle into a space. As you know, I ask staff not to park in the road just outside school but, in her case, I turn a blind eye.'

'I wonder what Adele Batty is plotting.' The two teachers watched the girl who lolled against the gate to the yard, surrounded by her usual crowd of admirers. She too had noticed Miss Summers' arrival and drew her followers' attention to it with a derisive jerk of her head. They saw Frankie Leonard, prompted by a poke from Adele, go over and speak to the woman. Something about the body language of both pupil and teacher told them that the girl was being insolent.

Mrs Barron sounded both puzzled and perturbed. 'It's not in Frankie's nature to be unpleasant. She's acting under orders from Adele. We're going to have to clip that young woman's wings before long. Oh God! Here comes Swindell to sort things out.'

They continued to watch as the two supply staff exchanged a few words. 'Mutual commiserations,' Mrs Barron observed. 'Come on, let's eat.'

Adele waited for the headmaster and his deputy to leave the main block and walk across the yard to the dining-room before she slipped through the gate, barely in time to catch the bus to town for her illegal meeting with Shaun Grant.

It was almost lunchtime before Martin Crossley found himself on the last stage of his train journey back to Cloughton. He wished he had driven, or at least checked the train times more carefully. He had known he would have to change at Sheffield and Leeds but had not expected to have to wait three-quarters of an hour in each place. Now his stomach was awash with coffee he had not even wanted when he was drinking it. It had been too cold and too wild, though, to sit out on the platforms.

He had hoped, when he had come to Cloughton on Monday evening for his induction day on Tuesday, that the weather there was an aberration even for Yorkshire in November, but the wind still terrorised. A glance through the window showed him three horses, huddled in the lee of a field wall but with manes flying into the air. When the train had stopped, seemingly for ever, just outside Leeds, he had seen a great tree, fallen across a household driveway, and had wondered how the flustered-looking man in a business suit would get to work.

When he had left his digs on Tuesday morning, Crossley had vowed that nothing would induce him to return to that poky dark room in the run-down B&B that had been recommended at the tourist information kiosk. He shuddered now at the thought of its greyish sheets, its bathroom along the landing with its yodelling occupant, and, when the aspiring musician had eventually let him in, its cracked washbasin and lethal-looking gas water heater. Now he was changing his mind. Somewhere else might be just as bad and time spent inspecting overnight accommodation would leave less for finding a suitable permanent place.

Not that he had any reason now for moving so far away. This morning's letter had put paid to any hopes he had had for their new start in Cloughton. It had also explained all the things that had been puzzling him, why all his detective work had failed to identify the man who had replaced him in Cherry's life. He felt his eyes fill and scrubbed his face angrily, thankful that the only other occupant of the long carriage sat several seats away.

He blew his nose and considered his position. Should he give back word to the Colin Hewitt Comprehensive? He had liked Colin Greenwood, though. He seemed that rare thing in education, a good man, and deserved better than to be let down at this stage of the school year. He would find a house in Cloughton and move into it. He could be miserable here as well as any-where.

Clement had spent a frustrating one and a half hours looking for

Shaun Grant. With waning enthusiasm he had visited the boy's home, his school and the amusement arcade behind the market. Finally, in despair, he had returned to consult the CI.

Browne's new instructions exceeded Clement's hopes. Uniformed officers were to take over his search whilst he was to interrupt Faisal Akram at Heptinstall & Hudson. So, now he had managed to get himself transferred to the more interesting of his shift's current enquiries. One object of his visit was to keep Akram from returning home in his lunch hour to obstruct the search there that Superintendent Carroll had sanctioned that morning.

Two young Pakistanis were on duty behind the counter and Clement approached the one who was not occupied with a customer. Sod's law ruled and he was unsurprised to be told that Akram was the other. A whispered consultation led to the customer being taken over by the colleague. Then Akram disappeared into a back region. Clement tensed, ready to chase, but he could hear Akram explaining to his superior that he had abandoned his customer. So much for his mother's proud assertion that the business was his own.

Clement listened idly to the business being transacted in the office. The customer had been recognised.

'It's Mr Crossley, isn't it. You were in a couple of months ago, I remember. You're the new teacher coming to the Colin Hewitt. Let me see – you wanted a small house in a good area and a bit of easily managed garden for when the babies come along. Right?'

'Wrong. You remembered well enough but things have changed, I'm afraid.'

Faisal Akram reappeared and went to his stool behind the counter to await Clement's questions.

'Isn't there somewhere a bit more private?' Akram shook his head, his face surly at this revelation of his lack of privilege. Clement took the customer's chair and asked without preliminaries, 'When was the last time you saw your sister?'

'Thursday evening.'

'What was she doing?'

'The usual things girls do when they're going away. Packing, checking things.'

Clement felt his way carefully. 'Most Pakistani families I know are very protective of their young women. Was no one travelling with Nazreen?'

Akram's head jerked up. 'Dad's taxi was taking her to the station. Asif was meeting her in Leicester. I –'

'So, why didn't Asif get in touch when she wasn't on the train?'

'I can't read minds. Why don't you ask him?'

As Akram's tone became more aggressive, Clement tried to sound sympathetic and reasonable. 'She would have had to change trains in Leeds and Sheffield. Were you happy to have her hanging around station platforms on her own?'

Akram appeared not to hear. Following his gaze, Clement realised that he was listening to his colleague's dealings with Mr Crossley. The enterprising salesman was doing his best to persuade his customer that he should soothe his sorrows with hard work and his sleepless nights with the resulting weariness, with the bonus of financial profit.

'Why not do up a semi-derelict property? I can offer you just the thing. A bit out of the way, but if you're not feeling sociable just now you won't mind that. It would be worth a fortune, this little place, with a bit more work done on it, and basically it's quite sound.' The salesman was on his knees, pulling files from a cabinet drawer.

Akram cut in. 'Shepherd's Rest? It isn't on the books any more.'

The man looked surprised. 'Who made the sale?'

'No one. It's been withdrawn from the books.'

Nothing daunted, Akram's colleague abandoned his first plan and began offering Crossley a choice of 'easy-maintenance' flats. 'Of course, you're coming to a new job. You'll need time to get the hang of it, especially at that place. You'll be looking for something easy to manage . . .'

Akram seemed to be availing himself of a lesson in sales technique. Clement raised his voice and repeated his question.

Akram's resentment was becoming more overt. 'She's capable of climbing out of one train into another. She isn't stupid!'

'Far from it, from what I've heard.'

'A bit too damned clever!'

'For your convenience, perhaps.' Clement had not expected the comment to soothe but was taken aback by such a display of bad temper in the man's own place of work. The manager came out of his sanctum and ordered both Clement and Akram to leave. Clement was happy to accept the banishment and offered Akram a choice. 'The station? Or the pub?'

Clement stayed on in the Oak and Acorn when Akram finally departed. It had been unclear whether his employer's dismissal of him held good for his immediate or his long-term future. Akram had issued threats to sue the Cloughton force if the episode in his office had cost him his job. He ordered another pint. His lunch hour had been spent in the course of duty and he deserved a quiet half-hour to gather his thoughts.

These revolved largely round the question of how he might finally jettison his search for the two young car thieves and become an accepted member of what might well turn out to be a murder enquiry. Ironically, the first person he saw as he was leaving the pub was Jonathan Stepney.

To the old ladies of Cloughton, Jonno was the one of the pair more to be feared, with his half-shaven head and the weird dyed tuft waving about on top. This week it was a fetching shade of purple, Clement noted. Ladies who had no objection to purple hair and jewellery were suspicious of the huge boots and loud voice and horrified by the foul language. Further acquaintance of the boys soon proved that the real villain was the more ordinary-looking Shaun. Though longish and greasy, his hair was still its natural brown but his father had frequently seen the inside of Armley jail and Shaun usually carried a knife.

Stepney was on the other side of the road, walking in Clement's direction. The DC moved to the edge of the kerb but the lights had just changed and a stream of traffic thwarted him. Waiting for it to pass, he caught the lad's eye. The last vehicle in the stream was a high-sided lorry that obliterated Clement's view across the road. When it had passed, Stepney was nowhere to be seen.

Clifford Summers apologised very profusely for being away from the house when DC Caroline Webster had called earlier in the day. She wondered why the old man should feel the need when he had had no reason to expect her. He was effusively friendly. 'Are you a friend of Cynthia's? It's very seldom I'm away from the house. I wish it weren't so. Would you like tea?'

Caroline hesitated and said, hoping he would not consider the implied question impolite, that it depended on how soon Cynthia was likely to appear.

'She'll be back directly school's over.' He glanced at his watch. 'In about twenty-five minutes.'

'Then I'd love some tea.' She could see that the old man's movements were painful as he propelled himself carefully to the kitchen but she hesitated to offer unwelcome help. Cynthia had evidently laid out a tray for him since Caroline could hear no clatter of crockery above the singing of the kettle.

After another minute, Mr Summers reappeared. 'Would you mind awfully just carrying the tray through and putting it on the table? I can manage it but maybe not without spilling.' Caroline went into the kitchen, praying that she herself would be able to deliver the heavy, ornate tray to the sitting-room with its embroidered cloth still spotless. She offered to pour the tea and saw that he expected this. It was the woman's job.

As they drank satisfying strong Indian – she had feared Earl Grey – he explained that this morning Cynthia had taken him to keep his monthly appoinment with his consultant at the Cloughton Royal Infirmary. Caroline prepared to be sympathetic as the gory details of his condition were expounded, but none was offered. They chattered instead about recent events in the town and his good fortune in having a daughter who was happy to give him such care as he needed.

His lively interest in the world around him included the affairs of the school as relayed to him by Cynthia. 'Teaching was not her first choice of career but it is a worthwhile one. I used to hope that she would be able to return to her medical studies but it seems unlikely now. As she says herself, she can't go on from where she left off in her course. Medical knowledge has moved on without her. Where did you meet her? Were you fellow students?'

'Actually, I haven't met your daughter but I've come to ask for her help.' With some embarrassment, Caroline displayed her warrant card and explained the purpose of her visit. He would wonder why she had not done so immediately. She could hardly reveal that she had at first assumed that his mental as well as his physical powers were impaired and that she had wanted to protect him from any unpleasantness.

She realised now that he was talking incessantly only because he so seldom had the chance and that he had made not a few astute observations. He was quite distressed to hear that his daughter's pupil was missing. To distract him, Caroline asked, 'Is your daughter the same Miss Summers mentioned in the *Clarion* in connection with the American rock singer who is to visit Cloughton?'

He laughed. 'She is indeed. It's quite extraordinary. She has such intellectual interests otherwise. She first went to one of the man's concerts many years ago with a school friend and was completely won over. Then, as a student, she went on a trip to New York to a concert and to attend a reception he gave to meet his fan club organisers from six or seven countries. Cynthia refuses to use the word "fan" and says she runs an appreciation society. And why shouldn't she enjoy such music? I quite like it myself now. It's grown on me.' Caroline confessed that, until she had read the article in the paper, she had never heard of the singer.

Mr Summers chuckled. 'I owe him a debt he knows nothing about. You probably think this is rather a big and grand house for just two of us.' Caroline had thought exactly that. 'Cynthia now insists that we keep it "for when the family visits". That's rather a change of heart for her. She thought the place took a lot of looking after and ate up too much money. Then, this Mr Robson called here one day to pick her up. It was two years ago, when he was doing a major English tour and Cynthia was helping with the arrangements. He went into raptures about the house, like Americans do about things that are English and old. He opened her eyes to its qualities. I'm grateful to him. I would have left the family home for Cynthia's sake. After all, she has given up a great deal for mine. But now I'm ending my days here with her willing agreement. It's not really for family visits. We never get them. One of my sons lives in Australia and the other lives down on the south coast and has a family of his own to keep him busy.'

When Cynthia arrived home a few minutes later, she found her father and DC Webster companionably listening to a falsetto voice giving an agile rendering of 'You'll really love the man I'm going to be'.

6

Like Clement, DS Taylor was feeling impatient with the slow progress made so far in the search for Nazreen Akram. Like him too, she felt that her present mission had some chance of moving things forward. She hoped that Amara Mahmood would not recently have changed her job.

Jennifer used this Tesco branch quite often. It was in the Pakistani quarter of the town and was a ready source of the ingredients required for the spicy Asian dishes she enjoyed making. There was a large proportion of Asian customers and she saw that more than half of the girls in the row of twenty checkout points were Asian too. There was no chance of picking out and observing Amara from a distance.

She sought help at the customer services desk and almost immediately the manager was brought out to her, anxious to co-operate. He agreed with no demur to release his employee and offered his own office for the interview. Amara proved to be a very plump girl with a double chin, an ample bosom and an Eastern air of serenity. Jennifer imagined her in the filmy draperies of her own culture and thought how much more they would flatter her than the navy serge trousers and neat checked shirt blouse that was the standard uniform here.

The buttons of Amara's blouse strained as she reached for blue and white plastic bags and helped her current customer to pack a mountain of purchases. Huge fibreboard signs hung above and around her, hemming her in and offering pet insurance, loan facilities and twenty-five per cent extra value – the latter rather a vague claim as it stood, unsupported. Jennifer shuddered and felt thankful for her own work. Whatever its discomforts and dangers, she breathed fresh air and seldom had to sit in one place for long.

As the customer moved away the manager caught his sales-girl's attention. He received the beaming smile that she seemed to offer universally. It produced dimples and expressed a good-will that made her attractive in spite of her bulk and the ugly plastic-rimmed spectacles she wore that half hid her delicate brows. Amara extricated herself from her little prison with some difficulty and a slimmer colleague slipped into her place.

Misled by the girl's amiable expression, Jennifer framed her questions with insufficient care and soon found Amara glaring at her. 'You don't understand the first thing about our custom. "How can we marry when we're not in love?" Only an English-woman would ask me that! What's "in love"? English people marry because they're besotted with one another. That's not love. Some of them do learn to love each other because, luckily, they turn out to be compatible. Others just endure or give up and part.'

'But if you don't feel anything for each other even at the beginning –'

Amara was growing seriously angry. 'We know that immediate feelings aren't important – not enough to risk the security of our children. How do English people know, going along with the emotions of the moment, that they won't feel exactly the same about somebody else after a short time? The English girls do what they like when they like. They say we spend our lives doing things we don't want to, just to placate our families. Our families have spent all our lives choosing what will be best for us. Arranged marriages make provision for plain girls like me, who have all the qualities that make good wives and mothers. They are qualities that last and partners are well matched in practical ways.'

In spite of herself, Jennifer found herself asking, 'Why is a girl with your intelligence and your vocabulary working here? Didn't Mr Greenwood think you would do as well in your A-level subjects as Nazreen?'

Amara smiled. 'But I asked my teachers not to argue with my parents. I am a true Pakistani woman. My career will be to marry Imran when he leaves the university and bring honour to his family by raising good children. At least I am English enough not to say "good sons".'

They smiled at each other. 'And Nazreen is not a true Pakistani?'

The girl was embarrassed. 'Nazreen is married to her ambition to be a doctor.'

There was a silence as they both reflected for a moment.

Jennifer framed her next question carefully. 'Could you just imagine for a moment that you were to refuse your husband? What would your family do?'

Amara answered promptly. 'Try to persuade me – because they have been thinking what is best ever since I was born. If I still refused – well, I suppose they would not force me but it would spoil everything.' For the first time Amara refused to meet Jennifer's gaze. 'I suppose you are wondering about Nazreen refusing Asif. Her father is . . .'

'Stricter than yours?'

'Oh, no. But mine is more polite, more willing to explain, more patient to let me think things over.'

'So, Mr Akram would be angry with Nazreen.'

'I think so.'

'Where do you think she is?' Jennifer let the silence continue for some time before she spoke again. 'What are you thinking?'

'I am imagining that Nazreen has refused Asif.'

'And?'

'It would depend how she did it. Whatever way, he would be angry. If she was disrespectful . . .'

'He might harm her?'

Amara shook her head slowly, as though unable to contemplate her friend's punishment. 'Nazreen knows her father. I think she would be careful . . .' She trailed off again into despondent silence.

'Would she face up to his anger, or would she be more likely to run away?'

'Where would she run? She is sixteen years old. She has no money. They would find her. They would not forget that she had disgraced them because they were glad to have her back. No, I don't think she has run away.'

'What about her family in Leicester? Might she have gone to them for protection?'

Amara was amazed at Jennifer's stupidity. 'But they would be even more angry. It would be their Asif that she had refused.'

'So, you know definitely that Nazreen has refused to marry Asif?'

Amara shook her head, seemed about to say more, then shook it again. Jennifer too was silent, weighing the information she had been given. 'Have you tried to persuade Nazreen to look at things your way?' Amara gave a half-smile. 'Do you think she will ever come round to your way of thinking?'

'Oh, no. Never.'

The quick denial was obviously immediately regretted. Now the silence became stubborn and Jennifer spoke sternly. 'My colleagues and I believe that Nazreen may be in danger. I believe that you share our fears. Are you sure that you've said everything that you can to help us?'

Amara removed the ugly spectacles to scrub at her eyes with her plump fists. 'Yes, everything. Everything that I can.'

Clement finished typing his day's report and trudged wearily up to Browne's office. There he found an equally exhausted-looking Caroline. For a few seconds he angled for a lift home, but she wished him goodnight and a pleasant run. 'At least the wind's dropped a bit.'

Crestfallen, he agreed and went to change into shorts and vest. He had first taken up running as a stringy youth who never made the football team and whose parents could not have afforded the strip if he had. He had set off wearing a pair of worn-out school plimsolls but he had financed himself by doing a paper round when he realised that good running shoes at least were a necessity.

Recently, he had become aware of another advantage of his chosen sport. These days, his advanced age of twenty-nine was over the hill for a top-flight soccer or rugby player, whilst runners went on racing into their forties and fifties and training even into the seventies.

There was no better way to get to know a neighbourhood. His singlet-clad figure often provoked amusement but rarely aggression. As a runner, he had explored districts of Cloughton where he might have feared to go as a policeman. Tonight, he was running home by the Willow Dean estate again. It was as sordid as it sounded idyllic. The two worst streets had been demolished now and their inhabitants rehoused in the Sainted City. They included the Grant and the Stepney families, but both Shaun and Jonathan sometimes revisited their old haunts.

Clement had built up quite a rapport with the gang of youths that congregated outside the row of shops there to plan their mischief. At first they had jeered, even thrown stones, though they had quickly learned better than to repeat such behaviour. Now, as they saw him coming, one or two lined up and ran alongside him, easily outstripping him since the distance they set themselves ended with the end of the precinct.

When they were ten yards in front, they turned to barrack him but these days their cat calls were good natured. Jonathan Stepney, who was not here tonight, was a good little mover. If he could ever get the lad away from the teasing of his mates, Clement intended to suggest that the two of them tried a real run together at a more realistic speed.

He reached his flat restored and exhilarated and feeling less tired than when he had set off. He drank a pint of water, showered and pulled on his dressing-gown. He was tempted to find some pretext for ringing Caroline, to assure himself that she had not fallen asleep at the wheel and run into a tree. Wisdom, however, prevailed. He filled in his running diary instead.

On Thursday morning, Clifford Summers read his paper silently after Cynthia had left for school. Though it contained little to interest him he continued doggedly, in the belief that a slackening of his grip on the world around him, local as well as global, could lead to that decaying of the mind that he dreaded more than any deterioration of the body.

Maybe he should try to understand the workings of the mind that found amusement in lighting a small, contained fire to trigger a smoke alarm that disrupted the procedures in two complete departments of the Infirmary yesterday morning. One of the zones affected contained two operating theatres! If his own appointment had not been at the opposite end of the series of buildings, he would perhaps have witnessed these events, been accosted by a reporter and suffered the embarrassment of having his words misquoted, his home address mentioned and his age revealed. He had pondered often on the apparent necessity in local publications of placing, in brackets, after each name, the age of each person concerned. He had seen nothing and had been besought for no comment. Thank the Lord for small mercies.

Cynthia appeared, looking flustered. 'It's the car. I don't know what's wrong with it. There was a clicking noise, on and off, yesterday and now it won't start. Oh well, at least it's safely in the garage rather than stranded near school. Now I shall have to catch the bus and be late. Mr Greenwood doesn't like people missing assembly but at least I'll be there for first lesson.'

A convenient local bus had delivered Cynthia to the bus station. There, a small crowd of Colin Hewitt students, unalarmed at the thought of missing assembly, noisily kicked a sturdy plastic cup. Others tried to take it from whichever child was dribbling it up and down the bus shelter.

Cynthia ignored them and joined the queue. Conscientious she might be, but no one, she told herself, who was not on the regular staff could be expected to be on duty out of school. She prayed that none of the children would address her as 'Miss' in front of the complaining queue.

The girls, she observed, were as usual more aggressive than the boys and the smaller had by far the most piercing squeals. A boy found a puddle where rainwater, and possibly more unspeakable fluids, had drained to the bottom of the slope in the angle of the wall that formed the shelter. He picked up the cup, filled it and flung the contents over his companions. Filling it a second time, he splashed liquid against the glass panels of the shelter, coming close to the adults in the queue but not quite daring to splatter them.

The small squealing girl approached a burly man and enquired the time in a surprisingly polite fashion. When the bus door slid open, however, she was the first aboard and her companions rudely jostled aside the first of the adults. Cynthia hardly knew how she felt about them except afraid. She did not disapprove exactly. All children were noisy and their boisterousness aroused envy in her as much as anger. If they had become seriously out of hand she could not have brought herself to remonstrate with them.

Since the children had charged up the stairs, she thankfully seated herself on the lower deck. Soon the bus approached the school and the youngsters half climbed, half fell down the stairs, the last boy swinging from the bracing bar above him by his hands. A fat passenger spoke to the lad sharply and he jumped down and alighted from the bus quietly. Cynthia's envy transferred itself to the fat woman as she followed her pupils and faced another school day.

As Mitchell entered the station foyer at about the same time, he held open the door for the harassed-looking, headscarfed woman who was leaving She scowled at him and hurried away, muttering.

Mitchell grinned at the desk sergeant. 'Another satisfied customer. What did she want?'

'The wind's blown her TV aerial down.'

'Well, I can see it's serious, but why us?'

The sergeant's mouth turned down at the corners. 'She's got to have it back up before the kids get home from school. She thought we were her best bet.' Mitchell cast up his eyes. 'That's nothing. I was on duty one Christmas Eve when a woman rang to ask how you basted a turkey.'

Mitchell grinned. 'You're a bit of a dab hand at the old roast and two veg, aren't you?'

The sergeant nodded. 'I told her what to do, then asked why she'd rung us. She said, "Well, sergeant, you knew, didn't you?"'

Distracted from his guilty hopes that Browne would again be absent from duty, Mitchell ran upstairs laughing. He discovered that his CI was closeted with his superintendent. Mitchell was to start proceedings and Browne would join the shift as soon as he could. 'Since I'm only minding the shop,' Mitchell told his officers grimly, 'we'll do things the CI's way. And, since I failed to deliver my report on the Leicester trip yesterday, I'll take first turn. Shakila and I interviewed a total of eleven members of Nazreen Akram's extended family.'

He described the fruitless encounters succinctly. 'Apart from enjoying a couple of laughs when Shakila made her farewells in Urdu and various people realised that their asides had been both understood and noted, we wasted our time. They all insist that Nazreen was expected. They all deny any knowledge of where she is now. Thanks for your call, Adrian. It arrived just in time. Asif didn't realise the cover story included him meeting Nazreen's train. He thinks on his feet, though. Said he set out for the station but his car broke down. When I saw it I almost believed him. What about Faisal? What else did he tell you?'

Clement too offered a brief summary, adding, 'They're not such a strict Muslim family as they'd have you think. It's just an excuse to keep their women down. We went to the local pub and he downed two pints that I'd paid for before he stormed out.'

'Stormed?'

'He thought he might lose his job because I made him lose his temper in the shop. Oh, by the way, there was a chap in there, coming to Col's Castle next term, looking for a house.'

'Shouldn't think that needs to go into your report.'

'The CI says everything goes in.'

'So he does. Is it there, Adrian?' Browne spoke from the doorway.

Clement was putting his notebook away. Realising that the answer that would please Browne would put him at odds with Mitchell, he gazed at his feet as he muttered, 'Yes, sir.'

Browne came forward to appropriate his chair and his briefing. 'Have you dealt with your trip to Leicester, Benny?' Mitchell nodded and scowled. 'It's a pity I missed it since I couldn't find a report on it when I looked through the file earlier.' Mitchell's scowl intensified.

The shift turned to Jennifer who was commenting on her encounter with Amara Mahmood. 'She knows more, I'm certain of it.' She looked across to Shakila who had raised her hand as if in class.

'She said Nazreen couldn't run away if she had no money?' Jennifer nodded. 'Amara herself must have at least a little. Are they very good friends? Could she be supporting Nazreen in a cheap B&B?'

'Or she might have hidden her wherever she lives herself.' The DC whose maiden speech this was offered it eagerly.

Jennifer had considered both ideas already. 'The girl seemed very level-headed, not anti-police, not anti-whites. I think she realises we are Nazreen's best chance of living her life according to her own plans for it. If she'd known where she is, I believe she'd have told me. I think there's something else, though. Something she knows that she thinks she ought not to tell us. I wonder if she might be more inclined to confide in Shakila.'

'Maybe she isn't anywhere.' They turned to Clement. 'Well,

not alive anyway. I got the feeling that Faisal isn't interested in looking for his sister. Maybe he knows where she is and maybe he knows she's dead.'

'For refusing to marry someone?' Clement looked disappointed at his CI's sceptical tone. 'Hardly a punishment that will teach her to behave better in future.'

The meeting was beginning to founder and Jennifer realised that the congregated officers were hardly listening to each other. Each was becoming more convinced that the Akram girl was dead, whilst they had neither a body to prove it, nor a convincing motive on anyone's part to justify spending the force's time and money in following it up.

The ANAH Project in Bradford was the proper organisation to deal with Nazreen's disappearance but no one wanted to relinquish it to them. Certainly none of them wished to be the officer who suggested it.

Jennifer knew that Browne, always scrupulously fair, would now invite Caroline to add her own comments to her report on the Summers. She knew too that his asperity in dealing with Mitchell was partly owing to his certainty that the briefing had already served any purpose it had had. She wished he had left Benny in charge. Then Caroline's right by custom would have been waived and they would all be out by now, looking for some fact that would keep the enquiry in their own court.

As Caroline began to speak, Jennifer made her a mental apology. The young DC had no intention of wasting time. Nor was the little she had to say without interest, though its relevance to the case, if case they had, seemed tenuous. The almost middle-aged woman, regarded as a saint by her father and a joke by her pupils, was apparently greatly valued by at least one person. Cynthia Summers was engaged to be married.

Jennifer grinned approval for her brevity at Caroline and wondered whether Mitchell's unwonted silence was because he was impatient to be active or because he was still smarting from Browne's reproof.

'Did I hear, sir, that we're going to dig up the Akrams' cellar floor?'

Browne glared at the uniformed officer whose contribution to the enquiry had been questioning the Akram family's neighbours. 'I wouldn't know what you've heard, Atkinson, but I suggest you read the file if you want the facts. Since not many of you seem to have had much truck with it recently' – Mitchell was favoured with another black look – 'I'd better mention the two most interesting discoveries made by the SOCO. There's a newly concreted cellar floor – which Superintendent Carroll has decided we are not, at least for the moment, going to spoil. My unsuccessful efforts to get him to change his mind made me late for this meeting, for which I apologise.

'The other useful find was a letter, torn into pieces, found in a waste bin. It was addressed to Mr Greenwood at the Colin Hewitt and said that Nazreen would be leaving school with effect from last Friday, the day we all lost track of her. In my view, that was her punishment for not –'

The telephone interrupted him and the team waited impatiently, getting no clues from Browne's brief questions and monosyllabic comments. His expression quizzical, the CI replaced the receiver and turned to face his team. 'Benny and Adrian, up to the school. They seem to have mislaid another youngster.'

In the region of twenty minutes past nine, as Mitchell abandoned his vehicle in the Colin Hewitt car park, he noticed a tallish, baldish, anorak-clad man closing his passenger door on a sulky-looking girl. He recognised and greeted the Education Welfare Officer. Having what he had described to Clement as 'a bit of action' to get on with had restored Mitchell's good humour and he beamed at the man. 'Collecting up the truants and getting them off the streets? Keep up the good work!'

The girl in the car glared at both newcomers and her minder turned to the DI. 'Just the opposite, actually.'

'What?'

He jerked his head at the girl. 'This one's been suspended. Her parents find the school's demand that they take some responsibility for their daughter utterly unreasonable. In protest, they deliver her here every morning, as usual. I'm just about to dump her back on them.'

Mitchell laughed. 'They have it all here, don't they?'

'This is the third time. The parents take care to be out, so the first day she turned up she sat all day in the head's office. Yesterday, I took her to her grandmother. Today, we're going to see how her father likes having her delivered to his place of work.'

'What does he do?'

'Calls himself a gents' outfitter. See you!' He drove off in a cloud of exhaust emissions to enjoy the projected confrontation.

'How can they know,' Clement asked as the two officers walked towards the school entrance, 'whether or not a child is really missing in the middle of this carry-on?'

Mitchell shrugged. 'I suppose you get a feel for it. Greenwood knows his kids, never calls us in for something he could sort out for himself. The less time we spend here, the less harm is done to the school's reputation.'

They found Colin Greenwood alone. As Mitchell had expected, he made their initial task easy, giving them a quick summary of the information he possessed so far. 'The girl's name is Frances Veronica Leonard. You can get all the details you want, photos and so on, from her file. Just ask my secretary to make photocopies. Frankie is in Year 10, what used to be the fourth form. She's skinny, cheeky and cheerful, no great brain but quick-witted, not stupid.'

'When was she last seen?'

'We know she was in school at lunchtime yesterday. Both Mavis Barron and I particularly noticed her as we were going to lunch. When the Leonard parents arrived this morning to say Frankie was missing I sent for her teachers for yesterday after-noon. I'm afraid none of the three of them could say for certain whether or not she was in class.'

Mitchell nodded, understanding, but Clement looked up from his notebook, startled. Greenwood smiled ruefully. 'Frankie sel-dom caused any trouble in the classroom and my colleagues' attention was entirely taken up with people who did. Not that those concerned admitted this in so many words.'

Clement added a further comment to his notes as Mitchell asked, 'You're starting from yesterday lunchtime because that's the last time the girl was seen?' Greenwood nodded. 'So she didn't go home yesterday afternoon?'

'It seems not.'

Mitchell was puzzled. 'But we only got the message . . .'

Greenwood let the question founder. 'You'd better meet the distraught parents.' He led the two policemen along the corridor to Mavis Barron's room where the door opened on to a cosy scene. A thin man sprawled comfortably in the only armchair. Grime in the wrinkles of his knuckles and deep in his fingernails spoke of dirty manual work, but the hands had been scrubbed and an effort had been made with a clean shirt and slicked-back hair.

A woman, presumably his wife, sat on a straight-backed chair and dandled a fat baby. It stared with round eyes at nothing in particular and leaked a spreading dampness on to its mother's lap. Mrs Leonard had bedraggled, over-permed hair and the sort of smile with which feckless people usually favour those they expect to look after them. A droopy-looking boy, ten or eleven years old and introduced as Stevie, lolled against his mother's legs and rested his head on her knees. 'He's poorly,' Mrs Leonard announced, in explanation of his presence. The boy was seeking relief from his alleged ailment by means of a rapid consumption of the chocolate digestive biscuits that Mrs Barron had arranged on a tray.

Invited to give details of their daughter's disappearance, the parents seemed faintly embarrassed and neither spoke. Mitchell decide that the father looked the more likely to answer a simple question and addressed him unsympathetically. 'When exactly did you get round to realising that you were one child short?'

Mr Leonard looked hopefully at Colin Greenwood, received no help, essayed an answer. 'I suppose it were when they went out for t'bus like. Marie and Kevin were scrapping till one of them said where were our Frankie.'

'This morning?'

He nodded, his manner easier now he had begun. 'Kev came in and yelled upstairs for her. Maureen' – he jerked his head towards his wife – 'told him to go back out before he missed it isself. You went upstairs, didn't you, Maur?' Still smiling, Mrs Leonard assured them that she had indeed made this effort.

'And Frankie wasn't there?' She shook her head. 'So, what then?'

'I had to get our Bev ready for nursery. Frankie usually does that and then our Pat drops her off on her way to work.'

'You stopped looking for Frankie?'

'I had to. Pat leaves at half-past eight and if Bev wasn't ready for her to take I'd have had her round my feet all day.'

Keeping a tight rein on himself, Mitchell asked, quietly, 'So – what – then?'

'Our Pat started making a fuss, climbed up to the top bunk. Said our Frankie hadn't been to bed.'

'Pat and Frankie share a bedroom and bunk beds?'

'Yes, with Marie and our Kelly in the other bunks.'

'In the same room?'

The mother had transferred her attention to the fractious baby. She jiggled it on her knee and the dampness spread to Stevie's shoulder. He wriggled the shoulder and reached for another biscuit. Duty done by her youngest she returned to the family's sleeping arrangements, since that was what Mitchell seemed to want. 'Katie here and Bev still have their cots in our room.'

Mitchell was rapidly counting children. 'It's easy to miss one when you've got eight.'

Mr Leonard wondered whether he could detect a note of criticism, then gave Mitchell the benefit of the doubt. 'Anyway, our Pat decided to wake me –'

'You'd slept through all this?' Mitchell's eyebrows shot up. 'Oh, well, I suppose it's easily done when you've had a skinful.'

After a short debate with himself, Mr Leonard decided to remain conciliatory. 'Any road, I suggested we come straight up here. We knew Mr Greenwood'd know what to do.'

7

The briefing that was eventually called for two o'clock that afternoon was conducted by neither Browne nor Mitchell. The superintendent himself was addressing the shift on the escalation of their workload. 'I say advisedly "of your workload" and not "of your case". We have no reason yet to suppose that the disappearances of the two girls are in any way connected. Certainly they attended the same school but that is the only common factor we have discovered.

'You all know better than I do that on the Willow Dean estate the report of a missing child does not mean the inevitable finding of a pathetic, small mutilated corpse as it might in another area . . .'

Caroline sighed and whispered to Jennifer, 'He's learned to get drunk on his own oratory.'

'Yes, but he's not as bad a case as either Petty or Kleever.'

Having paused fractionally to glance in the direction of the two women, Carroll continued. 'One result of feckless parenting seems, surprisingly but fortunately, to be a healthy resilience. Children from Willow Dean make their own rules. We have, all of us, spent hours going through the vitally necessary procedure for finding a child who has subsequently turned up, safe and cheerful, to exult in the notoriety the search for them has lent them.'

The shift felt justified in relaxing its attention and thinking its own thoughts. Jennifer noticed that the blown-up photograph of Nazreen that had appeared on the wall board was an enlargement of the school one in her file. She studied with interest a similarly sized picture of Frankie Leonard. One of the uniformed men had summed her up well. 'She looks a wick kid!'

It was an appealing face. The hair was chin-length and bedraggled, the eyes huge, the expression both alert and somehow wary. The cheeks were hollow and so was what could be seen of the chest. Jennifer would not have guessed from the picture that Frankie was almost fifteen.

Realising that the meeting had been passed over to Mitchell she began to listen again. 'Frankie was the second eldest of eight children, though the three-year-old is the illegitimate daughter of the eldest. The baby is the mother's child. Pat, the eldest, has spent some time in care and Kevin and Stevie, further down the school, are trouble-makers. But Keith Gordon called Frankie a happy little soul. He said she gets upset when she's referred to as "one of those Leonards". It's because she's different that the school called us straight away. Frankie isn't given to melodrama. Greenwood says she's the most responsible of the family, looks after the little ones at home and makes a good shot at her school work. Running off wouldn't be typical behaviour.'

'Maybe she's just had enough, thinks it's time she kicked over the traces a bit whilst someone else holds the family together.'

Mitchell had no compunction about disagreeing with his superintendent. 'No way. Responsible people stay responsible. And Greenwood thinks, wherever she is, she'll be worried about them all. He also said –'

'Stick your report in the file, Benny. We'll read the rest.' Mitchell glared at Carroll, indignant at having his soapbox pulled from under him. 'You have written a report?'

'Yes, sir.' Mitchell's eyes swivelled accusingly to Browne who ignored him.

'It's time for action. We haven't collected enough facts to debate yet.' Action sheets appeared and, considering the super-intendent's present mood, no one dared to voice dissatisfaction with his or her allotted tasks.

Mitchell, sent back to the school, was pleased to discover that Jennifer's brief was identical. 'We needn't spend any more time on Greenwood,' he told her. 'He's given us as much help as he can and, if anything else turns up, he'll come back to us.'

'So that leaves forty-two staff and something like eight hundred children. Where do we start?'

'The supplies.'

Jennifer looked doubtful. 'Won't they know even less than the others?'

'Maybe, but they might be less blinkered and less biased.'

'They'll just have a different bias. Do we take one each?'

Mitchell thought for a moment. 'No, we'll go together. A two-pronged attack will be more intimidating and with two views of an interview we'll have more chance of picking up on vital details than with one. It'll save time in the long run.'

Jennifer grinned at him. 'It'll be less tedious, you mean.'

They found Derek Swindell alone. Sue was having her hair done, he explained apologetically, as though no caller could be satisfied to see just himself. Taking them through to the living-room, he hurriedly pushed a paperback book under a cushion.

'Has Frankie turned up yet?' he asked, as they seated themselves.

'How did you know she was missing?'

'Mr Greenwood rang to ask if she was in my lesson.'

Jennifer took stock of the man as Mitchell spoke with him. Late thirties and not wearing well. Limp, fine, dark hair was thinning on the crown. His expression was half timid, half defiant, the sort of look she had frequently caught on her daughters' faces when they had indulged in some minor mischief. The heavy-lidded, pale blue eyes would look directly at neither of them.

The body language was all defensive. During Mitchell's questions the man sat with elbows on knees, forehead on one hand, gazing at the floor between his feet. From Swindell's answers, Mitchell learned that supply teaching was the worst of all worlds, that the essence of good teaching is knowing your children, which a supply teacher has little opportunity to do, that the secret of good discipline was keeping the children interested and busy. Mitchell allowed his witness to talk himself to a standstill on such generalities, making mental observations about him and pleased to see that Jennifer's opinions were being recorded in black and white.

Pressed for more specific answers, Swindell became more stilted. Yes, he was almost sure Frankie had been in his French class, the last before lunch. No, he had noticed nothing unusual about her behaviour then. 'Except that . . .'

'Go on.'

'Well, it wasn't particularly in that lesson, but I'd noticed lately

87

that she was coming more and more under the influence of another girl, Adele Batty.'

'And what sort of girl is she?'

Swindell cast his eyes to the ceiling. 'The worst sort. Loud, coarse, vulgar and a bully. Not that she often indulges in physical fights, inspector. She doesn't need to. She has that enviable something that makes people anxious to do what she says.'

'Including you, Mr Swindell?'

The man laughed unconvincingly. 'She'd like to think so. Certainly including Frankie. I think you need to consider whether she's run away because Adele is bullying her.'

'And that was the last time you saw Frankie?'

'Not quite. At lunchtime, I got back at more or less the same time as Cynthia. That's Miss . . .' Mitchell indicated that they were acquainted with Miss Summers. 'Adele was with her cronies by the gate. She definitely sent Frankie across to Cynthia to say something impertinent.'

'You overheard?'

'No, but Adele watched Frankie all the time. Frankie's attitude was half aggressive, half guilty, and poor Miss Summers' embarrassment was obvious. I understand she's very well up in her subject but she really can't handle the seniors.'

Mitchell suddenly lost all taste for the interview and brought it swiftly to an end. 'We'll see ourselves out.'

Obviously wondering how he had offended, Swindell trailed after them down the hall to the front door. 'I hope your next witness has a little more information to offer you.'

Mitchell did not return his ingratiating smile. 'And a little less humbug!'

'He'll report you for that,' Jennifer warned as they walked back to the car.

Mitchell was unabashed. 'Did you see the title of the book he shoved under that hideous cushion?'

'Yes. *Emotional Intelligence*. I've read it. It's quite interesting.'

Mitchell gaped at her, then dismissed the matter. 'Friend Derek doesn't know anything and he'd have been glad to take till teatime not telling it.'

In spite of the still blustery wind, Bob Crumb was enjoying his afternoon's work. He'd been doing it for close on forty years now. He didn't feel quite so much king of the road as when he'd first begun driving, screened off from hoi polloi in his cab with a conductor to be bothered with tickets and change and stroppy passengers. Still, most members of the public were pleasant and many were the times when they had told him something he hadn't known, or done something amusing that he could tell his mates at the club.

No two journeys were ever the same. Today, the older ladies were in their winter uniform, fur felt hats, padded raincoats and fur-lined, zipped-up suede boots, bought years ago and resurrected for the worst of every winter since. The youngsters, in contrast, were only half dressed but they never seemed to notice the cold and wind. He'd picked one up outside Col's Castle a couple of circuits ago. She'd been cheeky to one of the other passengers as she'd clattered upstairs for the couple of stages to town. Probably off to play the slot machines in the arcade.

He'd glanced up to the mirror that gave him a view of practically all the top deck. The lass had not been damaging the seat fabric. Sitting quite quietly, in fact, on the front left seat, the only one not quite in the range of his mirror. Just the shoulder of her green anorak he could see, but enough to know that she was behaving herself. There had been another passenger up there, sitting behind her, hopefully keeping an eye. He hadn't noticed either of them getting off but it was probably when the end-of-shift people got on outside the carpet factory.

Now, he had another whole circuit to do before there'd be any more kids on the loose. He braked at the crossing outside the library, then went round the car park intended as the site for the new supermarket to join the queue at the lights. Taking a left turn past the industrial complex, he started up the green bank, framed by mill chimneys, and topped by a hideous twee housing estate.

Past that, he came to the double mini-roundabout – two bloody white smarties! Let the bloody councillors who voted that in try to drive a double decker round it! A hundred yards past there came his terminus. On the corner, above the porch of the Catholic church, the Virgin held up her Child, exposing him to all weathers, including this freezing, squally November afternoon.

He liked the last bit. Four pubs and a chippie in forty yards. Going back to town, he took the short route, straight down the steep lane that was the old road out of town. A bit dicey when it was below freezing but all right so far this year.

Stopping at the lights again, he looked down into the well of the town. His eye followed the straightish course of the canal, rested on corrugated iron roofs, chimneys, tall flats and a satisfying number of trees. Glancing to his left, he noticed that the little sandwich bar was under new management. It had a new name too, the Nose Bag. Not very flattering to its customers. The wind was really getting up again. He was glad it was almost time to slip his module out of the ticket dispenser and knock off.

The lights changed, a motor cycle jumped them taking a course across Bob Crumb's path, just as a voluminous plastic sack was flattened by the mini-gale across his windscreen in front of him. Startled, he let his foot slip and his vehicle lurched sideways, entering the Nose Bag by way of the side wall.

Later that afternoon, Virginia Mitchell escorted her two older children back from school. As usual, she switched on her television set for the half-hour programme that Caitlin and the twins watched each weekday afternoon. Until recently, Declan too had looked at it, though affecting disdain. Now, however, he really had grown out of it and he cast his eyes melodramatically to the ceiling. 'P'raps you and me can have a sensible conversation in the kitchen.' He followed his mother hopefully. 'You haven't told me what you were talking about at Grandad Tom's.'

Virginia thought rapidly. 'Maybe Caitlin can join us too,' she suggested. 'Go and fetch her and I'll tell you both.' All three sat at the kitchen table as Virginia explained, simply and directly, that Granny Hannah was going to die. When the children asked why, she struggled to simplify what she barely comprehended for herself. Remembering a small electrical repair Mitchell had effected recently, she compared Hannah's motor neurones with the electrical junction box into which Declan had peered with much interest. 'Because the box had broken wires, it couldn't pass a message from the light switch to the bulb, telling it to light up. Granny Hannah's nerves are like the wires. They've got bad at passing messages, telling her body to walk and hold things and go on living.'

Caitlin looked mystified but Declan nodded sagely and asked, 'When will she die?'

Virginia resisted the temptation to say that no one knew. 'In about two years. That seems a very short time to us but it might seem quite a long time to you two.'

Now Caitlin had heard something she could relate to. 'A hamster dies in two years. Mrs Sampson says so. If a hamster had as many birthdays as a person, Mrs Sampson says, it would need one every eight days.' She wandered off to watch the rest of the television programme.

Declan had picked up his library book and was pretending to read whilst his mind absorbed the unwelcome news. After a moment, he looked up. 'Will she die when I'm watching her?'

Virginia considered. 'I don't think that's very likely.'

'Will we know she's dead? If she can't walk and hold things?'

'We'll call the doctor. He'll be able to tell.'

Declan returned to his book. Presently his eyes filled with tears that streaked his cheeks and dropped on to his book. Virginia took him on her lap and, briefly, they wept together.

Caroline jumped guiltily when Browne brought his coffee over to her table in the canteen. She apologised for her unsanctioned break without trying to justify it. Now, Browne laughed and settled himself opposite her. 'When it's a crime to take five minutes out to collect your thoughts, I suggest it's time to leave the force. Whilst you're on my shift, it isn't. I came looking for you.'

Caroline examined her conscience and took comfort from Browne's benign expression as he poked at floating sugar lumps with a spoon. 'I've been rereading your notes on your session with Cynthia Summers. It's very brief, and, from what I've heard, the lady is apt to chatter on. Also, she is reputed to have been fond of Nazreen. I'm surprised that she wasn't more help to us. Did you get interrupted?'

Caroline shook her head and took a tiny sip from her own cooling coffee. Putting her empty cup down might look like a hint that he should buy her another. Browne drummed his fingers, impatient for an answer, and Caroline forced her mind from such petty questions of etiquette. 'It was hard to keep her on the subject of Nazreen. I just put in the report what was relevant.'

'You often don't know what's relevant till the case is over.'

Chastened, Caroline searched her memory to supply her report's deficiencies. 'She seemed flustered when her father remarked that she was home early. That was because she'd told him she was teaching when I think she was meeting her unofficial fiancé.'

'What made you think that?'

'She was flushed and animated. She looked almost pretty. And she'd told me about the man last time I was there. All she said about Nazreen we already knew. She gave her a lesson twice a week if the girl could manage to be there for it and she has both given and lent her medical and biology textbooks. They didn't talk about anything but work, didn't want to waste the short time they had. She said that most people thought Nazreen should be in a different school. Cynthia didn't agree. She said that a doctor has to mix and be comfortable with all social classes. The school was good training for her in that sense, so long as she got her grades. She said, "I'm delighted to help on the academic front." Every so often, Nazreen would write a note of thanks. Once she brought chocolates.'

'So, what did the two of you talk about?'

'She talked about herself and her father, mostly. I listened because I thought she needed to be listened to. She was in her second year of medicine at Newcastle University when her father had a stroke. He went suddenly from fit and independent to weak and frail with no guarantee of a full recovery. Cynthia had her place held open for her at first and came home. There wasn't much time to consider alternatives. There was pressure to release his hospital bed and the staff expected her to take him, at least in the short term. He improved gradually for a while but he's as well as he's ever going to be now.'

'You obviously did a thorough interview. You need to put all that into the file so that we can all benefit from your impressions. Was she his only child?'

Caroline shook her head. 'There are two older brothers. One

92

went to work in Australia when the father was still well. The other claims four sons, unsuitable accommodation, his own bad health and the distance he lives from Cloughton stop him even having his father for holidays. Cynthia thinks he's sulking because he was always compared unfavourably with her when they were at school.'

Browne smiled at Caroline's indignant tone. 'Perhaps she took a fancy to help Nazreen because she feels their positions are parallel. You don't think you should have taken up social work?'

Whilst she tried to decide whether or not he was teasing her, Browne picked up his bleeping phone. He listened, then questioned tersely. 'Junction of Old Lane and Stebbings Street? Is she a white girl or an Asian?' The caller gave more details.

Browne rose, pushing back his chair. 'Body of a young girl found on a bus. You heard where. End of coffee break, I'm afraid. Pick up Benny and Jennifer and follow me there.'

'Which one have we found?' Caroline called to her CI's retreating back.

'Doesn't sound to me like either of them.'

Driven by Mitchell, the marked police car, with its siren wailing, arrived at the accident scene before Browne's. The traffic police were efficiently in charge of arrangements to separate the bus from the Nose Bag and two ambulances were about to depart with the walking wounded.

Mitchell, studying this very proper activity, could see no obvious reason for his own department's summons. Even if there had been fatalities, even if one of them was a young girl, there was no reason to suppose a connection with their own case. This was not work for the CID. Recognising Police Sergeant Anthea Riley, deep in conversation with an extremely short, bepectacled man, Mitchell tried to catch her eye and the two of them came towards him.

'This is Dr Beckham, sir. He was passing and stopped to help.' As Mitchell tried to decide whether this deference was sincere or ironical, he noticed that Anthea's gaze went beyond him. He ground his teeth. Browne had arrived. 'It was because of what he said about the dead girl that we called you in.'

'Where is she?' Browne looked up and down the pavement and over to the ambulances. 'Have the paramedics moved her?'

'We knew better than that, sir.' Anthea stepped back to let the doctor speak for himself.

Beckham handed over a card that identified him as belonging to a large group practice nearby. Browne put the card in his pocket and, with a raised eyebrow, invited the doctor to speak.

'She's still where we found her, on the upper deck. You can get up there fairly safely – the bus is firmly wedged into the wall. I saw the accident happen. The most valuable thing I managed to do was prevent a couple of well-meaning sandwich fillers in there from hauling the very bloody driver out of his cab, which is now part of the shop. An ambulance has taken him to the Infirmary. Then we helped the passengers through a window.' He pointed. 'That one. After I'd taken the remaining glass out and padded the frame with people's coats. Then Sergeant Riley and I climbed in from this side to check upstairs. We found the girl on the floor, in front of the left front seat.

'The thing is, though, I don't think she was injured in the crash. I think, by then, she'd been dead for about two hours.'

8

In time for his family's early supper, Mitchell opened his front door, sniffed and grimaced. He had remarked at breakfast time that he fancied a plate of bacon and mushrooms. If Virginia remembered to shop for them, he had intended to begin the day tomorrow with a royal feast. Breakfast was the meal he always cooked himself whilst she washed and dressed the twins.

She had not only found time to buy them. She was now cremating them for his evening meal. Regretfully, he addressed his elder son. 'Tea's almost ready, Declan. Set the table, please.' There was no response. 'Declan!'

The child looked up and blinked. 'Isn't reading funny? You open the book and there are little black letters on the page, but in your head there are moving pictures and you keep seeing the pictures and you forget you're holding the book.' He closed it and wandered over to the drawer that held cutlery whilst Mitchell, who could think of no reply to his son's remark, went into the kitchen to greet his wife.

'What's new?'

She grinned at him. 'I'm a kept woman. I've given in my notice as from the weekend.'

'My mother would have the twins, you know.'

'Benny, she's twelve years older than mine. She's brought up six children of her own. She deserves a bit of peace.'

'I suppose so, but you deserve better than to be at home all day with four kids.'

Virginia snatched the bacon from under the grill, blew out the flame and put the charred rashers in the oven to keep warm. 'I won't be at home. I'll probably be with Mum a good deal of the time. It wasn't a very satisfying job and doing it at home isn't going to work out. I've proved that in just a week.'

Mitchell reached into the fridge for a can, filled a glass from it and swallowed half the contents in a gulp. Virginia opened her mouth to remonstrate, then said instead, 'Child cases are the worst, aren't they?'

95

'For Pete's sake keep your eye on the cooker.' Mitchell raised his voice. 'Declan! You aren't reading that book again, are you?'

A busy rattling of plates began. Mitchell parked one ample haunch on a stool and nodded. 'Yes, they are, but it's not that.'

'So, what is it?'

Mitchell's forehead wrinkled. 'It's my whole career. I feel as if I'm stranded in the middle of a huge cliff face. The climbing's easy but it's too big to see the top. I'm scared that I might not be going up any more. I've no bearings.'

'You can't be too depressed if you can wax poetical.'

'I'm not complaining. I know it's as bad for you and worse for Tom, but no one seems sure who's in charge of the work. When I try to run things I get snapped at by your father and glared at by Jennifer. And I admit that my chief reason for trying to take over is my own ambition.'

'Plus your intense dislike of not doing exactly what you like when you like. With no one interfering.'

'Yes, that too. I don't know how to help Tom. He needs to be planning the case to give him something else to think about. He'd go crazy if all he had to do was stay at home and watch Hannah die. But it's difficult for him to . . . well, do it right when more than half his mind's at home, so I barge in. I can see Jennifer working herself up into lecture mode.'

Virginia laughed. 'Splendid. You can have an enormous row with her, then you'll both feel better.'

'Yes, for a while, but it won't cure anything. The case itself is weird. Two kids missing and we find the body of a completely different one.'

'Do you know who she is?'

'She's the one some people at the school were blaming for bullying Frankie Leonard.'

'What are her parents like?'

Mitchell shrugged. 'Wasn't my job. I'll have to look in the file.'

Virginia turned away from the cooker again and returned to the previous topic. 'Your trouble is, you've had a taste of being God and you'll never be happy again just being an angel.'

Mitchell agreed. Almost exactly a year ago he had been promoted to DI to further the personal ends of a corrupt senior officer. Moved to a substation nearer the Lancashire border, he had headed a case at least as complicated as his present one and he remembered now his euphoria at its successful conclusion. He beamed at his wife. 'You're quite right. Now the problem's identified, I'll deal with it. I want to sort things myself though. I'm not in the mood for a set-to with Jennifer.'

'Obviate it, then. Go and tell her you've taken your own medicine and she can leave you alone and get on with her own work. You're not the only frustrated member of Cloughton CID. Jen's only one step behind you because her own circumstances have hemmed her in. In her way, she's just as good a copper as you.'

Again, Mitchell agreed. 'If Jane's willing to stay with the girls, I'll invite her round for a drink later on.'

'No, not tonight.' Mitchell was surprised. Jennifer was perhaps more Ginny's friend than his own. He had expected her to second the invitation. 'I told Declan and Caitlin about Mum this afternoon.'

'And?'

'They took it well but Declan's going to dream about it. I don't want him feeling he's to wait till the visitor's gone before he can have our attention tonight.' She recounted the brief conversation and the questions their elder son had asked.

'I'd have got home somehow if I'd known – helped you explain.'

She smiled. 'Yes, I know, by telling them Granny Hannah will be dead soon, so they'll just have to face up to it. That actually might have been a good line with Kat but Declan's another kind of fish. I didn't deliberately wait till you were out. It just suddenly seemed the right moment. They both knew something was wrong and Declan politely reminded me that we'd promised to explain. I think this is ready now. Can you call the troops?'

Happy again, Mitchell concentrated on the before-meal routine with seat straps, bibs and arbitration on whose turn it was to eat from the Mr Men plate. He ate manfully and even stifled a laugh when Caitlin remarked, 'I don't like these black things. You said we were going to have mushrooms.'

*   *   *

Since he had lost his wife and baby son, Clement had not found it easy to sleep. For him, the recipe to achieve a restful night had two parts, a hard run and a huge mug of cocoa. It was not a beverage to which he often resorted and, of course, he had run out. Checking the exact time he was expected to appear the next morning, he went back into the station to change and pack his working clothes into his rucksack.

Mentally, he planned an eight mile route that would bring him to an open-all-night supermarket, not far from the precinct and about a mile from his flat. He reached it in forty-eight minutes, sweating copiously and, as usual, feeling relaxed and at peace with himself, as well as pleasantly tired.

When he realised that the person behind him in the checkout queue was Jonathan Stepney, he felt glad that his tin of cocoa was hidden in his wire basket by a half-dozen pack of Stella and a box of eggs. The boy's basket was loaded with tins of alcopop.

'Race you across the car park?' the boy enquired, his face lighting with recognition. Clement noted that he was wearing heavily studded jeans and enormous boots. It was not in his plan to outrun the lad and so he shook his head.

'I never run when I'm carrying eggs.' He let one eyelid fall in a droll wink. 'I've been wanting a word with you.'

'I've done nowt for you to be in a lather about!'

'You bloody have.' Stepney looked startled. 'The way you shift, you'll be entering one of my races one of these days and running the purple shorts off me.' Now the boy displayed a mixture of pleasure and embarrassment. Clement looked down at Stepney's basket. 'Go and put that disgusting stuff back and come and have a Stella with me. I'll give you a bit of coaching if you like. Then, when you beat me, at least I can claim some credit for it. Go on, Jonno. Give it a try.'

The boy was suspicious again. 'How d'you know my name?'

'We've a mutual friend called Shaun.'

'He's never been grassing?'

'Of course he hasn't. Your name just came up in the course of our interesting conversation.' Clement had paid for his purchases and the two of them sat companionably on the perimeter wall of the car park, each swigging from a can.

'You know my name. What's yours?'

'Sherlock.'

There was a considerable pause before Stepney grinned. 'Get it! Anyway, you can't coach me. I've no gear.'

'You got jogging pants?' The boy nodded. 'What size shoes?'

'Tens.'

A half-size smaller than his own. Clement was pleased. They'd manage nicely to begin with, with an extra pair of socks. 'That's lucky. I've got a pair of ten and a halves that always give me a blister. I was going to throw them away, but if you wore them it would save them going to waste.' Clement sometimes wished he lied with a little less fluency, but not very often.

The lad was becoming interested. 'Do you mean now?'

'No chance, I'm afraid. I'm in the middle of a case. At least, I've been sent to get a few hours' sleep first.'

'Looking for those girls?'

Clement nodded. 'Want another?' They pulled the rings off second cans. Their removal from the rucksack exposed Clement's tin of cocoa. Stepney eyed it wonderingly but made no comment, beyond, 'It'll have to be when the gang's not there.' Clement thought this was enough of a concession for the moment. 'Cloughie are playing away, Friday night. That's tomorrow. I could say I've no dosh and not go. Then we could have a jog round. I could show you the sights of Willow Dean.'

Clement nodded. 'OK. Work permitting, you're on.' He scrambled down from the wall and strode away. He was almost out of hearing by the time Stepney made his decision.

'About those girls.'

Clement whipped round. 'What about them?'

'Adele is Shaun's bit.'

'Who said we were looking for Adele?'

'You're not now. Copped it, hasn't she?'

'Who told you that?'

'Bush telephone.'

'So, if Adele was Shaun's bit, who's yours? Frankie?'

Stepney laughed. 'Dream on! Nice kid, Frankie.'

At something after two in the morning the Mitchells' bedroom door clicked open and a tousled dark head appeared round it. Virginia was awake in an instant. 'Is that how everybody dies, Mummy?'

'No, son. Everybody has his own death that is quite different from anyone else's.'

Virginia was startled. She had not expected Benny to wake. They both sat up and Declan wriggled under the duvet.

'So you and Mummy and me won't get wrong junction boxes?'

Mitchell looked puzzled. Virginia spoke in an undertone. 'Good question. We need to find out about the hereditary angle, don't we? I don't think it's occurred to Mum and Dad either. Whatever the facts, I think the answer you gave Declan holds good for all of us for now.'

'Any more questions, son?'

Declan grinned. 'Can we all three sleep in this bed till morning?'

A new picture had been added to the gallery behind Browne in the incident room. Adele Batty now smiled challengingly from her latest school photograph. Mitchell, who was fond of the genus children, even though the hordes of the offspring of his Irish Catholic relatives and four of his own had left him with few illusions about them, sensed that he would have found this one hard to like. The gathering in front of the picture was a large one. One child dead, from whatever cause, and another two missing from the same local school had produced two more DCs, half a dozen uniformed officers and a promise of more as required.

Browne turned away from the board to face his team. 'Dr Beckham believes that Adele was already dead when the bus crash happened. There was the beginning of lividity and there was no bleeding from a scalp wound behind the left ear. You can read all the details in his statement . . .'

Mitchell listened resentfully, remembering how Anthea Riley had treated him as an equal, reserving her 'sirs' for Browne. Dr Beckham too had quite obviously expected only Browne to accompany him to the upper deck of the bus as he had pointed out the evidence that justified his opinion. Admittedly, Browne himself had later taken his DI up the buckled staircase, carefully avoiding the twisted panels and rails, to look at the girl's body.

He saw it again now, in his imagination. She would have been pretty if she had not been so plump but the bulging cheeks and extra chin had made the striking features seem crowded into the middle of her face. The face had been strangely slack and expressionless. The hair was beautiful, thick and dark brown, clean and shiny. The girl's clothes were just a gesture in the direction of the school uniform worn by the school's more law-abiding pupils, but all was neat and clean, except where the jacket had been soiled by the debris on the floor and the skirt by the girl's urine. As he and Browne had descended to the street, ominous creaks had forced Mitchell to consider the idea that, in Beckham's view, his own thirteen stones disqualified him from a trip up those damaged stairs.

Browne was still talking. 'We identified Adele from a name-tape on her cardigan and the books in the duffel bag that was on the floor beside her. Damage to the front face of the bus is extensive on the lower deck and suggests that the driver has some unpleasant injuries. However, as the Nose Bag is a single-storey building, the upper deck was not completely stove in. That's about it. If and where we come in will depend on the PM. Questions? Comments?'

Mitchell's was the first. 'When's the PM?'

'First thing tomorrow.' Browne defended Ledgard against Mitchell's glower. 'It's a sudden death, not a suspicious one. There may have been an undetected heart condition or some other disease. We're on the alert because of Nazreen and Frankie, but we're not on a murder hunt – yet.'

'Has someone told the parents?'

Browne turned to Jennifer. 'Traffic have done it.'

Most officers were relieved. Mitchell was not among them. 'Pity, really, if it turns out to be a case. We've missed their first reactions.'

Browne was scooping up papers from his desk. 'All we can do meanwhile is continue looking for the other two. Your action sheets tell you who to talk to. They don't tell you what to say. The answer's not much. Don't interrupt unless your witness is way off beam, and maybe not even then. Above all, don't ask . . .'

His team chanted with him. '. . . leading questions to get support for your pet theories.'

The *Clarion's* front page on Friday had room to spare only for the three Colin Hewitt pupils. 'TWO GIRLS MISSING AND ONE DEAD', the headline screamed. Seemingly the editor disagreed with Superintendent Carroll and was convinced of a connection between the disappearances and the death.

Browne glanced at the copy that had been left on his desk. According to the leading article, the police were very concerned for the physical and moral safety of the two missing girls – true enough. They were acting on the presumption that the two missing girls were dead – definitely untrue. More than a hundred officers were currently employed on the enquiry – a gross exaggeration – but several promising lines of enquiry augured 'a speedy resolution of this distressing mystery' – wishful thinking! 'Augur' indeed! Browne smiled. The *Clarion* must have taken on some new Oxbridge wallah who talked like his daughter.

In various other parts of the town the article was being read with similar interest. By Sue Swindell, with some satisfaction. 'Looks as though some of the little devils are getting their comeuppance at last.'

By Shaun Grant, with cynical resignation. 'Give 'em another twenty-four hours and they'll have it all down to us.'

By Martin Crossley, with trepidation but no comment.

By the general populace, with salacious attention.

When the last of his team had departed, Browne sent out for coffee. He resented, as chief inspectors always had, having to sit at his desk when there was so much to be done. He knew, though, that the investigation would be less efficient if he were not there to assess and process all the information that came in. As the *Clarion* had reported, if inaccurately, there were plenty of officers out there. He was grateful for them, but their arrival only when the fates of three girls were at stake made him angry. If the men had been sent now, they must have been available before. If he had had them three days ago, things might not have come to their present pass.

He let his mind play over the current situation and the various members of his shift who were dealing with it. He had seen Clement's kick at the waste bin as the DC read his action sheet and realised he was still being excluded from what he considered the more exciting enquiry. The man should have learned by now that he couldn't pick and choose his jobs.

Not for the first time, Browne tried to weigh up the young DC – not all that young, actually. He seemed inoffensive, bland perhaps, even insipid. Jennifer Taylor made no secret of her contempt for him, slapping him down in discussions. Benny, though, seemed to think well of him, considered there was scope for his potential here in Cloughton.

Perhaps Clement had made too many new starts. Hadn't he begun his working life in some building society? A clerk with the Halifax, that was it. Then he'd joined the North Yorkshire force before moving again, this time to Cloughton. The last move was understandable. After the shock of losing his young wife and infant son it was natural that he should want to up sticks, be somewhere that didn't continually remind him of what was gone.

What he needed now was a good mate and there was no young male in the regular shift to offer his services. The team was almost too politically correct – more women than men since they'd co-opted Shakila for this enquiry. Some sort of relationship with a woman would be even better and, around last Christmas, Browne had thought there was something happening between Clement and Caroline but he could see that now she was finding him a nuisance.

A tap at the door was followed by the entry of a coffee tray, borne not by Karen from the canteen but by John Carroll. Browne blinked and slid his empty cup into his top drawer. The superintendent settled his spare frame comfortably and asked, 'How's Hannah?'

Guiltily, Browne realised that he had not thought about his wife for the last hour. It seemed his face had expressed his feelings and Carroll shook his head. 'Don't blame yourself for being distracted by the shop, Tom. It's likely just what Hannah wants. Your GP too, I'll bet.'

103

Browne nodded. 'The only possible answer is that she's getting steadily worse, but please don't stop asking.'

Browne had been wondering whether to pour the coffee but now Carroll proceeded to dispense his own largesse. 'So, what's the immediate situation?'

'Things are a bit better in a way. We know what we're dealing with. Benny and Ginny are rallying round . . .'

'And everyone at the shop, I hope.'

Browne smiled. 'Their solidarity is taking the form of no jokes at briefings, no objections to my instructions, apart from the odd kick at the bin . . .'

'We have left Benny in a pretty frustrating situation. Heading the team is being alternately held out to him and snatched away again.'

Browne nodded. 'At the accident scene yesterday I could feel his waves of resentment almost physically, though it wasn't Benny who kicked the bin.'

'So, where are we?'

Browne ticked off on his fingers. 'With the Akrams, still at square one. There's a team out asking about Frankie Leonard. Maybe we should be looking for a body.'

'You'd better start at the bus garage then.'

Browne managed a weak smile. 'We're doing nothing about Adele Batty, at least until after the PM.' Browne had noted the light of battle in his son-in-law's eye as he had made that ruling but he made no mention of it now. 'Several aspects of the accident scene are puzzling, besides what Beckham pointed out. I can't work out how the driver managed to crash the vehicle so firmly into the building. According to all the witnesses, it had been standing at the traffic lights only seconds before. He wouldn't have had the momentum . . .'

'Well, don't get fanciful and tell me the driver killed the girl and engineered the crash in an attempt to account for the body.'

'He'd hardly have risked killing himself. Beckham seemed to think he was in a bad way.'

'And he said the girl's wound hadn't bled?'

'There wasn't much blood anywhere, just small smears from superficial cuts. Not much in the way of injuries to passengers.

Beckham's coming in later this morning to give us a statement.'

Carroll drained his cup. 'I think you're right to leave the Battys
alone for the present. Any more on these thefts from doctors'
cars?'

'I've left Clement on it.'

Carroll grinned. 'So, he's the vandal attacking the bins.'

Dave Crumb had accepted a lift from his wife, on her way to the
Infirmary for her six thirty shift on Ward Five. This had brought
him to the Town Park, scene of his own current employment, at
an inconveniently early hour. He'd preferred that, however, to
two bus changes, and Pete's coffee stall would be open in a few
minutes. The full story of brother Bob and his body on the bus
should be good for a couple of free cups.

Now he knew that Bob's injuries were not as serious as the
doctors had first thought, he'd enjoy telling the tale until he had
to begin his own duties at eight o'clock. The park still lay in
darkness except for the path along the top side that had the
benefit of the floodlighting round the adult education centre. He
could see, sharp against it, the plinth on which a white marble
likeness of one of the town's long-dead benefactors reflected its
orange glow.

The row of drinking fountains beside it showed as just a huge
black oblong. Dave knew that, miraculously, one of the fountains
had survived the attacks of both time and vandals and still
worked. Last summer he had been one of the crew sent by the
Council to fill in the park's pond and turn it into another
flowerbed. It had not been a pleasant job, clearing the remains of
rusty old prams and drowned kittens. In July it had been hot.
The pond water had stunk as they siphoned it away but the little
fountain had provided drinkable water.

It was one of a row, each built into a separate, roofed, stone
shelter with an arched entrance, solid and Victorian. Across the
path from it was a seat of much more modern workmanship,
though, in Dave's opinion, they'd made it in keeping. Wooden
slats were supported by wrought ironwork. It looked very elegant but it wasn't very comfortable. Even so, Dave had chosen
to sit there to eat his sarnies.

It would be a bit parky sitting up there now. He was smiling at this clever pun when a handbell rang, Pete's signal to the men, busy turning trestles, hollow metal pipes and great sheets of canvas into market stalls, that the coffee was ready. Dave hurried to join them.

Mitchell was surprised to find the Leonards' house on a pleasant, tree-lined street, in the middle of a short terrace fronted by well-kept, small gardens. Number nine was marked off on either side by tall, neatly trimmed privet hedges, the neighbours' defences. Number nine had a low wall abutting the pavement, against which leaned an assortment of rotting planks and wood panels, the result, Mitchell surmised, of the removal of domestic fixtures and fittings. They had lain in their present position long enough for rough grass and weeds to grow through them. The well-proportioned stone bay window had its panes veiled on the inside by grubby, ragged-edged sheeting.

Before knocking, Mitchell walked to the end of the terrace and round to the back. Here the terraced houses had paved yards where tubs for flowers were arranged so as to leave parking space for modest saloons. The Leonards' area was adorned with a battered gate, off its hinges and lying on the flags.

Going back to the front street, he was approached by a woman who had emerged from the house next door. 'You the police?' Mitchell agreed that he was. 'That Kevin again? What's he done now?'

'Nothing I know about. I'm looking for Frankie.'

'She'll be at school. Probably the only one of the little beggars that is!'

Mitchell was puzzled. Had the Leonard parents not questioned their neighbours? Had his colleagues not done so? He explained the situation, heard that Mrs Barr had returned late the previous evening from a visit to see her new grandson and made a note that she had been missed. She looked askance at the decomposing wood and ragged curtains. 'Poor lass. If she was hiding away from all this in my place, I wouldn't let on. Look, I can leave my shopping till this afternoon if you want to talk to me when you've finished in there.' A derisory toss of her head indicated the Leonards' front door. 'Don't, whatever you do, eat or drink anything in there. Your system won't have developed a resistance to it. I'll have my kettle on.' She scurried back up her own garden path.

His second encounter with the family went very much as his short acquaintance with them had led Mitchell to expect. Mrs Leonard opened the door after his second knock, then backed away, leaving him to follow her into the main room. Depositing the baby on the grubby rug beside a bedraggled cat, she threw the stub of her cigarette into an overflowing ashtray, lit another one and instructed her second son to wake his father.

The languid Stevie, arms dangling over greasy chair arms, eyes glued to the television screen, ignored her. The mother's eyes appealed to Mitchell who kicked the boy's foot and jerked his own head towards the door. The boy slouched out. He was emaciated and Mitchell wondered whether he would have the energy to mount the stairs and whether he might genuinely be ill. He'd have to ask Greenwood. Suddenly he laughed at himself. Perhaps he was in good company with the Leonards.

The father, when he appeared, bleary and irritable, had one fixed idea. Frankie had run away because she was being bullied and he wasn't saying any more till Mr Greenwood was here.

What, Mitchell demanded, could be said with Mr Greenwood here and not without him? Mr Greenwood, it appeared, could stop the police twisting a justified complaint into grounds for slander. Mr Leonard knew the police and how they had it in for people like him but Mitchell could take it as gospel that Frankie was being bullied.

'If you know the police, maybe the police know you, Mr Leonard.'

'There you are!' The man turned to his wife as witness. 'What was I just saying?'

Pressed about the alleged bullying, both parents had shrugged. 'Well, it isn't us as hits her.'

Mitchell put his hands safely in his pockets. 'I didn't think it would be. That would be a bit too much effort.' In a few further minutes, he had established that the feckless pair knew little about Frankie's existence beyond that she was no trouble at school and that she made herself useful at home. He was wasting precious time on them.

When he returned to his car, he found a small girl leaning

against it. She seemed self-assured, about ten years old and sufficiently like Frankie in appearance for Mitchell to recognise a sister. She proved to be a young woman of few words and those to the point.

'I'm Marie. They think I'm at school.'

'Why aren't you?'

"Cause I'm looking for Frankie. Somebody's got to and they won't bother.'

The morning was cold and the child was scantily clad but Mitchell dared not take her into his car. 'I'm bothering – but I need more help than I've just had in there.' Man and child glared balefully at the peeling door with its grimy glass panel.

'What do you want to know?'

'I'll tell you something I've seen for myself. I bet this family is run by you and Frankie between you.'

He saw that he had won her over, though she did not smile. 'Just about.'

'So, who's been knocking Frankie about?'

The child shook her head. 'She wouldn't tell me. She *says* she was shoved out of the classroom and bumped into the wall.'

'But you don't believe her?'

'I know it happened but she had the bruises before that and she's got them on both sides.'

Frantically, Mitchell sought a way to regularise the discussion. Interviewing children was fraught with hazards but was a valuable exercise. They noticed things that their elders either missed altogether or took for granted and failed to mention and they volunteered information that more circumspect adults would keep back. Maybe he could take the child back into school and talk to her in the presence of a female teacher but that might inhibit her. Even without a chaperone, Marie might not be so communicative another time. He brushed aside his scruples.

'Who do you think did it?' She shrugged as though it were a matter of little importance. Worse things happened. 'Your father thinks that Frankie has run off because she's being bullied. Do you think she's frightened of somebody?'

Marie considered, then shook her head. 'Nah, Frankie's not a tinner. Are the police going to find her?'

'Yes.' He would keep his promise personally if routine procedure failed this child.

'How?'

'By asking hundreds of questions.'

Marie was disappointed, then scornful. 'What good's that? If somebody's hurt Frankie or frightened her off, they'll tell lies about it. Lots of people tell lies anyway, just for the hell of it.'

Mitchell kept his face straight. 'I see you appreciate our problems.'

His phone rang and he took a step or two away to answer it. Putting it away again, he opened the car door. 'That was my boss. I'll have to go.' As he drove up the street, he saw Marie slip into the garden of the sympathetic neighbour. He determined that he would be the one to break the news to her that her sister had been found.

9

Dave Crumb's stomach had been telling him for some time that he'd had breakfast too early. The gang's first job today had been to realign the stone slabs that comprised the steps from the main path down to the sunken rose garden. After the gales and rain that had held the work up earlier in the week, they had made good progress this morning.

The slabs now rose vertically and evenly. Dave thought that the expanding tree roots that had displaced them would do so again and said so. He was offended when his mate guffawed. 'Not in thy lifetime they waint. It'll be thy nippers as'll have to see to 'em next time.'

According to the gaffer, it would not be break time until the red and white tape that had cordoned off the area around the steps had been untied and the stakes pulled up and thrown into the back of the van. Dave pointed out that he had been on the job twenty minutes early. To prove it he indicated the used edging stones that he had chiselled clean whilst he waited for his mates with the heavy lifting tackle to arrive.

Excused clearing-up duty on these grounds, he wandered away, up the grassy slope. He'd have a slurp from the drinking fountain if it wasn't frozen up and eat his sarnies sitting on the fancy seat opposite. He'd have a good view from up there of the general effect of all their 'refurbishments', as the paper kept calling their repairs.

As he approached the bench, he saw that someone else had chosen the same picnic site. A blue-anoraked figure, hooded against the cold, was seated with its back to him. Looked like just a lass. Better call out. If he crept up on her she might think he was a dirty old man or something. This park had a bad enough reputation already.

The girl ignored him. Stuck-up little bitch! 'Where's yer manners, then? Can't you answer a civil question?' She sat unnaturally still. He went closer, touched her shoulder, then leaped back as the girl's body crumpled over the iron arm. His sandwich, with only one bite taken from it, fell on the grass, to be gratefully set upon by a mixed flock of sparrows and pigeons.

Dave half ran, half fell down the slope back to his companions. Somehow, they interpreted his gibbering. They had not seen the pathetic corpse and, after their labours, were ready for some light relief.

'Must be a curse on 'is bloody family. Yesterday their Bob were drivin' a bleedin' stiff around, now Dave's found isself another.'

''Ere, Dave, 'ow many more brothers 'ave yer?'

Mitchell's car threatened to be troublesome, starting only after a third assault on the ignition. Then, to atone, it moved sweetly into the line of vehicles travelling the main road. The mist that had earlier blotted out the valley and veiled the hillside had thinned and disappeared. Now, the day was sharp, colder but bright. He felt the sun lifting his spirits, even as he reminded himself that another child had died.

The car coughed as it made a turn, uphill and left, but the park gates were safely reached. They had been vandalised yet again and stood open, the left one swinging on its hinges and the other torn away from the gatepost with its bottom corner sunk into muddy, half-frozen grass. The large painted sign forbidding entry until such time as the council workmen should finish their improvements lay, face up, in the middle of the tarmacked path. Now it made ominous contact with the exhaust mounting as one of Mitchell's wheels passed over a corner of it.

Taking the path that ran alongside the college, he drew up, short of the drinking fountains, and got out to meet Browne. The two men looked down at the slight form, half sitting, half lying across the wooden slats and the whorls of wrought iron. The seat looked an inhospitable resting place, but Frankie Leonard was past minding about that. Mitchell turned and looked down the grassy hill to where, in the centre of the large flowerbed that had once been a pond, a tower of scaffolding rose around a defunct fountain surmounted by a white statue. Beside it, guarded by two uniformed police constables, were foreshortened figures, clad in yellow plastic crossed with silver reflective tape, huddled in a group.

Mitchell shivered and returned his attention to the young girl's body that had brought him here. Thankful that only Browne was his witness, he struggled against the tears that harm to a child always produced. He was not ashamed of them but he had grown weary of overhearing fellow officers express surprise that 'the macho bastard at least cares about something'.

Even if it had been filled with luxury and privilege, fifteen years would not have been much of a life. Frankie's had been spent in that dreadful house, watched over – or not – by two inadequates. The tears actually fell as Mitchell thought of spunky little Marie, facing the same disadvantages and deprived of her kindred spirit. It struck him that she had already faced the problem of her sister's absence, calmly taking matters into her own hands, accepting that nothing could be expected from her parents and that the police would disappoint her.

He brushed his face with the back of his hand. Marie would survive. She had learned at a tender age that you could rely on no one but yourself. He'd better attend to his own responsibilities. 'No obvious injuries to this girl either, as far as I can see. No books and bags this time, though.'

Receiving no reply, he glanced at his father-in-law and noted his greenish pallor. Tom was not squeamish and this was a very unmessy corpse. 'Another migraine?' Browne nodded. 'Aren't the pills any use?'

'I forgot to bring them with me.'

The superintendent's car appeared in the gateway and Mitchell heard, with reprehensible satisfaction, the clang that told him that the big VW's exhaust had also fallen foul of the torn-down noticeboard. 'What are you going to do?'

Browne smiled wanly. 'First, I think I'm going to be sick. Then, I'm going to take some of the leave that the super offered me earlier in the week.' He retired hastily behind the drinking fountain from where Mitchell heard him accomplish his first object.

Carroll insisted on driving Browne home himself. Mitchell hoped the reason for this was a consideration of his own ability to lead the present investigation in Browne's place. In the absence of both his superior officers, he was going to have to take responsibility for the immediately necessary procedures, whatever the outcome of their deliberations. He checked that the pathologist and a police surgeon were on their way and instructed the carload of uniformed officers that was just then arriving to tape off a sizeable area round the mock-Victorian seat. Carroll's car reappeared in a very few minutes, avoiding the offending sign this time by driving on to the grass. Mitchell diverted one of the PCs to its removal.

'Your father-in-law gave you a resounding vote of confidence, Benny!' was the superintendent's greeting. 'Of course, he's not on top form. That'll account for it.'

Mitchell hoped that the baring of his teeth passed for a grin. He had thought Carroll above this kind of infantile humour but he supposed it came with the job. That was something he would change when he'd climbed the next two rungs of the ladder – only one rung if the force ever got round to merging the two inspectors' ranks.

To his immense satisfaction, he found himself, at the beginning of the two o'clock briefing in Browne's office, with many caveats, in charge of his second murder investigation. He celebrated by trimming several inches from each of Browne's untidy trailing ivies.

When Jennifer offered to break the news of Frankie's death to the Leonard family, Mitchell was sorely tempted to accept. His reason was less a wish to avoid this harrowing task than a fear that he would be unable to refrain from giving the lackadaisical parents the tongue-lashing that he considered they deserved.

Arriving there, he was glad that he and his sergeant had gone along together to the ill-kept house on Spencer Terrace. They had found young Marie, conducting her own house-to-house enquiry, scornful of the efforts of the two constables whose work she was duplicating.

As if their conversation earlier in the day had been uninterrupted, the child pointed out to Mitchell, with some justification, 'I know which folk to believe.' The two officers delivered their bleak message to Marie, separately from her family, taking her into the marked Escort. There, with Jennifer's arm round her, she wept. Mitchell promised her, with a conviction that made her believe him, that his team would find out why her sister had died.

Marie's were the only tears for Frankie that Mitchell was to see.

*　　*　　*

113

When, some half-hour later, Jennifer, Caroline and Clement reported as instructed to Browne's office they found the desk heaped with sandwiches and the filing cabinet adorned with a coffee tray. Mitchell waved at them to be seated. 'Thank Karen, not me, and help yourselves. I'm not waiting on you. A working lunch is all we've time for, so what have we got and what strikes us?'

Caroline, promptly pouring coffee, spoke over her shoulder. 'We'd better make sure that the folk who are out looking for Nazreen have checked the other local parks.'

'I think it's high time we put more pressure on the Akram family. They're laughing as they watch the search. They're obviously not concerned about finding the girl, didn't report her missing, don't want to talk to us when we go to them.' Seeing how quickly the sandwiches were disappearing, Jennifer paused to fill her plate. 'Any normal parents would want reports every five minutes. Alive or dead, they know where she is.'

'It's exactly a week since they say she left for Leicester. It's a pity we didn't think to –'

'Ah, but we did.' Mitchell grinned at Clement. 'The CI thought of it before you. There's a mobile control van down at the station questioning regular weekend travellers, one at the other end in Leicester and one in Sheffield where she would have had to change trains. And we did a reconstruction this morning.'

'Is that where Shakila is?'

Mitchell nodded. 'The super said Akram needed his arm twisting to take part and drive her to the station. Threatened to charge the fare to us! He also said Shakila looked very fetching in a pink sari. I'll be taking her with me to the lab if she's back in time.'

'So that Dr Ledgard can ogle the pink sari?'

Mitchell gave Caroline a caricature of a smile. 'Because it'll be her first PM. Stop being facetious and pour us some more coffee. Anyone have any ideas about why the bodies of the other two were left in such plain view?'

'Over-confidence? Some advantage gained from early discovery? No means of moving them? Planned to but was disturbed?'

'You'd be a bit conspicuous carrying someone Adele's size in a fireman's lift while you climbed off a bus.'

Mitchell ignored Clement and picked up the second of

Caroline's string of suggestions. 'What has someone gained from our finding the bodies when we did – apart from putting egg on our faces because we didn't find Frankie till today?'

'We didn't know she was missing till yesterday and she might not have been on the park bench all the time.'

'Dr Ledgard thinks she died there.'

'When?'

'He wouldn't commit himself, of course, but he thinks she'd been dead forty-eight hours or so when he examined her. That takes us back to Wednesday morning and she was seen by lots of people just before lunch. Er . . . Don't you think I deserve that?' Mitchell addressed Caroline whose hand had frozen before it reached him with his refilled cup.

'Sorry. We thought Frankie was a runaway. Now we're treating both bodies as murder. We'll look a bit silly if it turns out to be a job for the public health department. Maybe it's not a crime we're dealing with but an epidemic, some awful disease.'

'A disease wouldn't dump people on a bus or a park bench.'

Caroline rounded on Clement. 'But it would. If it's a virus that causes heart failure or something, the girls would die wherever they happened to be. Adele died in just the place she usually is at school lunchtime, leaving the meal her parents had paid for and off to play the slot machines in town. And, if Frankie was being bullied, as her father insists, she might well have fled to the park as somewhere her tormentors wouldn't think of looking for her.'

Mitchell nodded. 'There's just a chance you're right. We'll look even sillier, though, if you're wrong and we've let the trail go cold, so we'll have an incident room set up this afternoon. We'll keep open minds, but we'll begin working on the assumption of murder of both girls by the same person – by the same apparent lack of means. If I'm wrong, I'll call you all together again to apologise.' He ignored the disbelieving murmurs.

'To go back to where we were, it would be less risky for someone just to dump Frankie in the park than to hang around digging a grave.'

'Could the men see the seat and the drinking fountains from the bottom of the hill where they were working?'

Mitchell shook his head. 'Probably not. We went down to see.

At the top of the slope, there's a dip before the path alongside the college. And, as one of the workmen said, they assumed any cars they heard were on the road outside. Anyway, their equipment was making a din.'

'Any significance in two brothers finding the bodies?'

'How could a bus driver not hear the struggle directly above him if someone attacked a healthy teenage girl?'

'And why, on a freezing cold morning, should his brother go and eat his sarnies away from the shelter of the back of a van where his pals were?'

'An impulse, he says. We'll get someone on to a possible connection between the Crumb family and the girls.'

'What about the parents?' Clement asked as he reached out for the last sandwich.

With a lightning strike, Mitchell beat him to it. 'As suspects, you mean?' He took a triumphant bite. 'I can't see the Leonards wanting to do Frankie any harm. When we told her her daughter was dead, the useless woman's first question was, "How will I manage now?"'

'What about Adele's?'

'Can't wait to get at them. I had a word with Barson from traffic who spoke to them yesterday. He didn't have much to tell me. She's an only child. They appeared suitably upset. Barson wasn't on the lookout for anything else at that point. Dr Ledgard has given both girls priority now, so, with luck, we'll have a cause of death before we knock off tonight. Meanwhile, the search for Nazreen goes on. I want you, Caroline, to go back to Cynthia Summers. Take her minutely through every last word she remembers that the girl has spoken to her. If Miss Summers was teaching her without payment, there must have been a good relationship between them. The girl would surely have felt free to confide in her.

'Adrian and Jennifer, you're going back to harry the Colin Hewitt Comprehensive. In the circumstances, I think Mr Greenwood will be happy for you to talk to anyone you like. Feel your way. Ask Mrs Barron to suggest which children might help us. Make sure you've got a suitable chaperone. With a bit of luck, the EWO will be in again.'

Mitchell was irritated by the two officers' mutual glances of antipathy. He ground his teeth silently. Sending Caroline with

Clement would only have produced unspoken reproaches from her. He was beginning to understand what a DCI's job was all about and he reflected briefly on the problems he himself had doubtless made for Browne over the years. His guilt was compounded as his gaze rested on the row of pathetically shorn ivy plants. In an act of contrition for his obstreperous past he watered them copiously.

Constable Shakila Nazir would have enjoyed the novelty of her morning activities if they had not been interrupted by a message from Mitchell outlining his plans for her afternoon. She was keen enough, of course, to see a post-mortem examination. Even though it would hardly be a pleasant spectacle, it would supply lessons she had to learn about the human body, the skills of a pathologist and the nature of forensic evidence.

However, she would have preferred this disturbing experience not to have been under Mitchell's eye. Before she had been called on to the enquiry into Nazreen's disappearance, he was the only individual on the shift that she had heard of and what she had heard had not inclined her to admire him.

The story of his getting his inspector's daughter pregnant and bringing her back from studying for a degree at Oxford University had been repeated and commented on throughout the Cloughton force until there was nothing further to say. Those who knew the couple only slightly were astonished that a clever girl like Virginia, attractive too, though not pretty, should have had any truck with him. Those who knew Virginia only by sight pitied her for being saddled with three further children and for having to live with a loud and decidedly unhandsome boor.

The Mitchell whom Shakila had met had been a pleasant surprise. He was all that his reputation promised, but no one had mentioned his intelligence, his willingness to give credit to his fellow officers or his patience and empathy with children. She thought he was probably a very fond father. He had little tolerance of disorder, weakness and general slackness, though and Shakila dreaded displaying any squeamishness this afternoon.

Her two-hour drive from Leicester meant a last-minute arrival and no time to stand about feeling nervous. Mitchell was waiting for her in the little reception office at the morgue. After she had scrambled into the protective clothing he handed her, he led her through a large, cold, tiled area, lined with fridges and littered with stretcher-trolleys.

The bodies of the two girls were already lying on tables in the lab itself, attended by the pathologist, his assistant and the Coroner's officer. Shakila watched with interest as Dr Ledgard examined the clothing that the bodies still wore, then removed it, piece by piece and stowed each away in its own sterile bag. He examined the first body, Adele's, externally from top to toe, lifting arms and legs, opening hands, turning the body on to its face. She became enthralled.

'What causes of death,' she heard Mitchell ask, 'won't show at this stage?'

Ledgard raised an eyebrow. 'Many and various. The most likely is a lethal injection.'

'And we'll find a puncture, if it's that?'

'Only if we're lucky or the injector was careless.'

Shakila was still willing Ledgard to hurry on to the first major incision, the ear–thyroid–ear–pubis cut that she had been told this pathologist favoured, after which she would know whether or not she would survive the ordeal with credit. She knew that Dr Ledgard had been informed that his examination was her first and she assumed that the flow of comment and instruction was chiefly for her benefit. 'Note the volume and character of the fluid effusions lying in the chest and abdomen,' he commanded, with a quick smile at her. The scalpel flashed under the strip lighting.

The said fluid effusions then absorbed his attention and Shakila knew he was no longer aware of her. She breathed a huge sigh of relief at having survived the worst moment and retained her dignity, then wished she had not as the stench filled her throat and nostrils. Dr Ledgard murmured into his microphone, '. . . lungs over-inflated . . . intense pulmonary oedema with pleural effusion . . .'

Shakila progressed from feeling thankful to feeling proud of herself. She watched, absorbed, as the pathologist took his specimens of fluid and tissue, accumulating a collection of sealed and labelled jars, all swiftly dispatched to the refrigerator. At last, she began to relax.

Having dismissed an air embolism as the cause of death, Dr

Ledgard was proceeding to a consideration of poison. 'We'll tie off both ends of the stomach and wash the exterior, then open it over a wide-necked jar. We don't want poison and pills washing down the drain.' As the contents of Adele's shockingly large stomach swilled into the bottle, Shakila was surrounded by swirling blackness. She fought desperately to stay on her feet.

Moments later, she became aware that she was being steadied by a surreptitious hand under her elbow. It was Mitchell's. When, recovering, she gave him a slight nod, he removed it discreetly. Ledgard turned from Adele's remains and rinsed his hands, leaving his assistant to tidy up and make all presentable again. He grinned round his audience. 'Thoroughly healthy, uninjured child. She ought to be sitting up and demanding to know why she's here. How about a coffee before the second half of the entertainment?'

'My constable hasn't even had lunch. I think I'll excuse her from Part Two.' When Shakila protested half-heartedly, he replied with a wink and a whispered, 'Don't push your luck.' Shakila vowed she would never hear a word against Mitchell again.

Back in Winter Street, Caroline once again found herself taking tea with Clifford Summers as they awaited Cynthia's return. However, he disappeared, promptly and tactfully, whilst she answered Caroline's questions.

Cynthia's greeting was more uncertain than her father's had been. 'I do assure you, Constable Webster, that I know nothing about Nazreen that I have not already divulged.' Her manner was quite agitated.

Caroline swallowed her impatience and reminded herself that the woman had spent her day facing a succession of rioting classes before braving Friday evening crowds as she shopped for the meal that she now had to cook. DI Mitchell thought it likely that, if Nazreen had confided in anyone at all, it would be in this woman. Caroline agreed with him and was prepared to take trouble with her. 'Well, at least drink a cup of tea before I try to jog your memory. Your father has been entertaining me. What a beautiful speaking voice he has. He could have been a radio newsreader, or an actor, maybe.'

Cynthia took her cup and seemed marginally more relaxed. 'He was a solicitor, actually, but he did acting as a hobby. He belonged to the Crown Street Players for years. I remember, when I was a girl, he had very enthusiastic reviews – not only in the *Clarion*, but in the *Yorkshire Post* too – when he played the title role in Oscar Wilde's *The Importance of Being Earnest*. It's so necessary, don't you think, to have a precise enunciation for Wilde?'

Caroline felt she could agree with this without compromising her integrity. She had neither read nor seen a play by Wilde, though she had at least heard of this one. Surely, though, clear enunciation was important for an actor, whatever the play.

Cynthia was warming to her subject. 'The Leeds paper said he was old for the part and, of course, he was. I've been told how successfully he played Lysander and Androcles as a young man but, even as a small child, I remember him as being rather old. He was forty-six when I was born.'

It occurred to Caroline that she had been thinking of this woman, with her infirm and dependent father, as being elderly herself. Cynthia reinforced this impression with her fussy, old-fashioned manners and way of speaking. Possibly, though, she was no more than thirty-four or thirty-five years old and maybe her engagement was not so odd. Physically, she was not unattractive, though the permanently anxious expression cancelled the impact of her faultless grooming and quite stylish clothes. Her name too belonged to another generation. Like Derek Swindell's.

Cynthia's discourse was cheerfully continuing on the subject of her father. 'Temporarily, his stroke robbed him of his lovely voice. His speech was slurred and he and I were both embarrassed until he regained control of it. As soon as he did, I knew he would survive. He still has many limitations, but he's Father again. Voices matter to both of us. I was first attracted to my fiancé by his voice, before I knew anything else about him.'

Caroline saw that here was another subject that would keep her witness happily chattering, but it was time to return to the purpose of her visit and she urged Cynthia to concentrate on remembering details of the coaching sessions. 'Just some tiny point might help us. Surely Nazreen said something about her ambitions, her future study plans, the work she was preparing for . . .'

'Well, sometimes, I suppose. She was going to apply to Newcastle and Edinburgh Universities. Their faculties of medicine have a good reputation and she mentioned that there were no Akrams in either of those places. We really didn't talk much in general because she was so keen to get on with the work. She had such a quick understanding, always asking questions about details the textbook missed out for the sake of simplicity. She was always very appreciative of the time I gave her, had always done the basic reading in preparation and completed the tasks I'd set the previous time.' Cynthia sighed. 'What a pleasant job teaching would be if more pupils were like Nazreen.'

'Did Nazreen have a pleasant speaking voice?' Caroline asked, on impulse.

Cynthia considered. 'Not particularly. It had the slight sing-song quality Asians have for speaking English.' She blinked. 'Constable Webster, we're speaking in the past tense. I don't think you'll find that Nazreen has shared the fate of those other two girls. She's not their type at all.'

As she climbed into her car, Caroline was still shaking her head. Even if she never read a paper or watched television, surely Cynthia's own experience had taught her that people do not always get what they deserve in this life. Very seldom, in fact. On the other hand, though Cynthia was less than ten years older than herself, she had been brought up by a father who was the same age as her own grandfather. Clifford Summers had taught his daughter what he believed – that, if you worked hard at school, you would get a good job and that, if you treated other people well, you would be treated well in return.

Caroline inserted her ignition key, then changed her mind and climbed out of the car again. She let the old man's chatter play itself back to her. He had mentioned, in passing, that a Mrs Aiken helped in the house and 'kept an eye out' for him when Cynthia taught a full day. Recently, this neighbour had taken Nazreen into her house and entertained her. Mr Summers had had a doctor's appointment, from which, he had been at pains to point out, he and his daughter should have returned in plenty of time for the girl's lesson. Unfortunately, the doctor had been called out to an emergency and they had had to keep their visitor

121

waiting for almost twenty minutes. It was a long shot but a recent twenty-minute conversation with the girl they were searching for had to be followed up.

Mrs Aiken was as willing to gossip about 'the little darkie' as Cynthia seemed anxious to avoid it. 'I'm not prejudiced, you know. Nothing against them as long as they behave themselves.' She was willing too to gossip about the Summers family, the rest of her neighbours and any other victim on whom she was allowed to cast her aspersions.

Cynthia was her particular choice. 'Nice as pie when she wants me to nanny the old man and looking down her nose when she doesn't. Never asks me in just for a cup of tea, mind. Just when I can make myself useful. And then she locks everything up.'

'Everything?'

'Huh, cabinet drawers, bedside cupboard, wardrobe . . .'

'So, you clean for them?'

She bristled. 'Do I look like a charlady?'

Caroline gave her a bland smile. 'I don't know. Is there a special way charladies look? I just assumed that, if you were in Miss Summers' room, you were there for a reason.'

After a pause for thought, Mrs Aiken nodded. 'Course I was. I was fetching something for the old man.'

'From Cynthia's room?'

'Yes, one of his books she'd been reading.'

'And you looked for it in the wardrobe?'

Too late, Caroline bit her tongue. Now she had alienated her witness and there was no way she was going to be able to persuade her to be helpful. She'd pass on the job to Shakila. Then, Mrs Aiken could show her virtuous tolerance of another little darkie.

10

Even at the end of Friday afternoon Mrs Barron was elegant in cherry red, maybe an attempt to cheer herself up. Surprisingly, the colour married well with the orange hair, though Jennifer, who knew instinctively about such things, could have told her that the lipstick was a mistake. She welcomed Jennifer to her office but seemed uncertain of what she could tell that would help the police.

'Tell me about Adele,' Jennifer suggested. 'Don't get the files out this afternoon. Just give me a flavour of the girl. We've got at least a partial picture of Frankie from her parents and brothers and sisters. I personally have heard just two opinions of Adele and those are contradictory.' Mrs Barron looked interested.

'Her parents describe a paragon of virtue whose teachers "have it in for her" because she has what they call "a bit of character". Mr Swindell tells us that she's fat, loud and vulgar. I expect the truth is somewhere between.'

Mrs Barron seemed to be anxiously seeking phrases that would neither commend nor condemn the girl unfairly. Jennifer wished all her witnesses were as fair and as articulate. 'Adele is – was – quite a complex character. All her school work is written neatly in fountain pen ink, when most of her class produce a scribble in ballpoint if we're lucky.

'She specialised in dumb insolence – asking clever questions of insecure teachers and then pointing out, to her classmates' amusement, that they'd contradicted themselves. Some of us had her marked out for a career in politics at some level. She was subversive, powerful, bullying – but not in any obvious physical way, at least not usually.'

'Mr Leonard claims she bullied Frankie.'

'She did. She made Frankie co-operate in her misbehaviour but she isn't responsible for Frankie's bruises. I could never decide whether the father or the brother Stephen was the culprit there. We took what steps we could. It's all recorded in the file we had copied for you. I don't think Adele has ever punched or hit another pupil but knowing she's permanently out of the way might have made life just about bearable for some of them.'

'Do you blame her parents?'

'To some extent. She was a very bright girl but she had no support from them. Not that she was neglected. On the contrary, she was very much indulged but there was nothing expected of her. It's a common problem here. People make the mistake of thinking our poor showing in public exams reflects poor teaching and low IQs, but we have our share of high-flyers. Nazreen isn't quite the rare bird she seems. Most of the clever children here have a lack of motivation, lousy role models, no one at home with any respect for learning.'

She stopped and smiled at Jennifer. 'Sorry. You've got me on my hobby horse.'

'But it was exactly what I asked for.'

Jennifer hoped she had managed to convey the spirit of this description when she reported back to Mitchell later that afternoon. 'They're being really helpful. You ask a question and you get a duplicated file as well as an oral answer. Greenwood arranged for us to speak to all the girls' main subject teachers but none of them knew as much as Mrs Barron herself. The rest have been asked to contact us if they've got anything that seems relevant. You don't want the whole shoot interviewed, do you?'

Mitchell grinned. 'Not today. Where's Adrian?'

'Still there as far as I know. They assumed we were following up one girl each and that worked well enough.'

Mitchell supposed it had. At least it would have prevented the school staff from realising that his officers couldn't always be civil to each other. 'Right. Go and tuck your girls into bed. Try to be back for debriefing.'

She nodded. 'You won't be seeing much of your tribe at the moment.'

Mitchell had been thinking the same. 'They're over with Hannah so that Tom can go to bed.'

'All of them?'

'Yes. Hannah likes having them there. Says it stops her having time to worry about herself.' There was little more to say, but Jennifer lingered. Mitchell laughed. 'All right. That's it, the blue sheet.'

Jennifer snatched it up and read quickly through the preliminary report on the two post-mortem examinations.

When Clement came in less than five minutes later Mitchell could see that he was full of a new theory. He would let him air it now and with luck he would have subsided before Jennifer came back. How boringly diplomatic he was becoming!

He smiled at himself and invited the DC to sit down. 'Just give me whatever you're bursting with and put the rest in your report. I could do with some good news.'

'Crossley!' announced Clement, cryptically.

'Is that the new man coming to replace Keith Gordon? What about him?'

'He was in school on Tuesday this week.'

'Right.'

'Then on Wednesday, when I was sent round to Heptinstall & Hudson to speak to Faisal Akram, he was in there, asking about houses.'

'That seems perfectly reasonable if he's coming to work here.' Mitchell wondered how long Clement would spin out the story.

'I mentioned it to Greenwood, just making polite conversation. Said I'd seen him there and Greenwood was surprised. It would have been more convenient for Keith Gordon to talk to the new man on Wednesday because he's got a full teaching day on Tuesdays. Crossley said that Tuesday was the only day his present head would allow him to take off because that's when he, Crossley I mean, has three of his free lessons.'

'So, he was staying an extra day to fix himself up and didn't want to be tied up at the school again.'

'I think that's what Greenwood thought. He seemed upset. Thought he was getting a good, keen, straightforward replacement for Mr Gordon and now he finds he's got a bad apple. I felt sorry for him.'

'Is it such a crime to want a day to yourself to get organised? It's not long to January if he's not got himself and his family sorted out with somewhere to live.'

Clement shook his head. 'It wasn't that. It was the lie that worried Mr Greenwood.'

'Well, it doesn't need to worry us, unless we find he was here last Friday and yesterday as well – and that he knew the three girls.'

Clement looked smug. 'I don't know where he was on Friday, but I do know that he lives in Leicester where Nazreen was supposed to turn up. Maybe she did go there and was intercepted by Martin Crossley. Could be that the Akrams, unpleasant though some of them seem to be, are innocently telling us the truth.'

Now Mitchell was interested. 'You didn't get his Leicester address?'

Clement shook his head. 'No, but I'm pretty sure the young man at Heptinstall & Hudson will have done.'

Mitchell smiled sweetly. 'Off you go then. They stay open late on Fridays.' Too late, Clement remembered that Mitchell was looking for a move out of his police house.

The officers who gathered for debriefing on Friday evening wanted to hear only one thing and Mitchell did not keep them in suspense. Picking up the single sheet that lay on his desk, he read from it the key sentence from the preliminary report on the post-mortem examination of their two victims. '"The pathological finding of intense pulmonary oedema supports an interpretation of the cause of death as fatal respiratory distress."'

Looking round at his team's frustrated expressions, he answered their unspoken question. 'Fortunately, I was given a translation. Both girls died because their lungs became waterlogged so that they couldn't breathe. Dr Ledgard couldn't find anything wrong with either of them.'

'Except that they're dead.'

'Yes, Caroline. Except that they're dead. No disease and no injury.'

'So, why . . .?'

'Don't ask. I don't know. He doesn't know. The only explanation he can come up with is some kind of poisoning. "Toxicological origins suspected but nothing found so far." Samples have gone to the lab in Wetherby. On Adele he found . . .' Mitchell paused as he looked for the place in his notes. 'He found "a needle-sized stab wound with evident subcutaneous bleeding."'

126

'So, both girls have been messing about with drugs?'

'At least someone has. Possibly. Adele wasn't giving herself a fix, though. The wound was just above her left shoulder blade.'

'Bony sort of place to inject into.'

'On Frankie it would have been. Adele was conveniently fleshy wherever her attacker chose to jab.'

There was a short silence as the team digested this. It was Clement who broke it. 'The car thefts!'

'I bet you're right.' Mitchell made no comment on this unwonted agreement between Clement and Sergeant Taylor. He felt cold. The only thing harder to take than the murder of a child was murder by a child. He listened to the shift's horrified conjectures.

'If we'd concentrated harder on the thefts we might have had it sorted out before all this happened.'

'Whoever it was could even have meant it as a joke, never intending that anyone should die.'

'For all we know, some Happy Harry's busy doing it again.'

Mitchell raised his hand to put a stop to their pointless self-reproaches. 'Adrian, you should have a list to hand of the victimised doctors. Ring them all and get an accurate list of everything their stolen cases contained. Do it now, man!' Mitchell's voice rose as Clement remained in his place.

The DC did his best to remove the smile of satisfaction that he knew was inappropriate. 'That was the first thing I did when you passed the enquiry on to me, sir. The lists are in the file. Been there for two days.'

Clement waited for Jonathan Stepney in the car park of the same all-night supermarket where the idea of this coaching session had been conceived. He shivered as he watched the mist rising again over the valley after the bright clear day. He peered through it as the minutes ticked by and was hailed as he was on the point of giving up on the lad. 'Don't know about a copper. You look more like a burglar out of a bloody cartoon!'

Clement supposed this was a fair description of the figure he cut in his black tracksters, thermal vest and balaclava that flattened his hair and covered his face all except for a circle in the middle. He forbore to comment on Jonathan's stained jogging pants and handed him a Tesco carrier bag containing two pairs of good quality running socks and a pair of running shoes with which he was loath to part.

The boy stared at them suspiciously, holding them up under the sodium light. 'Bloody 'ell, you said you were going to chuck 'em out.'

'Yes, but not because they're old. I told you, they rub my toes. Runners can wear anything they like on their bodies but they have to be very fussy about their feet.'

'So, what's wrong with these?' He held up the socks which were clearly new.

'They're a present from me. I'm so chuffed at getting somebody else off running. Hurry up and change your shoes. And don't be late next time. My boss doesn't allow me much spare time.'

Jonathan sat on the tarmac beside Clement's car to remove his dilapidated shoes and holey socks. He chose the gaudier pair of new socks and slipped the other into his pocket.

'You wear both pairs – the thin ones first, the thicker ones on top. And don't pull your laces too tight.'

Jonathan obeyed. 'Sorry I were late. A miracle 'appened. My old man got generous and offered to pay for me to go to t'match. I said it were a bit late 'cos I'd arranged to meet somebody. That got his suspicions up because I usually just mess about. I 'ad to listen to a lecture on not getting into bother. 'E let me go, though, when me mum told 'im she'd seen Shaun getting on t'football coach.'

Desperate to begin questioning the lad, Clement forced himself to chatter on about the importance of warming-up exercises. These caused Jonathan much amusement, but, behind the car park's boundary wall, away from the gaze of the late shoppers, he made a passable imitation of Clement's contortions. 'We're going to talk all the time we're running.'

'Oh aye?' Suspiciously.

'It's important. If you're too breathless to hold a conversation you're going at it too hard.' Clement began a slow jog, seeking to soothe his companion's slight antagonism by the introduction of a topic far removed from the deaths of his two schoolmates. 'Would you rather be watching the match with your mates?'

'Not really. I'm not footie mad but Shaun is.'

'Do you always do what Shaun wants?'

'I'm not doing now, am I?'

'No, but you told him a lie so you could be here.' Cloaked by the darkness, Clement blushed for the number of lies he himself had told in setting up their present meeting. 'Feet comfortable?'

'Feels like I'm wearing bloody bedroom slippers. Have you found out who killed those girls yet?' Clement stopped searching for a way to introduce the topic.

'Who says anybody killed them?'

Jonathan glanced over his shoulder from his position a couple of paces in front. 'Stands to reason, dunnit? They didn't die of nowt. Bit of a coincidence it'd be, two in a week.'

'I suppose so. I was wondering if they might have OD'd.'

Jonathan was indignant. 'Frankie was never on owt!'

'How do you know?'

'She wouldn't. She weren't that sort.'

'Was Adele?'

He didn't need to think about it. 'Nah. She got her kicks from jerking people about.'

'What people?'

'Most people. Her mum and dad, her teachers – some of 'em, anyway – other kids, lads who wanted to go out with her . . .'

'You didn't though? You fancied Frankie?'

'Yeah, but she didn't fancy me.' He caught his breath and Clement tactfully misunderstood.

'Bit fast for you? Let's slow down a bit then. From what I can gather, Frankie had a bit too much to do looking after her brothers and sisters to go chasing after any boys, you included.'

'You reckon?' Jonathan evidently liked this theory to account for the spurning of his affections. He trotted along, embroidering the theme himself. 'Yeah, p'raps I'd have been in with a chance, with Stevie being poorly, and when he got better I could have helped her keep an eye on him.'

So, Stevie was less trouble ill than well. 'Is Stevie usually a problem, then?'

'Worse than Kev, and he's only twelve.'

'So, what does he get up to? Same game as you and Shaun? Bit of nicking?' Jonathan came to a halt and leaned against a convenient lamp standard, gasping and protesting. 'Don't stop!' Clement ordered him, urgently. 'At least keep walking. Talk when you've got your breath back.' Clement held his. He could see from the stiff set of the lad's shoulders that he was offended and prayed that he had not ruined the tenuous relationship between them.

Between rasping breaths, Jonathan defended himself. 'I 'aven't nicked owt for ages now. Don't spend as much time with Shaun either. You didn't find owt in our flat, even though he did say I had to look after some stuff. I told him the old man had started searching my room every night since the last bother I was in.'

Their walk had slowed to a stroll and the breath was coming more easily. 'I could put you right on a few things, but if you don't believe me it's a waste of breath.'

'And, if you're carrying on with this game, you can't afford to waste any. OK, I believe you.'

'Well, it's not Shaun doing the cars. He says they don't carry enough to sell and he's too bright to take any stuff himself. I think he's a bit annoyed that he doesn't know who it is either. And neither of Frankie's brothers nick things. At least . . . at least they didn't when she was there to keep tabs on them. Stevie and Kevin are just always in fights. Stevie starts 'em and then Kev has to help out 'cos little brother hasn't the sense to pick on people his own size.'

'So, what's wrong with Stevie?'

Jonathan shrugged. 'Dunno but summat is. Ask your clever police doctors. Race you back to the car.' Laughing, he accelerated to a sprint for the remaining two hundred yards. Clement let him get there first.

11

Satisfied that he had done all that was possible for one day, Mitchell reached for the phone. 'Ginny? I'm on my way.'

'About time. If you see another body on the road, drive round it and keep going.'

'Ginny?' But she had disconnected, leaving Mitchell seriously alarmed. He had not heard any laughter in his wife's tone. And he thought he had heard Kat's voice in the background. The child seemed to have been programmed since before birth to shut her eyes and lie doggo from six each night to six each morning. If the situation at home had made Caitlin wakeful, then the volatile Declan was probably sleepwalking at the bottom of the garden.

Eight years of marriage to Virginia had left Mitchell believing that she would cope with any and every circumstance. She was a policeman's daughter and she had never before complained, in jest or in earnest, about the hours he had to work. She had understood the demands of the job from her early childhood. She had cheerfully borne and coped with four children, studying for her degree in and amongst. Later she had taken on a part-time job and still had energy to take a lively interest in his cases.

Her police background meant that she understood very well the need for complete confidentiality and Mitchell had enjoyed a greater freedom than most officers to air at home his view on his crime victims, his suspects and his superior officers. She was always a useful sounding board for his own ideas and, often, an intelligent source of suggestion for new lines of enquiry. Tonight, it seemed, she needed him to listen to her.

Driving home, he found his attitude to this new role was ambivalent. He didn't want to be Ginny's comfort and consolation. What was wrong with him? Was he really the self-centred, ill-mannered bastard that many officers in the Cloughton force considered him? If that was the case, tonight was not a suitable occasion for her to find it out. He could at least go through the motions for her. Tonight he would be the one to listen and to make suggestions and he would try to find time over the week-end to do some of the coping himself.

Filled with good intentions and not a little trepidation, he went into the house and found her in the kitchen. There was no sign of any of the children and Ginny greeted him cheerfully. 'I couldn't be bothered cooking supper. I rang up for an Indian.'

He was relieved. 'Fine. Go and sit down and I'll bring you a glass of something.'

'Make it beer. The curry's going to be hot.'

He nodded, filled trays with plates, cutlery, cans and glasses and followed her into the sitting-room. Glancing round, he willed himself not to tidy away the litter of toys in case she felt it was a reproach. When the doorbell rang, he leapt up. 'Stay there. I'll go.'

Carrying aromatic food in two carrier bags he found she had returned his trays to the kitchen. 'Benny, I can't cope with this.'

'I know. Look, I've got a lot on with your father being off work but I really will –'

'Shut up, man! It's you hovering and being tactful and solicit-ous that I can't cope with. For Pete's sake go and pick up the mess next door that you're itching to deal with while I put the food out. Then come and lecture me about taking smelly food all over the house. I can cope with that.'

Mitchell shot off to comply with the welcome request. Coming back, he collapsed into a kitchen chair and dug a fork into the heap of rice on his plate. For a time, they ate without speaking. Mitchell realised that the food, though comforting, was doing little to raise his energy level. 'It can't possibly be less than forty-eight hours since I got up this morning.'

She grinned at him. 'Tell me about it?'

Mitchell hesitated. Was he to take the request literally? 'What shall I tell you? For a start, I'm officially in charge of the enquiry so long as I refer every decision, except very minor ones, to Uncle John Carroll.'

Virginia laughed. 'So, you're God again instead of just an angel. How did you celebrate? Did you send the helicopter out with a thermal imager to find the little Pakistani girl?'

132

'She's not little but that's not a bad idea. Only problem is, we don't even know for sure which town to look in.'

'I wasn't serious. You had no trouble finding the bodies of the other two girls. If the same person had killed Nazreen, wouldn't she have been lying around on the surface too? Anyway, what have you been doing?'

'I spent the afternoon watching the PM but it didn't get us much further.' He described Dr Ledgard's activities and conclusions, sparing her some of the details in deference to their local take-away's commendable chicken Madras. 'Dr Beckham came in to give a statement but that didn't help us either.'

'Beckham's the one who helped at the bus crash?'

'Yes. His statement was full of "I continued auscultation for sounds of a heartbeat for five minutes," so I stuck it in the file. I meant to look that word up but I haven't had a minute. We've had some of the extra DCs re-searching the three girls' bedrooms. All women.'

Virginia raised an eyebrow. 'You think it's not proper to send men to search young girls' bedrooms?'

'Men might not see the significance of what they found.'

'Or what they didn't find.'

'Quite. I've seen Frankie's. It's minute, with two double bunks. Hardly room to climb out of bed and the four girls seemed to have their combs and flannels and so on as communal property.' His face screwed up in distaste. 'It was the only room in the house that was clean and reasonably tidy. Frankie's work, probably.'

Virginia laid down her fork, replete. 'So, what did you do for fun?'

Mitchell gave her a quizzical glance and stole the two juicy pieces of chicken she had pushed to the side of her plate. 'I suppose the bus driver was a bit of light relief. They let us see him for a few minutes today. He treated us to a very colourful account of the crash – gales blowing, motor-cycle maniacs hurtling, kids misbehaving and huge plastic sacks blinding him. Now that Ledgard suspects poison the driver's evidence isn't vital. He doesn't think it was one of the quick-acting things like cyanide so, although Adele died on the bus, it's not necessarily where the substance was administered.

'Bob Crumb was disappointed about that. Tried to whip up an

extra bit of drama, said he heard the girl kicking about when she first got on, saw her hand in his mirror, waving about. He was quite put out when he heard that his brother had been the one to find Frankie's body. The hospital wouldn't let the *Clarion* photographers in so the story's going out with a picture of Dave and not of him. We're trying to trace the people who were on the top deck of that bus but it's a long shot. People check destinations of buses, not licence plates. It's a frequent service too, so the time is less likely to pin it down. Thanks.'

He opened the second beer can that Virginia handed him, but, before he could raise it to his lips, in defiance of her admonitory glare at his glass, the kitchen door opened. Declan blinked in the bright light and regarded his parents under lowered lashes, uncertain of his reception.

'You've had your supper, Tiger.' Mitchell pointed to his son's usual chair. 'Five minutes' chat because I haven't seen you all day, then back upstairs at the double.' Encouraged, the child came to the table.

'Tell Daddy about your recorder lesson,' Virginia suggested.

With little enthusiasm, Declan told his father, 'I learned to do a trill.' Mitchell endeavoured to sound excited at his son's incomprehensible achievement but Declan seemed disinclined to continue the subject and changed it. 'You mended our junction boxes. Why can't they mend Granny Hannah's?'

'Mm.' Mitchell nodded his acceptance that this was a reasonable question. 'I'll tell you what. We'll send Mummy to bed, I'll put a drop of my beer in your lemonade . . .' Virginia rose obediently to fetch the bottle and another glass. '. . . and you and I will have a man-to-man discussion about junction boxes.'

Most of the other inhabitants of Cloughton were winding down to the close of their day. Clement stood in the shower, scrubbing himself vigorously and humming tunelessly. Things were going well. He'd managed to get quite a lot out of young Stepney when he thought about it. He'd enjoyed the lad's company too. He had been tempted to bring him back to the flat to wash off the sweat but decided it would be unwise. Instead, he had bought him a beer from the all-night supermarket and the two of them had sat on the wall, drinking and planning their next session.

Clement turned the shower up a notch and fantasised about cracking the car thefts and the murder enquiry with information given to him by his new friend. As he towelled himself, he changed the dream, this time tracking down Crossley in Leicester and proving his connection with the Akrams, perhaps even with Frankie Leonard and Adele Batty. As he climbed into bed, his imagination was screening a film that featured Caroline Webster as its female lead.

Caroline herself, a quarter of a mile away, had no need whatsoever of fantasy. Nor was she thinking of Clement. She was admiring her strong, slim, musician's fingers, particularly of her left hand, especially the third finger with its gold-mounted sapphire, guarded, one on each side, by two small opals. She was wondering if the events of her evening would still be real when she woke up in the morning.

Chief Inspector Thomas Browne, having slept for a good deal of the day, was wakeful. He wished he could get up and do something – do anything – but he was afraid of waking Hannah. Besides, there was nothing to do. For the moment, at least, there was no job to be responsible for. And there was nothing left undone in the house. Virginia had spent her day there, producing a standard of tidiness and cleanliness that he had only observed in her own when Benny had been busy.

In the miserable circumstances, they were all managing quite well and now Alex was coming. His son was returning home to gladden the heart of his dying mother and Browne heartily wished he would stay away.

Superintendent John Carroll, wearing striped winceyette pyjamas that would have amused his subordinates and startled his superior officers, was seeking the solace of a whisky nightcap and the sympathetic ear of his guest and former commander, now retired. He had a considerable number of worries to confide and his friend was proving an attentive audience. 'I feel I misread the situation. I've been in other places where runaway children were a common feature of the workload. They turn up whilst the search is still being organised, delighted with the fuss they've managed to cause.

'I've no qualms about the girl whose body we found first. It turned up before anyone knew she'd gone and we were doing all we could about Frankie, the second one, when we found her. It's the Pakistani girl I'm worried about. I put the brake on that one. I've got teams out combing the area now in what the local paper calls "a belated search" and I'm waiting for the DI to start screaming "I told you so!"' He winced as the former commander added soda to a replenished Laphroaig.

'Well, tell his chief inspector to slap him down.'

'Currently, he doesn't have a CI.' Briefly, Carroll described the Browne family's predicament. 'So, for the moment, Mitchell is in charge of the enquiry for all practical purposes. He'll lead the briefings and organise the team but all except minor decisions are to be in consultation with me.'

'But why don't you just draft in another CI? It would be much simpler – and more according to the book.'

'Officers of that rank are a bit thin on the ground here and, anyway, I want to hang on to Tom Browne. His men respect him and he's quiet but efficient. I think, when he's got over his guilt trip, he'll let the social services help with the care of his wife. His daughter's being very good too. She's DI Mitchell's wife.' The commander blinked. 'I want Tom's position to remain empty so that he can slot straight back into it when he feels ready.'

'And if he decides to devote himself to nursing his wife?'

'He'll be free within months anyway. Two years at most, he thinks. He and Mitchell make a good team.'

'So, what's he like, this Mitchell?'

'He keeps a much higher profile. He's exuberant, ebullient. He speaks plainly, believes, if something needs saying, sooner is better. He faces decisions and crises head on when others would be more circumspect.'

'Sounds dangerous.'

Carroll considered this. 'He is a bit like a bull in a china shop.' He grinned. 'Looks like one too, five feet nine square with an army-style short back and sides. He barges through life and people leap for cover – but they don't hate him. They moan about him, argue with him, then walk on water for him. Even his female sergeant who started here as a DC at the same time as he did will take orders from him.'

'Remarkable.'

'He has a presence that he's growing into. I bet it was a handicap when he was a cub but it'll sit nicely when he's a commander or an ACC.'

'You seem to have learnt a good deal about him in a very short time.'

'I keep my eyes open. That's what I'm good at.'

'And, sometimes, you see what you want to see. I think you're sticking your neck out for DI Mitchell because you like him.'

Carroll regarded the empty bottle mournfully. 'Rather that than what I fear.'

'Which is?'

'That I've just become part of the all that he carries before him.'

In her bedroom, in the house in Winter Street, Cynthia Summers was writing a letter.

'My very dearest Frederick, I do hope that you won't be offended by this notepaper but our little Cloughton stationer has run out of the Basildon Bond that I know you like to use.' Cynthia paused to sip from her bedtime cup of tea and to arrange the pillows more comfortably behind her. 'I'm sorry too that you're getting such short measure in my letters this week, but you'll understand how much I've had to do.'

She paused again, finished the tea, wrote another sentence or two. This week's letters hadn't been easy to write. They had been less of an outpouring, more of a duty. She needed to see Fred again. She fingered her engagement ring, turning it to the light and drawing comfort from the flash of its huge jewels. It had a big central garnet but, unlike Caroline, Cynthia wore hers on a gold chain round her neck where no one, especially not Father, could see it.

Eventually, she decided to leave the final few paragraphs till the next morning. She slid down between the sheets and began to review the names she had chosen for her and Fred's son and two daughters.

Just a few streets away, Derek Swindell was also busy writing, on many sheets of school file paper. The reams of paper, taken from the school stock room, were no more than he deserved after all the extra, unpaid hours he put in for that school. He'd better put his work away now. Sue would be back in a few minutes from her weekly night out with the girls and she'd expect him to have the kettle on. It would never do to have her seeing it and wanting to read it.

Amara Mahmood was not preparing for bed. An hour ago, she had begun her shift at the all-night supermarket and she would finish it at six in the morning. Would finish and go home at six, that is, if by then she had not brought the store's computer system to a standstill with her careless mismanagement of her own till.

Twice already she had had to appeal to a superior to cancel a botched transaction and once she had given a customer, fortunately a very honest young man, five pounds too much change. Imran would not be pleased with her if she lost her job. Nor would he be pleased if she went back to Sergeant Taylor and told her what she knew about her friend. But, the longer Nazreen was missing, the more likely it was that she needed the police to help her.

She made up her mind suddenly. She would go to the police station at the end of her shift. Her decision made, she knew she would now complete the rest of her night's work with her usual efficiency.

Colin Greenwood's choice of whisky was Glenfiddich. As he poured it into a tumbler, he was making a decision that was the opposite to Amara's. He had promised to let Inspector Mitchell know if he remembered any little thing that had happened in school this week that was unusual or remarkable. Remarkable in the context of the turbulent life of his school, he had meant. And Mr Greenwood had thought of one rather odd thing that had happened on Wednesday. But it was such a little thing, so unlikely to have any bearing on the inspector's investigation. And reporting it could easily do more harm than good.

12

Sergeant Taylor had seen very little of her daughters for some days. On Saturday morning, therefore, she roused the household early so that she and the girls could share their news and their breakfast. Six-year-old Lucy, resplendent in her new Pikachu dressing-gown, had an important announcement. 'I've got a boyfriend.'

Jennifer felt her mother-in-law's adverse reaction and gave her a warning glance. This was not an unhealthy precocity but artless chatter. Lucy was playing a game, being like the big girls. Her invention of a suitor to ape courtship was as innocent as nursing a doll and aping motherhood. She might contemplate worrying about it when Lucy could no longer be diverted from her amour by an extra slice of toast and honey.

The child had noticed and was quick to exploit this difference in attitudes between her elders. 'I'm going to marry him when I leave school.'

But Jane had picked up her cue quickly. 'Will you have me for a bridesmaid?'

When this produced screams of derisive laughter from Lucy, Judith hastened to console her grandmother. 'You can be one for me when I marry Sima.'

Lucy shook her head wildly and her mother sighed as long dark hair flew out wildly and wrapped itself around toast, butter and honey. 'That's silly. You can't marry a girl!'

Behind her hand, Jane muttered, 'By the time she's old enough, it'll probably have become quite a commonplace.' The remark woke an echo in Jennifer's mind. Who had said something very similar in the last few days? She was still trying to tease out the memory as she reluctantly sent her offspring away to wash and dress and herself set off for work.

The atmosphere in Browne's office, temporarily his own, seemed strange to Mitchell as he began his early briefing on Saturday. Jennifer was downstairs interviewing the witness who had been waiting for her when she had arrived at the station and Caroline was half-way to Leicester. There was just Clement left from his regular team. And, of course, Shakila, who seemed to have become part of it. There was, however, no shortage of officers for him to address. The numbers of extra personnel drafted on to the enquiry emphasised its seriousness. They were looking for a killer of two young girls certainly, and possibly three, and they were all facing him expectantly.

He glared back. 'I'll give you the good news. From the team with dogs that combed all four parks and the gardens in a half-mile radius around the Akrams' house – no result. From traffic division's street appeal – ditto. Teams of volunteers are still on the job. We couldn't have had a more thorough search. It's included the multi-storey car park behind the town hall that's being demolished. Chunks of concrete have been dismantled one at a time and taken away on lorries. We've looked in churches, industrial premises, the oil storage depot – everywhere, in fact, that anyone has suggested. We've an underwater unit checking the river, the canal and the boating lake in Crossley Park. No result so far from them. You'll have seen the posters we've scattered about. No response. Nothing yet from the mobile control vans. No comeback from the reconstruction. Door-to-door enquiries continue in ever-widening circles.'

He paused for breath. 'I'll keep the bad news to myself. It might depress you.'

To Clement, Mitchell looked far from depressed. The DI's face reminded him of his old school's star actor in their production of *Henry V* as he led his small army to the engagement at Agincourt against the might of the French. A line came back to him. 'We few, we happy few, we band of brothers.' Clement saw Mitchell looking at him and blushed furiously. Please God he had not spoken the line aloud! He concentrated on what the DI was saying.

'You've all heard about the new floor in the Akrams' otherwise dilapidated cellar. They account for it as the first step in making a games room for the boys, with a snooker table and so on. The super is talking about having it up if nothing transpires in the next twenty-four hours.' His eyes gleamed at the prospect.

Clement thought he would rather like to be there. He would have great pleasure in pinning the whole case on to the shifty

Faisal Akram, though there would be small comfort in finding yet another girl's body amongst the chunks of concrete. He jumped as he realised that Mitchell had handed the meeting over to him, having given him due credit for his consideration of Crossley as a possible suspect. 'I've sent Caroline down there to follow up your theory because I want you to lean on those lads from Sainted City about the drugs thefts. You're the one who'll best know how to tackle them. How did you get on at Heptinstall & Hudson, by the way? Did you get another chance to speak to Akram junior?'

Clement stood up. 'Faisal was out with a client. The other chap, Urfan Ali –'

'So you got pally enough to exchange names?'

'They wore badges. Ali didn't know where Faisal had gone. He was annoyed because they're supposed always to leave word.'

'OK. What about Crossley?'

'He certainly didn't intend being in Cloughton on Wednesday. I was at the estate agent's then to talk to Faisal, you'll remember. Crossley told Ali then that his school was shut because of a burst boiler and so he'd decided to come back here and look at some properties. He seems to have been having some sort of problem with his wife that came to a head between Tuesday and Wednesday and that changed all his requirements. He'd asked to see smallish houses with gardens, but on Wednesday he just wanted a small flat, even a bedsit.

'Ali said he hadn't given much time to finding properties for him to see because he had the impression that Crossley might decide not to come to Cloughton at all. He hadn't given a Leicester address, just the telephone number I gave you last night. He also gave a Cloughton number. I rang it several times and got no answer. The telephone people are getting us an address to match it.'

Mitchell nodded his approval. 'I've given Dr Ledgard photocopies of the lists you made of missing drugs. He's going to ring us too. In the meantime, get on to Shaun Grant and his hairy purple sidekick and get them to tell you who's in possession of the stuff, whatever it turns out to be.'

Clement looked doubtful. 'I'll see Grant in the interests of thoroughness but it'll be a waste of time. He tosses you a lie to keep questions at bay like his elders and betters in the thieving fraternity throw doped meat to guard dogs.' He ignored a mutter of 'Very poetic!' and continued, 'I'll take the sidekick for another run.'

'Not till you're off duty you won't.'

Clement grinned and sat down. He was not sure how much Shaun knew about the thefts from the doctors' cars but Jonno had said categorically that his mate was not this particular thief and that he himself knew nothing about it. Clement believed him but shrank from telling Mitchell that he knew the youngster wouldn't lie to him because he liked running. He might accept, though, that Jonno was too naïve to lie convincingly.

Shakila, sitting opposite to Clement, wondered what was making him smile. She was pleased with her lot. She had worked with this tight little team for just five days and already she felt part of it. If it included her, it had more women than men. Surely, though, there should be one from an ethnic minority. She was not sure about the racial proportions of the town population but they certainly justified the inclusion of at least one Asian in Cloughton's CID. She was determined that the representative Asian should be herself, and that as soon as possible.

She reflected that this was the way Caroline had wormed her way in, giving good value when she was transferred as an emergency measure. But had she herself only been used on this case because of her colour? She closed her mind to the disheartening thought. No one did well in life without taking advantage of incidental factors. Maybe Caroline too had had her share of luck.

Shakila liked Caroline, found her attractive. She dressed well, knew what suited her, though she hadn't the style of Sergeant Taylor. She had noticed that Clement seemed keen on Caroline but he had not had any success. Shakila wondered why. Clement was quite a catch, handsome, athletic, and yet somehow vulnerable. A heady combination.

She dismissed her wandering thoughts as Mitchell proceeded to her own short report. She rose to say that her notes on her house-to-house enquiries were in the file but they did not make very interesting reading. She added that, at Caroline's request, she had called on the Summers' neighbour, Mrs Aiken.

'Why did she pass it on?'

'She felt that she'd antagonised the woman, sir, and that someone else would get more out of her.'

'And did you?'

Shakila grinned. 'She blinked at me when she opened the door and then referred to Nazreen as "the other little darkie". She had nothing relevant to tell but I've done a report. What was interesting was that, when I was leaving, I saw Faisal Akram knocking at the Summers' door.'

When Jennifer had arrived at the station for what she had considered an early start to her day's work, the desk sergeant had informed her that a Miss Amara Mahmood had been waiting for her since just before seven o'clock. The girl had been given tea and sat patiently in the comfortable reception area. A voluminous and unflattering black woollen coat still swathed her ample form despite the efficient heating but her warm smile as she recognised Jennifer made her attractive.

It disappeared as the two shook hands and the girl bit her lip. She came to her point immediately. 'There's something I didn't tell you about Nazreen. I'm not even sure whether I should tell you now and I don't know where to begin.'

'Have you come here straight from your night shift?' The girl nodded. 'Then let's begin by finding you some breakfast. I'll just ask the desk sergeant to let my DI know where I am.'

As they went down the stone staircase and along the bleak tiled corridor to the canteen, Jennifer searched her memory for information on Muslim dietary rules. She was relieved to find the place warm and bustling and that Amara seemed more than happy to pile her tray with scrambled eggs, toast, little pots of jam and a huge mug of hot chocolate. Food, as her figure testified, was her solace.

It would have been courteous to eat with her witness but Jennifer had for once breakfasted heartily at home and compromised by taking a cafetière of Kenyan Dark. Amara ate with relish but was still finding it difficult to begin her story. Jennifer helped her out, thankful that she had managed to work out what her smaller daughter's chatter had reminded her of. Rebecca Sparks had said that Nazreen followed her teacher about 'as though they were in love with each other'. Rebecca had been deriding Nazreen's actions and attitude but the remark had surely implied some kind of response from the mistress.

'Have you come to tell me that Nazreen was refusing to marry Asif because she was in a relationship with another woman?'

Amara stopped chewing, lowered her eyes, raised them again to meet Jennifer's, then closed them and nodded. Jennifer felt that she was overcome not with embarrassment at the subject but with thankfulness that she had not needed to break Nazreen's confidence. She wasted no further time in recriminations. 'Now I know, tell me all you can about it.'

Amara attacked the remains of her breakfast with renewed enthusiasm and now talked willingly. 'I think really I've known since we were small children that Nazreen wasn't quite like other girls. I knew it was something to do with her attitude to them but when we were small I didn't know any words for it.' She chewed and reviewed her memories. 'At junior school we both had long hair and I was very proud of mine. Nazreen hated hers so much that she shut herself in the toilet one day and cut chunks of it off as close to her scalp as she could. She was in disgrace for months for not wanting to be a pretty little girl.'

Amara spread thick jam on cooling toast and wiped her fingers fastidiously. 'When we were in the last year at junior school we had a new girl in our class, a white girl, all ribbons and ringlets. Nazreen became her friend, her exclusive friend. I was quite jealous – but only in a normal way. At playtime, Nazreen used to hold her hand and stroke her hair. She seemed to know that other people would think it was wrong – they always hid out of the way somewhere. I used to spy on them. I was furious because Jackie had cut me out. She didn't stay at the school for very long. I forget what job her father did but the family was always moving house.

'Soon, Nazreen and I were best friends again. When we went to the Colin Hewitt, though, there was another girl, a Pakistani girl this time, that Nazreen had the same kind of friendship with. I understood what was going on by then but the rest of the class didn't seem to. Nazreen was never pretty but Rizwana was. The others thought that Nazreen hung around in hopes of catching one of Rizwana's cast-off boyfriends. Nazreen was having to hide her feelings all the time and she got angry and depressed. That was when she confided in me.'

Amara paused to drain the chocolate in the big shallow cup in two huge draughts. Jennifer saw that she had come to the next part of her account and that it was awkward for her to explain. She offered to refill the cup and, when it was returned to her, the frothy contents overflowing into the saucer, Amara sipped without speaking.

'Did you try to help Nazreen, give her advice?' The silence continued for a while. Jennifer waited.

'I did, but I don't know whether it was good advice. In fact, I knew it wasn't. I told her she was just afraid of men, perhaps because she had such a religious home. Mine keeps all the rules but her father and grandfather and Shahid are always at the mosque. Even while I was saying it, and hoping it might be true, I knew it wasn't. She said she was going to tell her mother but I begged her not to rush it. Once her mother was told, she'd know for good. Nazreen couldn't take it back. In our religion, homosexuality is abnormal and completely banned.'

There was another long silence, until Jennifer asked, 'What happened about Rizwana?'

Amara shrugged, not embarrassed by this question. 'It just faded out in the same sort of way that the boy-girl relationships of the others did.'

Jennifer smiled. 'Did you have lots of boyfriends?'

The girl looked startled. 'Of course not. I always knew I was to marry Imran.'

'So, what next for Nazreen?' Amara was biting her lip again. 'You've talked to me quite readily so far. Why are you getting tied up now? Is it because Nazreen's latest relationship is with a teacher at your school?'

Now Amara's tone was almost angry. 'I needn't have worried about this. I needn't even have come!'

'Yes, you should. Something someone else said put the idea into my head but I had to have it confirmed. I need you to tell me everything you know now.'

Amara drained the last of the chocolate and considered her options. Jennifer restrained her impatience with difficulty. Waited. Suddenly the girl squared her shoulders, though her tone when she spoke again was rueful. 'I've made a lot of trouble for both of them now, whether I tell you any more or not. I don't know much, actually.'

'Well then, it won't be long before you can go home to your well-earned rest with a clear conscience.'

The next words came out in a rush, as though Amara was afraid she would lose her nerve. 'This is my impression. Nazreen always started it. When she touched Jackie, I never saw Jackie touch back.'

'You mentioned Rizwana's cast-off boyfriends. Are you sure you were right about that friendship?'

'Oh, yes. She cast them all off, but there were always boys hanging around her because she's lovely to look at and fun to be with. Most people thought she was just being kind to Nazreen. They were both very careful in school. They were both Muslims. They knew they could be in a lot of trouble – but not as much as Miss Pearson will be in now,' she added, echoing Jennifer's thought. 'And it isn't fair.'

'What do you mean?'

'Because Miss Pearson ignored Nazreen at first.'

'At first? Tell me how this last relationship began.'

'The beginning is all I know about. Miss Pearson only came to the Colin Hewitt last Christmas, when we were in Year 11, and I left in the summer. Nazreen liked her – was attracted to her straight away. I warned her that if . . . Well, Miss Pearson could lose her job. I thought Nazreen had seen sense. She still hung around the woman a bit but she's a good tennis player and people expected it.'

'Miss Pearson teaches games?'

'And junior biology. Anyway, it cooled off. I wondered if Miss Pearson had snubbed her and I was pleased.'

'So, what's the situation now?'

'I'm not sure but I was wrong about it all fizzling out. I saw them during the summer holiday, going into a house in Clarkson Street. If Nazreen's grandfather finds out, Miss Pearson could be in danger too.'

Caroline knew that her day in Leicester had to be a complete success. It had been obvious how much Mitchell had wanted to make the trip himself. He would be highly critical of any slips she and PC Smithson made. Smithson had been eager to drive Caroline's new Peugeot 206 GTI. She regarded cars as merely an efficient way of getting to where she wanted to be and was happy to let him, leaving her free to plan her day.

When they approached the city centre she directed him first to the main Charles Street station to let the Leicester force know that Cloughton had arrived on its patch. She was impressed by the imposing building on the rather bleak and dusty junction. A uniformed officer at the desk supplied Martin Crossley's school telephone number, the address and a scribbled map. He also offered the home address and the loan of a street guide with a slip of paper in the appropriate page. Caroline refused coffee and saw that Smithson was disappointed.

She telephoned the school first and found the secretary in the office. Bored with stocktaking, the woman offered more information than Caroline had expected. Crossley had spent the previous Tuesday visiting a Yorkshire school by arrangement between the two heads. They were afraid he might have met with an accident or been taken ill there, since he had failed to return to St Mark's and no message had been received. Was Caroline a friend? Did she know what had happened? They had rung and visited Mr Crossley's home but no one was there.

When Caroline introduced herself in her official capacity, the secretary referred her immediately to the headmaster. She telephoned him at home and he reluctantly agreed to meet the two officers later in the day. Caroline conveyed the news to Smithson.

'Time for a coffee?' he suggested hopefully.

Caroline shook her head. 'Time to see if and when friend Crossley has been at home and whatever else the neighbours can tell us.' She handed the address and the street guide to Smithson, who promptly handed them back.

'It's a new estate of modern boxes, not far out of town. My daughter's got one of 'em. Daft little pillars holding up the porch, loads of gables – looks like bloody Toytown!'

The weather, having had its fun earlier in the week with first gales and then mist, was now aping late April. The sky was blue and the air mild, so that bare branches and empty flowerbeds in suburban Leicester gardens seemed inappropriate. The two officers arrived after less than ten minutes' driving and Caroline saw what Smithson had meant. The houses were all grandiose on a tiny scale so that it seemed odd that adult-sized people came in and out of them. Crossley's house was in the middle of the estate, detached from its immediate neighbours by a gap just wide enough for a slim person to walk between with his hands by his sides. Its front garden consisted of a tiny mound set with alpines that already had nowhere else to spread.

Ringing the bell and hammering on the door brought no response from within but the two officers were quickly approached by both the woman from the house next door and a youth from across the road. The woman reached them first. 'Whatever are you two doing here together?' She stopped just short of Caroline and began to apologise. 'I thought you were Cherry. You look like her – well, a bit, anyway. Same build, same colour hair.' Since Caroline was unremarkable in both respects she supposed she could be easily mistaken for a good many other women from a distance.

The boy was more canny. 'They're coppers. You can always tell.'

The woman's eyes glinted and Smithson turned a deadpan face on the youth. 'Thank you. You've been very helpful.' With perfect seriousness, he noted down the number of the house from the garden of which the lad had appeared. 'And you are?'

Preferring to remain anonymous, the boy retreated and Caroline turned to the woman. 'Perhaps you can give us some help, Mrs . . .?'

'She can get inside and put the bloody kettle on!' Smithson told her. He chuckled at Caroline's horrified expression. 'We've just had our first piece of luck,' he told her. 'Meet my daughter, Helen.'

When Clement left the Cloughton station, he set out for the car park of the all-night supermarket. He knew Jonathan had taken to hanging around there, partly in an attempt to avoid the gang that had got him into so much trouble and partly in the hope of another encounter with himself. Sure enough, as he parked, he could see the lad, perched on the boundary wall, kicking his heels against the bricks – and the pricks. Another few minutes of it and the shoddy fashion shoes would disintegrate.

'Come for a Stella?' the boy asked hopefully.

Clement wagged a finger. 'If you're going to be a serious runner, beer has to be an occasional treat.'

'That why you guzzle bloody cocoa?'

Clement was angry with himself for blushing. 'Jonno, does Shaun know who's doing the doctors' cars?'

'I think he might.'

'Why?'

'Because he hasn't said he does.'

'Eh?'

'If Shaun doesn't know summat, he pretends he does. He doesn't like not knowing. But, when he does know, he sort o' hugs it to himself.'

Clement paused to sort this out. 'Right. Thanks for the tip.'

'Hey!' Jonathan was alarmed. 'If you tell him I said that I'm dead.'

'Trust me, Jonno?'

'Yeah, you're OK – for a copper.'

'So, where will I find Shaun?'

Jonathan shrugged, then relented. 'There's no match this affs with them playing last night. Likely he'll be stripping his bike down.'

Clement was surprised. 'Shaun's a cyclist?'

'Motor bike. One o' them scrambler things. Takes it to that place just outside Keighley with them little tracks over the moor.'

'Does he now?'

Jonathan bridled. 'It's not illegal. It's off the road.'

'You're quite right. I'll go and ask him to give me some lessons, and, before you insult me with a warning, as far as he's concerned, I haven't seen you.'

As promised, Clement found Shaun Grant kneeling on the flags at the back of St Oswald's House, fitting the last metal jigsaw piece into the frame of his bike. He glowered at his visitor. 'What am I supposed to've done now?'

'I know it's not you.'

Shaun sat back on his heels. 'Well, that's a first. What haven't I done?'

'Those GPs' cars.'

'So, why're you here?'

'Because someone as sharp as you will know who's busy on

150

your patch – and to see if you're offering lessons on that.' He nodded at the bike. 'You've made a good job of fettling it.'

'Am I supposed to be flattered? What do you know about it?'

'That you scramble through mud and that that bike is immaculately clean. Who's doing the cars, Shaun?'

'According to you last Tuesday, it was me.'

Clement dropped to the flags beside the boy. 'Ah, but I'm prepared to admit when I'm wrong.'

To show he was not consorting with the law, Shaun stood up and put the bike between himself and Clement. 'You working yourself up to another compliment? I hope you're not going to tell me what a good grass I'd make. Mind you, the only way you'll get there is by somebody telling you. You've had a nice little chat with him already this week. You can't recognise your villain even when you're talking to him.'

Clement was frantically rehearsing all the questioning he had done in the last few days. 'What do you mean?'

But Shaun had leapt on his bike and, even as Clement began to scramble to his feet, had become merely a dot on the horizon.

13

At twelve o'clock on Saturday, Mitchell decided to go home for lunch. He would finish sorting out his thoughts on Amara Mahmood's revelations to Jennifer by explaining them to Virginia. His heart sank as she produced her 'casserole' with an apologetic explanation. 'I thought there'd only be me. Never mind. I'll throw in a tin of beans.' He averted his eyes as she carried out this threat.

'Had an interesting morning?' she asked brightly as she ladled out her disgusting-looking potage with the microwaved beans stirred in.

'It had its fascinating moments. Before she left for Leicester, Caroline gave me a sealed envelope to be delivered to Adrian.'

'Oh dear.'

Mitchell chewed, found the contents of his bowl delicious and contrived not to express his wonder. Instead, he repeated the gist of what Jennifer had passed on to him and his account lasted until the end of the meal. He laid down his spoon and fork. 'That was good,' he ventured. 'I don't suppose you kept the recipe.'

She replied with a straight face. 'I've made it hundreds of times. The recipe's simple. Empty the dregs from the fridge into a dish, stir and heat. You don't usually like it.' Her tone changed as an idea struck her. 'You've got all this stuff on Nazreen. You haven't heard any whispers about a similar relationship between Adele and Frankie? That would fuse your two cases into one.'

'Aren't they a bit young?'

'According to what you've said, Nazreen had worked out her sexual orientation when she was still at junior school.'

Mitchell considered the idea whilst his hands made coffee. 'Wouldn't Greenwood have mentioned it to us?'

'He said nothing about Nazreen in that respect.'

'True, but from what I've heard about her I'd expect Nazreen to have been discreet. I think Adele was less so.'

'Of course, you only have Amara's word for any of it.'

'You're right again. We're going to have to see Greenwood

again, and Mrs Barron and this Pearson woman.' Timing the five minutes he always allowed his coffee to stand before pushing the plunger, he realised how quiet the house was. 'Where are the kids?'

'You've noticed that four members of the family are missing? Well done. But then, you are a detective. Your mother's got them. Says she quite understands we have to spend a lot of time with my people just now but she'll have them today so the twins remember who she is. She picked them up after breakfast. All to be returned at seven.'

'I'll have a long lunch break, then. I'll be lucky if I'm home before midnight by the time the troops have come in with their reports. How's your mother?'

Virginia shook her head. 'I'm keeping out of the way today. Alex was arriving this morning.'

'He's your brother. You haven't seen him for two years!'

'Mm. He isn't like your brothers though. If he were Dominic or Pat or Seamus I'd be thankful to share my responsibilities but Alex is just another problem.' She gave a mirthless laugh. 'At least he'll be useful as a counter-irritation.'

'Is that really all you feel for him?'

Virginia considered. 'It's difficult to know what I feel. I could never get past his waves of resentment of me and the guilt he caused me because Mum and Dad really did give up on him in the end and concentrate on me.'

'I've never thought of your father as a quitter before. I'm surprised he gave up his job so quickly and easily too.'

Virginia wrapped her hands round her coffee mug and scowled at him. 'You aren't in his place. If he were the one who's ill he'd have stuck it out much longer, though if he'd had this particular disease it couldn't have been very long. He's affected by its psychological impact, but, because he's not ill himself, he has no access to protection and hope from his own body.'

Mitchell refilled his cup, then stared at her. 'Come again?' He waited as his wife sought simpler words for her complicated observation.

'My mother and father can't share a common view of the situation. My mother is bringing reality together with hope and creating an illusion. My father sees reality as stark reality. He feels divided in his loyalty, him and his anxiety against Mum

153

and her illusion. He feels he should offer constant moral support but all he has are grief and worry. She can face things far better on her own. Then he feels shut out, and that he's letting her down.'

'Where did you get all that from?'

'From watching them. You try living with all that and see how long you last.'

Mitchell let her words sink in, then said, apologetically, 'I didn't mean to criticise.'

'And I didn't mean to lecture. In any case, there are plenty of practical matters to keep Dad busy. Social services could help Mum a lot but their resources are limited and, unfortunately, it's the people who make the biggest nuisances of themselves who get what there is. He can use his nervous energy pleading her cause.'

By mutual consent they abandoned the subject and began to discuss their house-hunting plans. After some time the telephone rang. They both sprang up and Mitchell reached it first. 'It's for me. Caroline from Leicester.'

He listened and smiled. 'That's even more interesting than you think. Call in at HQ when you get back and I'll explain.' He replaced the receiver and grinned at his wife. 'In just a few hours, as you predicted, this case has gone from being a miscellaneous collection of unpleasant events to having a fairly consistent theme.'

H.P. Josephs MA (Cantab) had chosen to meet Caroline at the school. He offered her only a perfunctory handshake when she was ushered into his study, followed by 'Thanks at least for coming in an unmarked car.' Smithson he eyed with particular disfavour and for once Caroline wished that she too was wearing a uniform with which to offend the unwelcoming headmaster. They were less the headmaster's allies than destroyers of his school's fine reputation. 'What has Mr Crossley done,' he demanded, 'and what has it to do with us?'

Caroline's reply was cool. 'We are interested in Mr Crossley as a possible witness of a crime committed recently in Yorkshire. Our interest in him sharpened when, like you, we were unable to find him.'

154

'I suppose my secretary volunteered the information?' Josephs remembered his manners and offered coffee. Once more Caroline disappointed Smithson. 'The sooner we have what we need, the sooner we can leave you to get on with your usual routine. Perhaps we could see Mr Crossley's file.'

Mr Josephs' face closed a little further. 'There can be no question of that.'

'Do you mind telling us what your objections are?'

'With pleasure. So far as any of us is aware, Mr Crossley has broken no law and his business is none of yours. I will give you his address.'

'Thank you. We have it – and his telephone number.'

Mr Josephs acknowledged this with a single nod. 'Nor have I any objection to telling you that he teaches history, is thirty-four years old, is head of Year 11 at St Mark's – that is the GCSE year . . .'

Caroline gave him a reciprocal single nod. 'Thank you, but again I knew that. Do you feel able to tell us why he is leaving St Mark's?' Smithson's gesture suggested it would be in search of a more sympathetic headmaster. She frowned at him and turned back to Josephs.

'I assume it's because he himself is aspiring to a headship. His next step is to take charge of a larger section of preferably a bigger school. St Mark's already has those slots filled. Mr Crossley has a good honours degree and has the experience of having been an adequate year head. I doubt if he will find those useful qualifications in a school such as the Colin Hewitt Comprehensive. I think he will find it difficult to impose himself there.'

'Thank you. That's the first thing you've told us that we couldn't have found out elsewhere.'

'Then I regret my indiscretion.'

Caroline was rapidly tiring of the head's word games. She would try someone else. 'Does Mr Crossley have a particular friend on the staff?'

'I have never made my colleagues' personal affairs my business.'

Caroline smiled as sweetly as if she had met with the man's fullest co-operation. 'Then, I'm afraid we shall have to consult other staff who may be less careful with the reputation of St Mark's than you are.'

Josephs sighed impatiently. 'If he's in I'll ask Mr Johnson to speak to you. He lives across the road, so he may as well come and meet you here.'

Terry Johnson waved away their apologies for interrupting his Saturday morning. He was as forthcoming as Josephs had been reticent. He settled himself with Caroline and Smithson in a bay in the school library, surrounded by shelves of venerable volumes. 'The head doesn't like Martin. His appearance is too trendy, his way with the pupils is too familiar. In fact, he's generally considered "the wrong type for St Mark's".'

'Mr Josephs seems to think he's the wrong type for the comprehensive too.'

Johnson shrugged. 'We lead a sheltered life here. The kids' parents want them to get on. If we punish them and they're unwise enough to report it at home they get an extra swipe from Dad. I remember –'

'I get the picture. None of you have been put to the test.'

'Except academically.'

Smithson looked up from his notebook. 'I don't reckon working for H.P. Josephs MA would give me a sheltered life.'

Johnson grinned. 'He's all bluster and clever quips. He hasn't any bite if you stand up to him.' There followed a silence in which Caroline felt that Mr Johnson was working himself up to some question or observation. He asked, after some moments, 'Why are the police wanting Martin?'

Caroline repeated the excuse she had given to Josephs. 'But now we're concerned because no one seems to know where he is.'

'That's bothering me too. I can see that a few more days spent in Cloughton, getting the hang of things, would be useful, but you'd think he would ring up and say he's ill or something.'

'His story in Cloughton was that St Mark's has closed because of a burst boiler.'

'Dream on.' Johnson grinned but sobered quickly. 'This is very odd.'

'Not typical of Mr Crossley?'

'Well . . . not under normal circumstances.'

'And his circumstances were in some way not normal? If

there's something you're not telling us, I think you should. We're not investigating unauthorised absenteeism. In Cloughton we're on a murder enquiry.'

'But that can't have anything to do with Martin. He doesn't know anyone there. He said so. He's only been there twice, once for his interview in September and then on Tuesday for this visit.' He looked to Caroline for another question but she merely stared at him, refusing to help him out.

After some seconds he continued. 'Look, Martin was very upset when he left Leicester on Monday evening. There's been trouble between him and Cherry for some time –'

'His wife?'

Johnson nodded. 'He told me she wanted what she called "time out" to think the marriage through. I'm not sure whether Martin agreed to it, or whether she just left him or whether she ever meant to come back. She was always on at him to better himself. He thought, if he bought a really smart house in Cloughton, it could be a fresh start for him and Cherry and the job would be a stepping stone to a deputy headship.'

'So, he stayed on in Cloughton to pave the way.'

'Well, no.' Johnson swallowed the coffee he had brought in with him. It was cold and left a revolting slimy skin on his top lip. For the first time, he met Caroline's eye. She hoped this meant he had decided to tell the whole story. 'When he came back home, late on Tuesday, he found Cherry had pushed a letter through the door. She said she was living with someone and wasn't coming back. Martin rang me, well after midnight, absolutely out of his tree. I went round and did what I could to sober him up.'

'He hadn't suspected there was another man?'

'That's just what he had suspected, but it wasn't. It was another woman.'

Sergeant Taylor was finding neither the person of Lesley Pearson nor the situation between her and Nazreen Akram as she supposed they would be. The nine-year-old Jackie and teenaged Rizwana had been described by Amara Mahmood as feminine, decorative types. Jennifer had expected Miss Pearson to be young, slim, blonde and doll-like.

She was certainly slim, to the point of a thinness that was evident even as she sat in Mrs Barron's office enveloped in a fleecy tracksuit. Jennifer estimated her age as at least in the mid-thirties, the dark hair, pulled severely into a ponytail, being streaked with grey. The woman was neither aggressive nor ashamed and seemed to ask her first question merely to clarify the situation. 'Did you tell Mrs Barron why you wanted to talk to me?'

Jennifer shook her head. 'But I shall have to ask her again what she's noticed about Nazreen's friendships and attitudes. I think you must face the likelihood of the rest of the staff finding out your sexual orientation. Mrs Barron is astute and observant. You may find that she has been aware of it all the time.'

'And didn't tell you?' Jennifer too was surprised that it had taken so long for someone to point out this situation to them. As she mentally framed her first question, Lesley Pearson spoke again. 'Before you ask, I don't know where Nazreen is. If I'd had any idea I would have come to you days ago.' She fished in her pocket. 'Here's my key. You're welcome to look round my flat. If there's any other way I can help, please ask.'

Jennifer took the key and slipped it into the envelope file on Miss Pearson, supplied by the ever-obliging school office staff. 'Weren't you committing professional suicide by beginning a relationship with Nazreen?'

'I wasn't breaking the law.' The woman's tone was even. 'I've been aware of my inclinations for some considerable time but this is the first physical relationship I've had. And I certainly did not begin it.' Jennifer waited, confident that the whole story would follow.

It did, almost immediately. 'I was an only child. My father died when I was four. I believed for years that the reason I couldn't relate to men was because I'd been brought up with no father and no brothers. My mother and I were all things to each other for a long time but she didn't hold me back and seemed quite happy for me when I left home in Manchester and took a job in Sheffield. I learned a lot about myself there. I thought I'd be able to keep things from my mother, avoid upsetting her.'

'You were sure she'd be upset?'

Miss Pearson shook her head as though she had expected more sense from a police officer. 'Have you got children?' Jennifer nodded. 'Would you be glad to think they wouldn't grow up in the accepted way?'

Jennifer felt a moment's panic as she thought of three-year-old Judith and her little friend Sima. She shook it away and concentrated on her witness. 'But you told her.'

'It wasn't a conscious decision. I just, one day, found myself doing it. We'd always shared our hopes and problems. She did her best to accept it, drew up a sort of unspoken arrangement with me that we wouldn't mention it in front of her relations and neighbours. She said she would keep hoping that I would straighten out one day. She couldn't use the proper terms, talked to me about being "that way inclined" and "one of those". We've been uneasy with each other ever since because she refused to deal with the issue.'

Having let her explore her position, Jennifer brought Miss Pearson back to the present point. 'When did you first notice Nazreen? Did you teach her?'

'Yes, some biology. She plays tennis for the school so we had contact there too. I was attracted to her but I would never have approached a pupil.'

'But you must have done.' Jennifer's tone was gentle so that the contradiction was not an accusation.

Lesley Pearson shook her head. 'One night, Nazreen just looked up my number in the phone book and rang me. She said she loved me and that she was sure I felt the same way. She said she thought I would find it easier to talk if we couldn't see each other for that first approach. I felt as if she were years older than me. She suggested that we should meet at my flat and told me when it would be possible for her to get away from home. And she called a spade a spade.'

'You mean she was quite sexually explicit?'

'Yes, but never indecent. It was so refreshing after all Mother's euphemisms and evasions and false hopes.'

'Was? Are you assuming that Nazreen is dead?'

Miss Pearson looked surprised. 'Oh, no. It's just that the euphoria evaporated. She was soon telling me her plans for the future. I could stay here at the Colin Hewitt until she finished A levels and then I would get another job in whichever university city she chose to study medicine.'

'Or whichever one accepted her.'

159

'No, she didn't see it that way round. We would share a flat, she said. I felt as though I had been completely taken over and I was in a position where it would have been dangerous to upset her.' Her face had flushed angrily and she paused to take a hold of herself. 'Oh well, now everything she could have taken from me has gone and I shall not continue to meet her when . . . if she comes back.'

Mitchell had not looked forward to returning to the office after his afternoon at home. Having piled his desk high with reports and filled his coffee pot to the brim, he gritted his teeth, dragged his envious mind away from the more exciting exploits of his ground forces and determinedly began to read.

He willed one of the team to return. His mind worked better when he pitted it against someone else's. Doggedly he continued and, after a while, he realised he was beginning to enjoy himself. He was commander of the battle strategy. They were testing out his theories and tomorrow he could send the troops out again, matching his men carefully to the tasks they were most fitted for.

Presently, having finished his second mug of coffee, he laid aside all the paperwork except for the reports brought in that day and began to make a list of all the questions that these had raised. As seven o'clock approached, the hour appointed for today's debriefing, he had worked himself into a thoroughly good mood. He had called only the small regular team. He was tempted to take them to the Fleece and let beer loosen their tongues but, unsure of his reasons, he put off this plan.

He wandered to the window to pull down the blind and noticed the healthy-looking pale green shoots on the short, spiky stems of Browne's ivies. He wondered whether they were the results of his ill-natured pruning or his penitent watering.

Clement arrived first and sat glumly waiting for the proceedings to begin. Mitchell wondered whether his state of mind was caused by a lack of results from his efforts with the Sainted City gang or the contents of Caroline's letter. Jennifer appeared moments later. He was pleased to see her sit in the chair next to Clement. Perhaps her goodwill was the result of having, for once, been able to put her daughters to bed herself.

The next tap on the door surprised Mitchell. He had expected Caroline to be late, having started her journey from Leicester in heavy traffic. It was Shakila who came in. She had had no specific instructions to attend and she sat down, half defiant, half appeasing, but determined to remain part of this inner circle. Mitchell beamed at her and watched her relax. He was glad they had not adjourned to the pub. Then he would have missed this gesture and Shakila would have gone away disappointed, possibly bitter.

He began the debriefing, making no comment on her presence, and, two minutes later, Caroline came in with a murmured apology. She slipped into the seat on the far side of Clement. Their eyes met, then both looked away. It must have been the afternoon's work that had depressed him. Mitchell invited him to share his bad news.

'How did you know?'

'Your face is a picture.'

Clement gave a brief account of his conversations with each of the boys, finishing with a droll description of himself trying to rise from an uncomfortable squat on the stone flags as Shaun Grant rode off into the sunset. 'I've kept an eye open all afternoon but I haven't found him and his mother doesn't know where he's gone.'

Jennifer grinned at him. 'He always comes back. You'll get him eventually.'

Mitchell tried not to look surprised and rushed on with his business. 'Dr Ledgard called about the missing drugs. There's nothing on the list that would be worth selling. The amounts of heroin are only enough for temporary emergencies and, all lumped together, would make no one a fortune. Quite a lot of the items are downers – barbiturates, tranquillisers. There was very little, according to Ledgard, that would give anyone a good time. More like a good sleep.'

'What about a long sleep?'

'Ledgard's doubtful. The stuff was mostly in pills and tablets and you couldn't have powdered and dissolved and injected them very easily – though he is arranging for tests to be done for anything on the lists that could possibly have caused the death of either of the girls.'

Caroline, refreshed by a few minutes out of the driving seat, asked, 'Why did you say my report was more interesting than I realised?'

'I'll let Jennifer tell you.'

Jennifer made her account of Amara's evidence as brief as possible, since it was new only to Caroline. She dealt with Lesley Pearson at greater length, adding, 'Till this afternoon, I'd been uneasy with Rebecca Sparks' story. I couldn't see Nazreen setting up such an elaborate system to get the teaching she needed in spite of all the family opposition. All that seems quite in keeping with this new picture of her. Whatever's going on, I'm beginning to get the impression that she's in charge of it. She seems to have made all the running in a relationship when she was only about ten years old. Then she had the neck to ring her teacher out of the blue and start making plans for her life for years ahead.'

'If all our witnesses are telling the truth.'

'At least they all seem to agree with one another.'

Mitchell nodded. 'Right. We've lost the academically gifted but timid victim of an Asian culture. We still have to find her though. She's only sixteen.'

'If Lesley Pearson wanted to get rid of Nazreen,' Clement wondered, 'how could she have done it?'

Jennifer shook her head but replied without her usual animosity. 'If Miss Pearson had removed her, she'd hardly have presented me with her motive all tied up with ribbon.'

Mitchell considered. 'Would it have been any more dangerous than letting us work it out for ourselves? She knew we'd talked to Amara and she couldn't pretend to be madly in love and concerned for the girl's safety when she'd failed to come forward with what she knew.'

Jennifer glanced at her notes. 'She said she hadn't seen Nazreen since the day before the purported trip to Leicester. She was getting on the school bus to go home. The girl hadn't told her she was going away and they hadn't arranged to meet. She thought she'd see her in school the next day and felt no great enthusiasm at the prospect. So, what did Caroline find that was so interesting?'

Caroline glanced apologetically at Clement. 'I thought I'd just been sent to check on a series of coincidences, and eliminate a not very serious suspect. I found out, though, that Martin Crossley has good reason to have a grudge against lesbians.' She gave the gist of what Crossley's friend Terry Johnson had told, ticking off the points on her fingers. She was not wearing her engagement ring. 'So,' she finished, 'he's off balance because his wife has left him, he's under pressure at work and he's not to be found.'

'He might be.' Caroline turned to Mitchell. 'We eventually got a reply to the Cloughton number that Adrian was given at Heptinstall & Hudson. It's a grotty bed and breakfast place and Crossley's expected back there tonight. Any more from Leicester?'

'Just that Mrs Jackman, Smithson's daughter Helen, said that Cherry Crossley had an Asian friend. She saw quite a lot of her before she disappeared from the house a couple of weeks ago.'

'What sort of friend?' 'Did she imply it was a lover?' 'Could it have been Nazreen?' 'But her family keeps a close eye on her and she has to go to school.' 'She could say she was meeting Asif.' 'It would have been easier for Cherry Crossley to come to Cloughton.' 'What do we know about Cherry?'

Their shouted questions and comments overlapped until Mitchell held up a huge hand. 'Don't let's weave fairy stories. We'll have Crossley in for a chat and see if we can pick up his wife. It occurs to me, by the way, that there's someone with easy access to drugs that we haven't considered with respect to any of the girls.'

'You mean Grandfather Akram?' Shakila quickly apologised for interrupting.

Mitchell laughed. 'You'll lose your good manners if you stick around here for long. Yes, I mean Grandad Akram.'

'Do you also mean,' Jennifer demanded, 'that you're making the deaths and disappearance a job lot? What would Akram senior have to gain from injecting Adele and Frankie?'

'Shakila?'

The girl lowered her lashes, then gathered herself and met Mitchell's teasing grin. 'I've been checking the files. It was Smithson who first talked to him. Akram boasted to him about his two other sons in Leicester. One's a GP, the other's an anaesthetist at a Leicester hospital – although, after the tales Mrs Akram told about Faisal and her husband, Smithson added a note that it might be a gross exaggeration. He didn't seem proud of Nazreen. Said she wouldn't be considered clever in a better school, though she would make a reasonably intelligent wife for Asif, his cousin's grandson.'

'Do you want to follow this up tomorrow?'

Shakila was tempted but shook her head. 'He'll say more if you send a man. What I would like to do is ask Cynthia Summers why Faisal came to call.'

'That all right with you, Caroline?'

'Fine. They must be sick of the sight of me.'

'And I'm sick of the sight of all of you, for today at least. Go home, go to bed, go to the pub – whatever, provided you're in here with the whole case solved at the usual time tomorrow.' Jennifer gave a huge sigh. 'What's that for?'

'We seem to be finding either the means or the motive for almost everyone we've questioned. We haven't narrowed things down much.'

'Whatever's wrong with that? Just how I like my cases – suspects galore.'

Just before nine o'clock, DC Caroline Webster was sitting at her piano, wrestling with a tricky passage in a Schubert Impromptu. It had been a good day, she felt. The debriefing had been upbeat and everyone seemed happy that the enquiry was now progressing quickly. There was plenty to do, of course. 'Suspects galore' as Mitchell had said. Now they simply had to follow all of them until just the one did not lead them to a dead end.

On days that went badly she set her sights lower and soothed herself by playing pieces that were well within her capacity. Her evening, she reminded herself, was to be more difficult than her day. She took the Impromptu from the music rest and replaced it in her Schubert folder on the bookcase. Then, returning to the piano, she began to play Chopin from memory and had lost herself in the music when the doorbell rang. She let Clement in and offered him a choice of wine or coffee.

He shook his head. 'Not yet. Finish what you were playing.' She returned to the piano and began again on the Chopin. The piece was undemanding, calming them both. 'Is it a waltz?' he asked as she finished playing and turned to him.

'Well, there are three beats in a bar but I don't think we're supposed to dance to it. It's the E flat Nocturne.'

'So, what's a nocturne?'

'It's night music.'

Clement sank into an armchair. 'Yes, remembering my O level Latin, it must be. Play some more.' His tone made the words a polite request.

Obediently she played again whilst he listened in silence, perfectly still. When the piece finished this time, she closed the lid over the keys. 'That really was a waltz, the C sharp minor. Now we'd better talk whilst I open a bottle.'

Suddenly, Clement knew that the talk would finally dash his hopes. He ignored the hint, tried to divert her. 'You could have been a concert pianist.' It was common knowledge in the station that Caroline had left a prestigious music school, the name of which had meant nothing to Clement, because she thought she would find the camaraderie of the police force more attractive than the competition of the concert hall.

Now she smiled. 'Perhaps. I doubt it and I don't think you're the best judge. Besides, playing only fulfils one side of my nature. I have to be active too. I have to feel I'm doing my bit for mankind in a practical way. And this is the right way round. You have to admit it's easier to fit playing the piano into the life of a DC than to fit a few stints as a special constable into the life of a professional musician.'

They both laughed and Caroline poured wine. 'Don't drink it yet. It's not warm enough. Let's get the business over and then we can enjoy it. You knew, didn't you, that my invitation tonight wasn't a come-on? I deliberately made it formal. I would have preferred not to have made it in writing but I realised that I'd be on my way to Leicester before you'd finished your sweaty marathon to work.' She grinned at him, then was serious again. 'This isn't very easy for either of us, is it?'

Clement sighed. 'I thought, when you agreed to come to the police Christmas ball with me . . .'

Caroline searched her mind for a way to explain her delight when he had offered his invitation. She had realised it was a sign that he was prepared to put his personal tragedy into the past. He would never forget his dead wife and child but he was beginning to look to his future. If she put this into words he would think she had pitied him.

He seemed to read her thoughts. 'You were sorry for me!'

'On the contrary, I was glad for you. Glad you could see a way forward without Joanne.'

'But not with you.'

'Not permanently. I thought you'd understood that.'

'Not altogether. Not then, but I've understood the brush-off you've been giving me ever since.'

'This isn't a brush-off, Adrian. This is final. There's someone else –'

With unexpected understanding, he interrupted. 'It's the music, isn't it? Does he play the piano? Is he someone you knew at college?'

She shook her head. 'I met him in Cloughton a couple of years ago. He was a suspect in a nasty multiple murder enquiry. But, yes, he is a musician. He plays a lot of things but chiefly the organ, professionally.'

'Why didn't you tell me before?'

She lifted her hands, bewildered herself. 'I didn't know before. I knew how I felt, of course, but I didn't know he felt the same. We got engaged yesterday. A week ago, although we'd enjoyed time and music together and . . .' She blushed. 'Well, you know. I just thought he was too involved in his career ever to consider marriage.'

Clement found that, on his own account, he was disappointed but not bitter. He could be glad for her. 'Congratulations. Why aren't you wearing your ring?'

'I wanted to make you understand first.'

That brought tears which he brushed away furtively. From somewhere he produced a jocular tone. 'You've kept it pretty dark. There hasn't been a whisper at the station.'

Caroline replied with a flash of irritation. 'It makes things a bit awkward when every last secret about the man you want to marry is written up in a police file for any officer to read.'

He wondered how to placate her. 'Why don't you play something else?'

Caroline considered the idea and rejected it. 'No, let's get drunk.'

166

14

When Mitchell arrived in the foyer of the station early on Sunday morning he found a member of the public in angry conversation with Sergeant Decker on the desk.

'. . . I've caught him this time, good and proper. I'll teach him to keep his thieving little paws off my things. I've been telling you folk long enough –'

'I know, but,' Decker sounded apologetic, 'knowing's one thing and proving's another. I can see how annoying it is to have your property constantly broken into but we've too much on with more serious matters to go looking –'

'There's no looking to do!' their visitor roared. 'I've caught the young villain myself with his fingers in the biscuit packet.' His voice broke and continued hoarse and he decided to stop shouting. 'It's not the biscuits themselves. All kids lift grub when they see it lying around – but he had to break into the shed to know the flaming things were there.'

'I sympathise, but we simply haven't the manpower to be watching out for petty –'

The voice roared and broke again. 'Will you listen to me? I'm not asking you to catch him. Turned the key on him myself. He's safely in the shed, unless he's kicked it completely to bits in his temper. All I'm asking is for one of your uniforms to give him a good kick up the backside. Got better boots for it than me.'

An idea struck Mitchell and he strode over to join in the argument. 'Someone's broken into your shed during the night? You caught him there and locked him in?'

'At last.' The man beamed at Mitchell. 'Someone with a grain of intelligence.'

'Is the lad blond with a scar across his right eyebrow?'

'He's blond all right. Can't say I've gazed into his eyes. He's little and talks big – like a lot of little chaps, young and old.'

'I'll come with you, Mr . . .?'

'Sawyer.'

'Right. Let's see if I can help.'

Shaun was at the window, watching their approach across the allotments. When they released him he neither ran nor cowered but eyed Mitchell, taking his measure. 'You the other one's mate?'

Mitchell too was short for a policeman but it had never affected his self-esteem. 'I'm the other one's boss.'

'I only sleep here when my mam or the rozzers are after me. I haven't nicked anything.'

'I believe you. I wonder though why you felt the need to reassure me.'

Shaun gave up his attempt to stare his accusers out and dropped his eyes. Mitchell let the silence last until the boy was subdued but not humiliated. 'There's something you need to know, Shaun.'

'Are you telling me this little bugger's well known to you?'

Mitchell quelled the belligerent shed owner with a look. 'Our doctor found a needle mark on Adele's back, the mark of an injection.'

'She never injected! She never used at all.' In Adele's defence he had regained his aggression.

'I'll take your word for it. She isn't likely to have injected herself between her shoulder blades anyway. So, someone with access to drugs and a syringe did the job for her. Who do you know who had some, Shaun?'

'Did Frankie have marks as well?'

'I can't tell you.'

'Seems to me you can pick and choose what you tell.'

'You're right, we can, but in this case I can't tell you because we don't know. The fact that our pathologist could find no evidence doesn't mean that no injection was given.'

Mr Sawyer had completely forgotten his abused shed and was listening open-mouthed. Mitchell knew he was out on a limb. If Shaun failed to respond to his appeal he would be in deep discredit with Superintendent Carroll and furious with himself for having miscalculated. He sensed, though, that the lad's attachment to Adele, though temporary, was powerful. 'How about coming back to the station and giving us a bit of help?'

Clement's Sunday morning run to work was along his favourite course, passing the supermarket a mile from his home. Though it was only just getting light, the faithful Jonathan was sitting on the wall.

Clement was about to wave and pass when the boy stood up, balancing precariously on the decorative brickwork, one leg in the air. He pointed urgently towards his foot and Clement saw that he was wearing the new socks and trainers, the latter gleaming silver in a mixture of supermarket floodlighting and the encroaching light of day.

Clement went to stand below him, running on the spot so as not to break his rhythm. 'You're not ready for the full distance yet. You can come a couple of miles with me.'

Jonathan leapt lightly to the ground. 'Done my warm-up. Twice through because you were longer than I expected.'

They set off together and ran in silence for some minutes. Clement did his best to stop his mind rerunning last night's conversation with Caroline.

'Cracked your case yet?' Jonathan asked. He was into a third mile and proud that he was not even breathing heavily as he kept pace with his trainer.

'What my case needs,' Clement told him, 'is for you or one of your mates to have seen Frankie after the end of morning school – or some other magic trick would do, I suppose.'

Jonathan produced a grin that split his face in half. 'Abracadabra!'

'What did you say?'

Obligingly, Jonathan repeated the word.

Sergeant Decker had called Shakila to the desk when he saw her arriving through the revolving door of the foyer. 'Message from the DI. He's downstairs with a witness and the briefing's been delayed until ten thirty. In the meantime, he wants you to go to see the Summers. He says you know about it.'

Shakila nodded, beamed and went out again, walking round

the rest of the circle that the door kept completing, into the second spring-like day of this November week.

When the old man let her in there was no sign of Cynthia and Shakila hoped that Sunday was not the day she slept in. Then she remembered that Caroline had stressed how much her father depended on her. He was up, looking spruce and smart. She must be about somewhere.

In the living-room the television set was broadcasting a church service and Shakila felt her eyes drawn to it. She had been to very few Christian services. Nor had she made enough Moslem observances to please her parents. She had never felt that either form of worship had much relevance to police officers. Sometimes, she imagined an international, maybe even an interplanetary god, out in space somewhere, wondering how all the peculiar creatures he had created could have discovered so many facets of him and managed to respond to him in so many different ways. She blinked, realised she was being offered coffee. She refused politely and asked if she could speak to Cynthia.

'Certainly. She went upstairs after breakfast. She's busy making some arrangements for the Rick Robson concert that's being planned in the Victoria Hall. I wonder if you'd mind going up to her there? I'm sure she won't mind being interrupted. I do have a push button to bring her down.' He indicated it on the wall by the fireplace. 'I don't want to ring it, though, because I seldom disturb her when she's busy. If she hears it she'll come rushing down thinking something's wrong. I'm afraid her room is two floors up.'

Shakila assured him that she was quite equal to two flights of stairs and ran up the first to prove it. She took the second more circumspectly, not to save breath but to have time to look about her. All was neat, clean and old-fashioned. The top landing had three doors, two of them open. She could see that the rooms were empty except for stored articles. Their floor space was quite extensive but each had limited headroom because of the slope of the roof.

The room in the centre of the roof had its door closed with a line of light showing beneath. There was no sound of movement from within. Shakila knocked.

There was a moment's silence before a voice asked, 'Who is

it?' Shakila identified herself. The voice, carefully controlled, spoke again. 'I do beg your pardon, constable. I'm just changing. I won't keep you more than a minute.'

Shakila heard much opening of doors and drawers and wondered why the same clothes would not do for eating breakfast, making arrangements for a concert and answering police questions about her pupils. It occurred to her that Sunday was an odd day to contact people about a concert. Surely the officials who would make decisions about such things would not be at work. Cynthia probably liked to have everything done by letter and distrusted agreements made over the telephone.

She heard a small clicking sound like a key turning and smiled. She had studied the case file till she almost knew it off by heart and remembered Mrs Aiken's complaint to Caroline that Cynthia's possessions were always locked away. She supposed Cynthia would have to do it habitually since she would not know, during the week, whether or not she would be at school, leaving the interfering Aiken woman in charge of her father and with the run of their house.

Eventually the door opened and Shakila was ushered into a comfortable armchair from where she took stock of the room. Cynthia was filling a small kettle at the washbasin in the corner. She was wearing well-cut jeans and had the hips to look good in them but the effect was ruined by a fussy blouse. On the desk there was no evidence of letter-writing, but just a fat book that looked like a diary, fastened with a miniature lock. Perhaps the woman had a lock fetish.

On the bedside table there was a photograph of a man whose face was faintly familiar to Shakila. Again, she mentally recapped the case notes. 'Is that your fiancé? I have a feeling that I might have met him.'

Cynthia blushed deeply and shook her head. 'I doubt it. Fred has been working in America for some time.'

Shakila felt somehow impelled to worry at the subject. 'You don't wear a ring.'

Cynthia fingered the frilly neckline of her blouse, pulling out a long gold chain on which an expensive-looking ring was threaded. 'We're waiting for the right moment to tell Father. We think that either he'll panic because he thinks he'll be left on his own or he'll worry because he thinks we won't want him with us after the wedding.'

'The ring's beautiful. Is the stone a ruby?'

'It's a garnet, Fred's favourite. The jeweller who made it wasn't happy. He said it was very unusual to set semi-precious stones with good diamonds and that it would make the ring difficult to sell profitably. We laughed. Selling is hardly one's first consideration when one is choosing an engagement ring.' She slipped the ring back inside her clothing and the subject seemed to be closed. 'What did you want with me this morning?'

'We're interested in one of your visitors.'

Cynthia looked surprised. 'Why?'

Shakila had expected to be asked whom. 'You'll understand that, until we've found Nazreen, we're interested in every aspect of the Akram family. Yesterday Faisal was seen going into your house.'

'I suppose Mrs Aiken told you that.' Shakila waited in silence for Cynthia to continue. 'We wondered ourselves why he had come. His excuse was that he was returning a textbook that I'd lent Nazreen – in case I might be needing it, he said. He was very chatty, though. He seemed very interested in our quiet life, saw Father's chess set and said he played, even asked if he might call again, on Father, to have a game.'

'Did you talk about Nazreen?'

'He only said they were very worried about her. I thought it strange. To me, they appear so little worried that I suspect they know perfectly well where she is.'

'Do you know?' Cynthia seemed not to resent the question, merely shaking her head. 'Do you teach Nazreen up here?'

'Yes, so that Father can still watch television. He needs the sound up rather loud lately.'

Shakila wandered over to the bookcase. She had no object in the movement except finding an excuse to stay. She felt that, if she could find the right question to ask, there was something here for her to find. 'Which was the book Faisal returned?'

Cynthia pointed to a fat textbook and Shakila pulled it out, trying to show just an idle interest. It opened easily, presumably at the page from which Nazreen had been working. Shakila saw at once that something had been written in ink in the right-hand margin. It seemed to her unlikely that Cynthia would write in a book, except perhaps for a faint pencil note to be rubbed out once the fact or idea had been filed away in the proper place. She handed the book to its owner, pointing without comment to the defacement. The writing was tiny, not easy to read. Cynthia unlocked a desk drawer and took out a small magnifying glass.

'Is it valuable?' Cynthia looked puzzled. 'The glass. You have it locked away.'

'Ah, you don't know Mrs Aiken.'

Shakila chose not to contradict her and watched as the glass magnified two words. 'Shepherd's Rest'. She looked at the diagrams on the double page spread, of the male and female reproductive organs. Were the words some kind of obscene joke? Not of Cynthia's, certainly. Of Nazreen's? But why should the girl risk offending this woman who was so useful to her?

She glanced at Cynthia and felt that the puzzlement on the woman's face was what she was really feeling. 'Is that Nazreen's writing?'

'It's so small that it's difficult to be sure, but I'd say so.' Cynthia agreed willingly to let the DC take the textbook away with her. 'I suggest you go and ask Faisal about it.'

Shakila glanced at her watch. Nearly time for the postponed briefing. She would have to defer that pleasure.

Mitchell was very angry but not with Shaun Grant. He read through the notes he had made on what the boy had told him. 'I find all this quite easy to believe, more's the pity, but you'll have to give me chapter and verse before I can act on it. How do you know about it?'

'Frankie told Adele. Adele told me.'

'Sorry, you'll have to do better than that. I need all the details. I could offer you a cup of police coffee whilst you're thinking about it, provided you promise to drink it and not throw it in my face.'

Shaun grinned and nodded. 'OK. Frankie noticed the big change in Stevie and thought he was on drugs. Stevie had been hanging around me and she thought I'd been supplying him. She told Adele and Adele got on to me. Adele liked Frankie and

173

gave me what for. I had to let her search my room before she'd believe me and then she wasn't sure.' He bit his lip hard.

'So, it got back to Frankie? Then what?'

'Frankie believed me. We had to find out where Stevie was getting the stuff. I told her to keep a close eye on him, follow him to the bathroom, to his bedroom, when he went out with his mates. She wanted to get Kev to help, for obvious reasons, but we decided not. Stevie never did go out with his mates. He just lay in a chair in front of the telly. I kept an eye on Kev myself but I didn't think it was him. Him and Stevie are always on for a fight but they're neither of 'em into nicking.' Smithson slipped quietly into the room and placed three thick mugs on the sticky, fly-strewn table.

'Then, one night last week, Frankie heard her mum and dad arguing. Her mum wanted to take Stevie to casualty at the Infirmary. She'd already had him to the doctor's and she was really worried about him. She wouldn't give in, even when old Leonard started slapping her about. They started shouting. He said did they want him back how he was before, always causing them trouble. In the end, she cottoned on to what he was up to.'

'Which was?'

'Are you thick or something?'

'I'm not allowed to guess. I have to follow up evidence.'

'Like what I tell you?' The idea afforded Shaun some amusement. 'OK. Old Leonard was sick of being hassled by all the people who expected him to make Stevie behave himself, so he was pinching the docs' bags, sorting out the downers, grinding them up and feeding them to Stevie in anything that covered the taste.'

'And Frankie told Adele who told you. So, what did you do?'

'Minded my own business.' Suddenly the canteen cup crashed into the saucer, spilling hot coffee over the desk and Shaun's knees. 'The bastard!'

In the corridor outside, Mitchell met Clement with an embarrassed Jonathan Stepney in tow. Clement made to take Mitchell's place in the interview room he assumed was empty but the DI held up his ham of a hand to prevent it, throwing over his shoulder, 'My office.'

Clement grinned at Jonathan. 'Can't be in my honour. Must be in yours.'

Jonathan Stepney found his interview as alarming as he had expected. Mitchell tried to put him at his ease. 'All you have to do is repeat what you've already told DC Clement.'

'You mean Sherlock here?'

Clement blushed as Mitchell agreed. Jonathan was probably quailing at the thought of having to remember the substance of an hour's conversation. He wondered, on his own account, how much bother he would be in if the boy forgot himself and repeated the bits that concerned Mitchell.

They exchanged agonised glances and Clement tried to rescue the situation. 'Can you tell us about seeing Frankie at the beginning of the school lunch hour last Wednesday?' After a silence, he offered a further prompt. 'You said she was with Adele, in the playground, not far from the gate.' Jonathan nodded, thankful to have the words found for him.

'Could you speak to the tape, please?'

'What do I say to it?'

Clement bit his lip. 'Inspector Mitchell just wants you to answer aloud so that we have a taped record of what you've told us.'

The boy nodded and spoke slowly and loudly to the machine as the British do to foreigners. 'I agree with what Sherlock here has just said.'

'Sherlock is your name for DC Clement?'

Jonathan nodded, remembered and said, 'Sorry. Yes.' After a while, he became accustomed to the situation and forgot the recording. He seemed anxious to explain not his absence from but his presence at school. 'My mum had flu so I couldn't hang around in the flat. Anyway, Wednesday is double games and RE with Mr Gordon.'

'You enjoy RE?'

'I like Mr Gordon.'

'So, go back to Frankie.'

The boy scratched his head. 'There isn't much to tell. We'd written rude essays for Miss Summers on Tuesday, about – well, sex, like, and we wanted to know what she'd do about it. She was just coming in for the afternoon while we stood there. Adele told Frankie to go and ask her if she'd marked 'em. Frankie didn't want to. She doesn't really like being stroppy. Adele's a bit of a cow. She was having a go at Frankie for being a tinner and trying to get old Summers to start crying because she daren't tell us off for all the sex stuff we'd written.'

'Did Miss Summers often cry?'

'We'd only seen her once. After that Adele did all she could think of to make her do it again.'

'Then what?'

Jonathan shrugged. Mitchell pointed to the tape recorder and the boy muttered, 'Don't know.' He added, after a moment, 'I were starving, I'd gone for dinner. When Frankie didn't come, I thought she'd gone with Adele to play the slot machines in the arcade. Her and Shaun meet there every dinner.'

'Why not meet in school?'

Jonathan thought about the question. 'Well, Shaun's usually laykin' and, if they're both at school, it makes a trip out to break the day up.'

'Does she go by bus?' This time, Mitchell accepted Jonathan's nod. He was disappointed. Clement had led him to expect more. Why was the DC looking so smug?

Clement sat forward. 'Who did you sit with at dinner, Jonno?'

'Kev Leonard. At least, he come and sat with me.'

'And what did you talk about?'

'Oh, yeah, I forgot that bit. He said what a creep Frankie was. He seen her helping old Summers carry exercise books out to her car.'

Now even Clement was becoming impatient. 'And?'

'And she'd said after that she was nipping home to sort summat out wi' Stevie and her dad.'

Having dispatched Clement to deliver both Shaun and Jonathan to their respective parents, Mitchell sat, gathering his thoughts. He was trying to stop them straying to his home situation and keep them on the best deployment of his men. At the tap on his door, he looked up to greet Jennifer, but it was John Carroll who breezed in and dropped into Mitchell's most comfortable chair.

'The mountain has come to Mahomet, though, since you were referring all but minor decisions to me, I don't suppose you have much to tell me.'

In the last couple of years, Mitchell had learned to be just a little circumspect. He began the account of his activities with the drugs thefts, that case having broken so recently that he could legitimately claim not to have had time yet to report on it. 'You'll remember, one doctor's bag was dumped in a skip in Orange Road, just round the corner from Spencer Terrace and very convenient for Leonard. They're comparing the prints from it with Leonard's now.

'There are a couple of men at the house but I don't expect they'll find anything. That and the garden were searched as soon as Frankie went missing, but I've had a call to say Leonard's locker at Purling's where, nominally, he works is a treasure trove of bottles, jars and packets. Those are being printed now and Leonard's in cell four. It's the smelliest today. I suggested that the swilling out after last night's D&D should leave a few whiffs behind. Not that that won't make him feel quite at home.

'Young Grant thought that Leonard had used some of the stuff to shut the girls up but I'm pretty sure not. Sounds a bit of a decisive course for a spineless lump like Leonard.'

'Wasn't the way he was dealing with Stevie decisive?'

'No way. He thought he could just jack it in if things got awkward.'

'Why did it take so long to get Stepney's information? I thought Clement had been working on him for a while.'

'Clement's still learning. He asked the lads about Wednesday and Thursday in general. Jonno hasn't the nous to realise that something not specifically asked for might be relevant. Adrian and I have been taking it in turns just now with some very specific questions.' The words were cheerfully flippant but the tone was abstracted.

'I'm trying to work out why you don't sound your usual smug . . .' Carroll stopped, remembering Mitchell's domestic circumstances. Mitchell however had banished his worries and was now a hundred per cent involved in his work.

'It bothers me that we've almost lost sight of our murder investigation. We've spent a lot of time and resources on the Akram girl and not enough on finding who's responsible for killing Adele and Frankie – especially now we're discovering what a bossy clever boots Nazreen is.'

'I think that was the right way round. The fact that we're finding she is much more bold and resourceful than we thought doesn't mean she's not in danger. She has it in her power to disgrace her family and betray her partner and she may be the object of a powerful desire for revenge in such people as Martin Crossley. Our first priority has to be to find her.'

The telephone rang. Carroll, nearest to it, picked it up and listened. 'There's a Derek Swindell downstairs, asking for you.'

Mitchell groaned. 'Tell Decker it's Smithson's turn to have his time wasted.'

Carroll grinned and repeated the message. 'Any other commands?'

'Yes, stay on. The team should be here in a couple of minutes. Listening to us squabbling should give you a pretty good idea of where we're at.'

'How kind.' The superintendent indicated that Mitchell would still be in charge of the briefing by settling himself further back in the best chair as Clement knocked and came in. The DC sat down next to Carroll without either looking at Mitchell or greeting Superintendent Carroll. Mitchell, who had been about to apologise to Clement for stealing his witness and thank him for softening Grant up for him, instead sat tight-lipped.

Jennifer and Shakila came in together, felt the disapproving atmosphere, muttered a general good morning and they all waited in silence until Caroline hurried in, breathless. Jennifer immediately noticed her ring and, momentarily, the case was forgotten. She beamed at Caroline and reached out to shake Clement's hand. 'Congratulations, both of you.'

Having anticipated this gaffe from one or other of the team, Caroline had prepared a face-saver to rescue both Clement and Jennifer. 'I'd have jumped at an offer from Adrian, but Cavill beat him to it.'

Mitchell and Jennifer blinked and Jennifer asked, 'Cavill Jackson?'

Mitchell grunted. 'There'd hardly be two blokes in a town this size with such a bloody silly name!'

There were further murmured felicitations to which Jennifer added, 'I want an exclusive, as soon as we're out of here!'

Caroline gave Clement a rueful grin that said 'What did I tell you?'

Now Mitchell understood the reason for Clement's unsociable mien, he hastened to placate him. 'For a change I've some good news for you. Thanks to some hard work behind the scenes from Adrian, we've got a cough for the drugs thefts.'

Clement was surprised. 'Leonard's not denying it?'

Mitchell cast up his eyes. 'Just asked us what else he could have done.' The congratulations were now for Clement till Mitchell jerked them out of their complacency. 'Now we've only got to find out who killed two girls and find another one, before we can all go home till next time.'

They listened more soberly to the rest of Mitchell's report. Leonard was in a cell. Dr Ledgard was currently persuading Mrs Leonard to agree to Stevie having the blood test that would be necessary for the prosecution of her husband.

Mitchell paused and frowned at Jennifer. 'Is there something significant in that folder you're clutching?'

Jennifer looked at it, seeming surprised to find it on her lap. 'Decker handed it to me. He found it in the foyer, down by the seat where Swindell sat waiting for Smithson. We weren't absolutely certain it was his. I looked inside to check.' She grinned. 'A few key words caught my eye. I'm afraid I couldn't resist beginning to read it. Then I thought you should see it.'

Mitchell took the file, withdrew a wad of printed sheets and read aloud the heading on the top one. '*New Millennium Mitty* by Derek P. Swindell.'

'It gave me the creeps. It seems to be about a man who keeps on killing his wife.'

'You mean a series of wives?'

'No, it seems to be the same one.'

'I'll save it to read in bed. What did Swindell want, anyway?'

'You'll have to ask Smithson when he's finished with him. He told Decker it was a piece of evidence that he felt, reluctantly, he should give against a colleague.'

Mitchell dropped the file on his desk. 'It might be more to the point to hear what Faisal Akram wanted with the Summers pair.' Shakila gave a concise summary of her conversation with

Cynthia and produced the textbook that Nazreen's brother had returned to her.

Mitchell contemplated the garish cross section diagram of a penis. 'Looks like Miss Summers dealt with sex at every educational level. Do you think we could commandeer the pile of rude essays Stepney told us about as essential evidence?' He caught Carroll's eye. 'The biro scribble says "Shepherd's Rest". Does that mean anything to anyone?'

Clement made a slight movement but, when Mitchell invited him to speak, he shook his head. 'Sorry, it's gone. I think it does connect with something. Perhaps it'll come back.'

Mitchell nodded. 'Don't beat your brains or you'll lose it for good but when it surfaces, get in here and let me know.'

'Sounds like the name of a pub,' Caroline observed.

'It is a pub.' They turned to Jennifer. 'It's right up on the moors at Widdings. I used to go there sometimes with Paul.'

'Fancy a sentimental journey?' Mitchell saw Carroll wince but he and Jennifer understood one another.

'What am I looking for?'

'Anything you find. We aren't letting up in the least on the routine searching for Nazreen but let's concentrate for today on the other two.'

'What can you do that you haven't already tried?'

Mitchell was grateful to Jennifer. At least his sergeant didn't find him wanting. 'Well then, let's try some things again and do them better. Where do we start?'

'Back at basics?' suggested Carroll. When no one presumed to ask him to clarify his remark, he did so anyway. 'It's Ledgard's best guess that two girls have been poisoned and that the poison was injected.' He paused for general agreement. 'So, we're looking for someone who had the poison and a supply of hypodermics and could get within jabbing distance of the two girls, either in private – or in public without attracting too much attention.'

'Like Mr Markov and the spiked umbrella? Hey, nobody's reported any ricin missing, have they?'

Mitchell shot Clement a warning glance. 'It'll certainly be easier when we know what the stuff was.' He looked speculatively at his superintendent. 'Anyone you can lean on at the lab?'

'Done it. They still haven't found anything but they'll keep looking.'

'And we don't know whether the poison was quick- or slow-acting . . .'

'So, we don't know how long before death it was administered . . .'

'Which is why we haven't got very far!'

Mitchell was quite unconcerned by his team's lack of good manners, delighted that they were all thinking together. 'How far have we got? We've looked fairly carefully at the families, parents, uncles.'

'Aunts,' put in Clement, indignantly.

'If the Leonards bumped off young Frankie,' Mitchell continued, 'they were cutting their own throats. She looked after them all.'

'What about an uncle who'd accepted Frankie's favours and wanted to shut her up?'

'Frankie was a virgin.'

Mitchell looked approvingly at Shakila. 'I'm glad somebody keeps reading the files. Anyway, there are no uncles. Mrs Leonard told Temple, who's their liaison officer, that she and her husband were both only children and were determined for that reason to have a big family.' He snorted. 'More likely she meant her old man wasn't going to spend good beer money on contraception.' His glare round the room dared anyone to comment on the size of his own family.

'What about the Battys? The CI allocated Janet Jones to them. She thinks their grief was a bit perfunctory but quite genuine. They didn't spend a lot of time with Adele but they spent a lot of money on her. Lots of uncles for Adele but they all live in south London and we can't find any traces of any of them being up here.'

'Anyway, it's surely got to be somebody with a grudge against both girls.' Caroline looked up to check with Mitchell. 'Assuming a quick-acting poison, Adele's killer must have been on the top deck of that bus. We appealed for travellers on that route, didn't we? Much response?'

Mitchell's answer was more precise than she expected. 'Eighty-four calls from people using that route on Thursday afternoon. Seven from people on that particular journey – when

Adele must have first boarded the bus, I mean, not when the accident happened. All seven travelled on the lower deck. Two of them glanced up when they were waiting to get on at the stop after the school. Adele caught their attention by waving to someone – not to either of them. One of these two thought there was someone in the seat behind her but could give no details. Just an impression. You should all know this. It's in the file.'

Caroline looked chastened. 'Should I talk to Bob Crumb again?'

'Think you'd get any more out of him?' Mitchell looked doubtful.

Caroline nodded. 'He was quite lively when I spoke to him, indignant because his brother's photo was in the paper and not his own, but he drooped quite quickly and the nurse sent me away. They'd run all their tests and knew that his head injuries were less serious than they'd first thought. They said he was very shocked though and slightly concussed. They thought he might find his memories of Thursday afternoon would come back to him in bits and pieces.' She shot Mitchell a wicked glance. 'You should know that. It's all in the file.'

Carroll gave a shout of laughter in which Mitchell had the grace to join. 'You'd better get there quickly before he's had time to convince himself that all the embroidering he's done for his visitors is the truth. Adrian, Shakila's fixed for you to see Grandad Akram.' He grinned at Shakila and wondered if she were blushing under the smooth dark skin. 'Now I'm tethered to a desk, you're my only messenger boy. She tells me the Akram men don't bother talking to women.'

'Does that mean I can choose a job for Shakila, then?'

'She's learning the file by heart. I'm going to test her on last night's homework.'

Half of the team was already through the door when Clement stopped them. 'Wait a minute! I've just realised that I know what Shepherd's Rest is, though I don't know where. Last Wednesday, at Heptinstall's, I was half listening to Faisal Akram and half to Ali and Crossley. When Crossley let on that his wife wouldn't be joining him in Cloughton, Ali started trying to talk him into taking on a derelict place and doing it up. Sort of dual purpose. He'd make a profit and it would give him something to think about instead of licking his wounds.'

'Ali sounds an enterprising salesman. There can't be much demand for ruins.'

'Or else a marriage guidance counsellor manqué.'

'Can we get back to Shepherd's Rest?'

'We haven't left it. That was the property on offer, but Ali couldn't find the details in the file. Then Faisal said that the owner had taken it off the market.'

'And you think Akram had taken it off himself and dumped his sister there? Where is it?' Clement's shrug signalled ignorance. 'Well, get off pronto and find out!'

15

Mitchell, waiting impatiently for Clement to arrive with Faisal Akram, had eventually to be satisfied with a telephone call. 'Sorry, sir. Faisal's out with a client. His boss was furious because he hadn't left word where he was and, now he knows he took Shepherd's Rest out of the files, he's gone into orbit. I had to threaten to arrest him before he'd tell me where the place is. It's up at High Stubbs, near the wind farm.'

Mitchell scribbled the address and grid reference and left the frustrated Clement to wait for Akram and bring him back to the station. 'Don't let him contact his sister, and keep in touch. He might have some keys we'd find useful.'

'I thought the place was derelict.'

'If we're right, there'll be somewhere he's got the girl banged up.'

Caroline was no more enthusiastic than Clement had been to miss the rescue attempt and Mitchell watched her depart reluctantly to keep her appointment with Bob Crumb. He decided to take both Jennifer and Shakila to Shepherd's Rest. If he found another body, he would need his sergeant, but if he found a badly frightened, hysterical schoolgirl, sobbing in Urdu, he would need Shakila.

He dropped the map on Jennifer's knees and followed her directions, though the wind farm could be clearly seen on the horizon when they were still several miles away, the windmills looking like children's toys. None of the three officers had attention to spare for the bleak beauty of the moors, though Jennifer remarked enthusiastically, as they passed it. 'There's brilliant water skiing on that reservoir in summer.' In his mirror, Mitchell saw Shakila blink as she absorbed yet another new aspect of the sergeant.

After bouncing over a series of cattle grids, Jennifer ordered Mitchell to stop on the narrow ribbon of road at a cobbled lay-by. The windmills now were very close but they still seemed insubstantial compared with their traditional couterparts. Even in the strong wind blowing off the moor their blades made a soft swishing sound they could hear only between gusts.

The sizeable building they were making for lay a couple of hundred yards away across sheep-nibbled grass. Jennifer tried to keep the map from taking off into the wind as she marked their parking spot with a finger. 'There's a stony track that's probably negotiable by car, leading right up to the place from further up the road. We can take that if we want them to know we're coming. If not, there's a footpath, though no more than a trod, starting with that stile.'

Mitchell chose the footpath leading towards the building and skirting a drystone wall that bounded it on one side. As they got closer, piles of substantial stone blocks suggested that some reclaiming had already been done. A new door and some windows had been fitted and the roof repaired, though there was no machinery to indicate that work was continuing. Nevertheless, if Nazreen was here, she was not living in the discomfort they had imagined.

He turned back to the two women. 'Looks as though the previous owner's money ran out.'

Jennifer grinned. 'Looks like the resting place of rather a sophisticated shepherd, even in this state.'

'Are we going in?' Shakila was eager for action.

Mitchell hardened his heart. 'You aren't. We need a lookout. If Faisal gets wind of this trip he could arrive with a whole posse of Akrams whilst Clement's sitting pretty, mopping up Heptinstall & Hudson coffee.'

Shakila rather sulkily took the pair of binoculars Mitchell handed her and perched on the wall to get a good view of both paths from the road. Mitchell smiled. So, there were things the new girl still had to learn. Motioning Jennifer to follow, he picked his way to the front of the house, examined the new door and hammered on it.

A voice enquired, 'Who is it?'

Mitchell cast up his eyes. 'She sounds like a maiden aunt checking that it's only the vicar she's letting in. Well, thank goodness she is still at home.' He raised his voice. 'It's the police, Detective Inspector Mitchell and Sergeant Taylor from Cloughton station.'

The voice requested calmly, 'Could you come to the window,

please, and show me your identification?' Jennifer stepped over the uneven, stone-littered flags and saw, through a smeared pane, the face she recognised from the photograph in the girl's school file. She held up her warrant and Nazreen nodded and disappeared.

Feeling that he needed to regain the initiative, Mitchell shouted to her, 'Stand back from that door, please!' He took several steps backwards and prepared his shoulder for impact with it.

For the first time, the voice from within sounded agitated. 'Don't damage anything! Please. If you wait a minute I'll unlock it.'

Mitchell ground his teeth. Jennifer laughed. Shakila crept up behind them to see what was happening. There was the sound of a key turning sweetly in the lock, then the door opened and they saw a tall young woman, dignified in an emerald green sari and an old army-type blanket, worn as an enveloping cloak.

She regarded her visitors in silence for a moment, then smiled. 'Thank you for coming. You worked things out as quickly as I hoped you would.'

By the time he had to report his morning's progress to the superintendent, Mitchell had had a chance to arrange his facts into a semi-logical order. He felt quite proud of his lucid exposition. 'The two conflicting factors are that Nazreen's a Muslim by tradition and background but a lesbian by nature. To make things worse, she's a clever girl in a culture that looks for quite other qualities in women. The only member of the family who is prepared to understand is Faisal.'

'But I thought –'

'Yes, so did we. Faisal's an old trouper, could play Hamlet. In Nazreen's plan he played the bad guy.'

'I still don't see the point of the plan.'

'Neither did we till she explained. She admitted her true nature to Faisal years ago. They got on well because she helped him with his school work without making him feel stupid. He looked after her because, although she's bright, she wasn't old enough, in the beginning, to understand the furore it would cause if they confided in the rest of the family. Later, there were wedding plans in the air, so the balloon was going up anyway.

'They decided she should talk to her grandfather. He'd never been particularly sympathetic to her in general, but she thought, as a doctor, he'd understand it was something beyond her control and he would have the authority to stop the family punishing her.'

'And she found he was more jealous of the family reputation than any of the others?'

'That's right. At least, though, he didn't tell them. He thought the fewer people who knew, the less likely it was to become common knowledge. There was some half-hearted discussion of a deal on the lines of Nazreen pretending to be straight, going through with the marriage and getting her grandfather's support for a university education.'

'Bit rough on Asif.'

'Tell me about it! So, she dreamed up this plot with Faisal. He went to his grandfather, pretending to have found out and to be shocked. Said he could use this property that no one was showing any interest in. Suggested they kept her there with enough food and blankets to keep her alive but not comfortable till she gave in.

'The place is actually in much better shape than he said and he fixed her up with a Calor gas heater and a junk shop table. He smuggled books from her bedroom and paper and pens. It was quite cosy in daylight but she must be pretty strong-willed to have spent nights there on her own.'

Carroll frowned. 'But I can't see what she's achieved beyond making monkeys out of us and holding up the investigation of a much more serious crime.'

'She doesn't care much about that but I don't think she actually intended it. The point is, she and Faisal thought it was quite possible that, to save the family from that particular sort of disgrace, Dr Akram would really harm, even kill her. It's been known. It's not so far-fetched. The punishment Faisal suggested left things in his control. Nazreen was counting on the school making a fuss. The family thought a letter to Greenwood, saying she was leaving, would be enough. Faisal intercepted it.

'That got us involved and made sure we understood the situation. So, if any harm were to come to her now, the family

187

will be carefully investigated. The only option left to them is to let her finish her studies, make excuses to Asif and get her to a university miles away where no one knows them. Which is just what she wants.'

'She could have ended up in that position just by appealing to the ANAH in Bradford.'

Mitchell was not so sure. 'Well, in any case that would have denied her all the fun of jerking us about. I get the distinct impression that she's enjoyed her little adventure.'

With Nazreen safely delivered into the bosom of her manipulating and manipulated family, Mitchell had one more object to achieve before setting about another long evening's work. Leaving a message with the desk sergeant in the foyer, he turned the car towards home.

The streets around him were gloomy, in the middle of a mini non-season with the glory of autumn over and the excitement of Christmas not yet generated. In the usual tawdry way the shops were aping seasonal goodwill and merely adding to the aura of depression.

Mitchell parked on his own street and unlatched the front gate. His two youngest children were playing on the front lawn, muffled in thick leggings and fleece tops. He realised the sun had gone in since lunch and that he was shivering in his light jacket. Sinead flung herself towards him whilst Michael continued to sit gazing at a small creature that was crawling over his shoe. Swinging his younger daughter up on to his shoulders, he walked across to Declan who sat on the steps of the minute paved terrace in front of the police house.

'I'm keeping an eye on the twins.'

Mitchell nodded approbation. 'And where's your mother?'

Declan grinned. 'Keeping an eye on me, I think, and making sure Kat doesn't eat the biscuits.'

'I could use someone like you down at the station,' Mitchell told him, adding hastily, as he saw his son preparing to take him seriously, 'but Granny Hannah needs us.' He lifted Sinead down and took her hand. 'Bring Michael in and I'll tell your mother I'm home.' He hoped Ginny would capitulate without too long an argument and saw that she was coming out to meet him.

188

'I've got to sort things out with Alex for my own sake as well as for my parents'?' She raised an eyebrow.

'I never said a word.'

'Well, I've been thinking, and, besides, it's all in your face. Into the car, you folk. I don't suppose your father has all afternoon to play with.'

Mitchell had stayed with his in-laws just long enough to see that, temporarily at least, things between Alex and his sister and parents were going smoothly. He was convinced that Virginia always told the truth, at least so far as she saw it. He had had trouble in taking her seriously though, when she insisted that the main cause of contention between herself and her brother had been the fact that she had been three years younger and consistently slightly taller throughout a good part of their childhood. When, after two terms at Durham University, he had come home measuring five feet eleven and a half inches to her five feet ten, their relationship, she insisted, had improved. Virginia was one inch taller than himself, which was of no concern to him whatsoever. And, come to think of it, Hannah was slightly taller than Tom too. Or, she had been until the onset of this horrific disease.

There were still a few minutes left before the appointed time for his debriefing. Mitchell pulled out Derek Swindell's story and began to leaf through it.

'He remained at the kitchen table, the vestige of a smile lighting his eyes as his lips soundlessly recited the little parody he had composed, just for his own amusement, of the well-known Elizabeth Barrett Browning poem. His version began, "How can I kill thee? Let me count the ways."

'He had a book upstairs, the only object he had ever stolen. It was a textbook, written for forensic pathologists. He had found it in a sale at the library of books that people no longer borrowed. The other books he wanted, he had queued and paid for, but this one he would use in secret and it had seemed important to smuggle it out. He had learned from it enough to write several verses in mockery of Mrs Browning's poem and, in his fantasies, he had killed his wife many times and by many methods.

'Today, he would use carbon monoxide. Inside his head, he

persuaded Sue into the garage to advise him about the exact place to put up an extra shelf. He had left a spanner ready on a ledge behind the door and had studied the book to find just how much force would be needed for the tap behind the ear that would stun her. He carried her into the front of the car, closed the door and fixed the hose to the end of the exhaust. He dragged its other end carefully round to the front passenger window, where he trapped it, not too tightly, into the crack where the window was not quite closed. It remained only to close the gap at the bottom of the garage door with old rolled towels, retrieved from under his work bench. He added another roll of wadding on the house side of the door leading from the integral garage into the hall. All he had to do now was wait.'

Mitchell blinked and looked up. This man was definitely unbalanced. Who was Mitty? Was Swindell's attempt to get Miss Summers involved in their enquiries meant to divert suspicion from himself? There couldn't have been much love lost between Adele and Swindell. 'Fat, coarse and vulgar', he'd called her. She'd have been more than a match for him, though. He tried to imagine the man in charge of a lesson orchestrated by Adele. He must have hated her.

Had he mentally rolled together the objects of his hatred at home and at school? If so, where did Frankie fit in?

He was still wondering when, at six o'clock, Superintendent Carroll appeared for the second time that day at a team meeting. Jennifer half rose to offer him the only comfortable chair but he waved her down again. 'I'm not staying. Just a word of appreciation. A missing girl found and a series of drugs thefts sorted out in one weekend. Well done – especially as all the current extra manpower is deployed on the other part of our enquiry. These two successes are down to the regular CID contingent.'

This was not what the said contingent was used to. They appreciated the superintendent's acknowledgement of their efforts but his two predecessors had given them no practice in finding a proper response to it. Without intending to be ungracious, Mitchell shook his head. 'The point is, we're supposed to be dealing with a double murder enquiry and we've hardly even scratched the surface of it.'

Carroll's expression was crestfallen. 'Well, at least for the moment you can concentrate on it.' He turned on his heel and left them looking ruefully at each other.

Jennifer was annoyed with Mitchell. 'It's not fair either to us or to yourself to say we haven't really started. We've done a tremendous amount of groundwork. The super wasn't only complimentary, he was right. We've had two other cases distracting us. Now we can get to grips with the one that's left.'

Mitchell grinned. 'All right. You asked for it. Adrian, go and get the files.'

'There's more than one can carry. I'll give you a hand.' Jennifer followed Clement out.

To stop himself commenting on this unwonted co-operation, Mitchell asked his one remaining team member, 'Where's Caroline?' Then shook his head. 'Forget it. You've been with Jennifer and me most of the day. I don't suppose you've seen her.'

Shakila grinned. 'Actually, we sneaked out to the Fleece for a G&T together whilst you were out this afternoon. Bob Crumb had gone down the pub with his mates by the time she arrived at his house. His wife said they were beginning at the Crown but they would probably have moved on. She cooks their main Sunday meal at about five o'clock. Caroline opted to go back there then rather than chase him round. In the meantime she went to a call-out down at the women's refuge but uniforms are dealing with that now.'

Thumps from outside the room indicated the arrival of the files. Clement dropped his considerable share on Mitchell's desk. 'Why isn't all this in a computer file?'

'It is. You can go and look at it on a screen if you like. Come back when the machine gives you an answer. Personally, I prefer bits of paper.' Clement considered the idea, then opted for the companionship of the office.

Jennifer grinned at Shakila who was fielding odd papers escaping from the pile she clutched. 'I thought I'd spend an hour or two later tonight asking the computer what it thinks.'

Mitchell was grateful. 'Fine, if Jane doesn't mind. Now, we'll try to avoid rereading our own reports and see if we can throw fresh light on each other's.'

There was silence for some while, except for ponderous

breathing, rustlings of paper and occasional scratchings of ball pen on notepad.

Clement was the first to look up, though the rest were glad to follow his lead. Mitchell accepted this natural break. 'Let's see what we've got then. Adrian?'

'I was looking at Caroline's chat to Mrs Aiken and wondering why Cynthia Summers keeps everything locked up.'

'Makes her feel important.'

'Caroline said Mrs A herself was the reason.'

'If the rest of the work she brings home to mark is on a level with the essays that Jonno's lot handed in she'd want to lock it away from her father. He thinks she's a good teacher.'

'So does Nazreen.' Mitchell held up a hand to stop the chorus of simultaneous comment. 'Anything else, Adrian?'

'Well, still on Summers, we haven't dicovered why she was in school on the day Frankie disappeared. She hadn't been called in and it keeps cropping up. Colin Greenwood rang to mention it, then Jonno and today that jerk Swindell came in telling tales about her according to this note from Smithson.'

'Greenwood was quite happy about it. Said she often spent hours in the library preparing brilliant lessons that she never taught because she couldn't make herself heard. Said he wished a few more would follow her example.' Mitchell grinned. 'Mrs Barron said she'd thought about paying her for her notes and teaching from them herself. Jennifer?

His sergeant looked worried. 'We seem to have it in for Cynthia tonight. I was looking at another of Caroline's sessions with her. She objected – rightly, as we know now – to Caroline using the past tense when talking about Nazreen. She suggested she didn't think we'd find that Nazreen had shared the fate of the other girls because she didn't deserve to die. That suggests she thought the other two did.'

As they thought about this, Caroline came in. Mitchell pushed a stool towards her. 'Did you see Bob Crumb?'

She grimaced. 'Yes, eventually. I only got one more fact out of him but it was interesting. He says that one of the Colin Hewitt staff was on the bus on Thursday lunchtime. A woman. He noticed that she went upstairs. That morning she'd arrived on the school bus that he was also driving. We had a ten-minute diversion then on the evil of split shifts. The woman doesn't usually catch the school special and, in the morning, she sat on the lower deck to avoid the kids. They were acting about and she made no attempt to restrain them – he called her a useless streak of pump water.'

'Does that sound to you like Cynthia Summers?'

'Cynthia? It might if I were a teaching colleague, I suppose.'

'Did you ask where she got off the bus – at lunchtime?'

'Yes, but he couldn't say. He was busy in flurries. He had the impression though that Adele and this teacher were the only two passengers to go upstairs.' Caroline realised they were all hanging on her words. 'Do we think it was her?'

Jennifer saw Mitchell's doubtful expression and shared his opinion. 'It's all a bit nebulous.'

'Does that mean vague?'

Jennifer ignored him. 'We don't have to guess about who was on the bus. Just wheel the possibles in front of Bob Crumb.'

'True. I don't think the rest justifies a raid on Winter Street tonight but we'll bring Cynthia in in the morning for another word.'

Shakila had said nothing for some time. Her attention was drifting, her eyes unfocused. She had spent too much time this morning out in the fresh air with the wind in her face. It had been pleasant but it made the present warmth and comfort soporific, especially when she had unwisely indulged in the large gin that Caroline had offered her. She blinked, tried to shake herself awake and found she was staring at the previous day's *Clarion* that was sticking out of Mitchell's waste bin, and, in particular, at the photograph of a man. She reached for it and straightened out the pages to reveal the whole face and the accompanying article.

'Poor girl. You'd think she could afford her own paper.'

Shakila ignored Clement and continued to read. Rick Robson, who was to give a concert in Cloughton next July, had brought his new fiancée to London to celebrate their engagement and to see the sights. He had landed at Heathrow early on Friday morning. A small group of fans had waited in the rain outside his hotel. As always he had spent time with them, posing with his fiancée but refusing to talk about their wedding plans. Shakila thrust the sheet at Clement. 'Who's Rick Robson?'

'You really can't afford the rag then? He's a geriatric rock star

193

from Wisconsin who's coming here next year to give a dreary concert at the Victoria Hall because dreary Cynthia Summers is the organiser of his British fan club.'

'Dreary Cynthia says he's her fiancé. She showed me a framed print of that photo this morning, except hers has a loving greeting penned on.'

Mitchell frowned. 'Are you sure?' Shakila nodded, now fully awake.

'Could we take Bob Crumb with us to pay a courtesy call on Cynthia to tell her we've found Nazreen?' Jennifer suggested.

'Faisal may have done it already.'

Mitchell raised an eyebrow, though Clement's tone was not aggressive. 'Well, we aren't to know that, are we?' He dialled and spoke to Mrs Crumb. For Mitchell, the tone was persuasive rather than peremptory as he requested that her husband should take a short ride in a police car to try to identify the person he had described to DC Webster. His tone soon changed. 'Well, I shall need him to do it first thing in the morning –' High-pitched invective interrupted him. 'In that case we'll bring her to him. Thank you. That's very kind.' The receiver slammed down and he glared as they endeavoured to hide their grins.

'At least we call a hangover a hangover and work through it. Was he drunk when you talked to him? I hope he's going to tell the same story when he's sober.'

Caroline shook her head. 'He was sober this afternoon. Well, soberer than he'd intended, anyway. His mates were taking him out to celebrate his recovery but one of them had brought him home early from the Crown where it was supposed to start. His wife had to get him out of bed to talk to me. If she said he'd been overdoing things I think she meant just that. Do we ring Cynthia and tell her we'll pick her up in the morning?'

'Definitely not.' The telephone rang. This time Mitchell listened patiently, contributing only, 'Interesting . . . Bloody stupid thing to do . . . Ginny and Hannah never mentioned it . . . Ah, that's why. Surely they'd be familiar to him . . . They don't leave it unlocked, do they?' Each question seemed to need a lengthy reply. 'Thanks. Could you just repeat that number?'

He laughed at their curious faces. 'Dr Ledgard. You probably recognised the dulcet tones. Maybe Shakila isn't the only one who should read the paper more carefully. Remember a paragraph on Thursday about a hospital fire hoax?' None of them did. 'There was a hoax alarm in the theatre block. Ledgard's just had a call from the anaesthetist who's been doing a bit of adding up and getting the wrong total. They got the patient out of theatre and cleared it. There were hordes of women in greens about, supposedly helping. There was more to worry about than who they all were.

'Later, he found he was low on a drug called sux-something or other. He knew he'd ordered twenty packets the week before. He'd locked them up, but in a busy hospital there's always an open cupboard or the right moment to get access to a useful key. Anyway, when he had a spare minute, he was watching the TV news with the latest on our enquiry. He's just rung Ledgard to say that this drug would do the job and leave no trace. He's even read fairly recently in the *Journal of the Forensic Science Society* about a murder case in Japan where it was used.'

'So, how are we going to prove it if there's no trace?'

Mitchell shrugged. 'You're asking the wrong person.'

'Are we still looking at Cynthia?'

'She's got the right background.' The telephone rang yet again. This time Mitchell answered in high good humour. 'Mrs Who?' He grinned at Shakila. 'Mrs Aiken – wanting to speak to the little darkie.'

Shakila prepared herself to be patient but the message was brief. 'You did right, Mrs Aiken. Have you sent for an ambulance? No, we'll do it now. Remind me of Miss Summers' car registration. Make? Colour? Can you grab a coat and wait outside?' She replaced the receiver and immediately picked it up again. 'Ambulance please. Immediately or sooner to 15, Winter Street.'

She turned to Mitchell. 'Miss Summers has made off in her own car without her father and without asking Mrs Aiken to keep an eye on him. She went and peered through the window – with the best of motives, of course. The old man's lying on the front room floor. Oh, and Cynthia asked for her key back last night, the one she used to leave with her for emergencies, so Mrs A can't go in and help him.'

'Open Sesame!' Mitchell declared melodramatically. 'But I hope the old codger's all right.'

With everything hooting and flashing they reached Winter

Street in seven minutes. Outside the house, they found not one but a crowd of a dozen women. Mitchell glared at them and his nod singled out Mrs Aiken. 'Have you tried all the doors?'

She nodded. 'All locked. And the windows, except the bathroom.' She pointed and eyed Mitchell speculatively. 'You wouldn't get through there even if you knocked all the glass out.'

Mitchell agreed. He applied his shoulder to the front door. Mrs Aiken's friends breathed down his neck. After a minute, the erstwhile immovable object gave way to the irresistible force. Mitchell stepped forward into the doorway, the women hard on his heels. He roared at them in something approaching the Queen's English, letting his tone do the swearing. They edged back a little way.

Shakila looked up and down the street and saw no sign yet of reinforcements. She stepped over to Mrs Aiken and whispered in her ear.

Mrs Aiken beamed. 'Certainly, love. I'll do most things if I'm asked nice.' She turned to her small army. 'Come on, you can squeeze into my place. I'll soon have the kettle on.' They followed her like lambs.

'I'll speak to you later,' Mitchell told Shakila, and hurried to join his sergeant.

Jennifer was kneeling by the old man and gave a brief shake of her head as Mitchell came up. 'They might resuscitate him if they're quick but he's not breathing.'

Thankfully they heard the ambulance bell. Jennifer ran out to direct and brief the paramedics, giving them Mitchell's best shot at pronouncing the name of the drug that might have been used. They seemed to understand.

With the medical emergency handed over to the experts, Mitchell reviewed his options and determined to get Shakila permanently transferred to his team as soon as he could. She was bilingual and so able to communicate easily with much of the Asian population of the town. She was able to persuade salacious voyeurs to organise their own peaceable dispersal. She even had the file off by heart almost as soon as the reports came in. It would be unrealistic to expect quite such keenness once she'd wormed her way into CID but she wouldn't be satisfied with that for long. He wondered if he were contemplating the future first British Asian female chief constable, and suspected that, when she looked in the mirror, so did she.

Now, she was looking at him deferentially. 'Cynthia's bed-sitting-room's on the top floor, sir. Mr Summers sent me up this morning. Everything will be locked.'

Mitchell shrugged. 'I've a pocket full of little gimmicks that aren't too destructive and Jennifer has an amazing collection of keys. She's been collecting them since she was a child. I think she's almost got to the stage where she's got more than she can easily catalogue and retrieve.' He had taken the stairs at a run, partly because of the urgency of the occasion but partly in hopes of leaving Shakila either behind or breathless.

She replied evenly, her nose almost touching his shoulder blade. 'It sounds an interesting hobby.'

One of Mitchell's gimmicks opened Cynthia's bedroom door without much trouble. Another was finally successful in opening the wardrobe. It took three minutes for Jennifer to find a key that would open the desk drawers. They contained nothing but letters, more than nine hundred of them, each one addressed to Frederick Robinson Esq. and sealed with old-fashioned sealing wax, stamped with a monogram formed from the letters CR. Cynthia Robinson?

The lock of the fat diary that still lay on top of the desk was unassailable.

16

Cynthia had intended to park some streets away from Fred's hotel. Once she had put his fiancée to sleep, it would be better if her Fiat were not seen on the impressive forecourt. In the end, however, she had found it impossible to find anywhere else where she was allowed to leave it. She would never complain again about parking in Cloughton. She felt faintly anxious now. The little car looked conspicuously modest compared with the maroon Jaguar and the silver Mercedes on either side of it.

She entered the foyer, refusing to be overawed by the lofty proportions, the huge stuffed and buttoned sofas or the glamorous clientele. As Fred's wife, she must accustom herself to such people and such surroundings. She approached the reception counter and felt that she could cope with the supercilious girl with some dignity. 'I would like to speak to Mr Frederick Robinson. He may be using his professional name, Rick Robson.'

The girl was snubbingly polite as she explained that Mr Robson had to be security conscious. It was not possible to allow people he did not know . . .

Cynthia held up a hand and wondered if she could achieve a smile that was not ingratiating. 'Please tell him that Miss Cynthia Summers is here to see him.' She offered her driving licence and her passport as proof of her identity before they could be demanded. Reluctantly, the girl picked up the telephone.

She blinked as she received an unexpected answer and her manner changed slightly. 'Mr Robson says you're to go up. The lift is through that door and on the left. The porter will . . .' She stopped and turned towards an elegantly suited man who had come up to stand beside Cynthia. 'Yes, Mr James?'

'I'm looking for a Miss Summers who is here to see a Mr Robson.' He turned to her. 'Would you be she?'

Approving his proper use of the nominative case, Cynthia admitted to being Miss Summers. Now, she received the girl's most radiant smile. 'I was just directing Miss Summers to the lift.'

Mr James took Cynthia's elbow. 'Mr Robson will be engaged for just a few more minutes. I'm his manager. Mr Robson has asked me to offer you some refreshment. If you would come with me, he will ring down to the desk as soon as he is free and Natasha will bring you the message. I think you will be comfortable here.' He settled her on one of the stuffed sofas and pulled up a small table within reach.

The girl's jaw had dropped. Quickly, she rearranged her face into the required smile, then unfolded the slip of paper with her name on it that he had palmed to her. As he settled himself beside the provincial little woman, Natasha heard him ask, 'May I take your bag for you?' and her reply, 'Its contents are rather important. I'd prefer to keep it with me, thank you.'

Mr James was patiently expressing a sympathetic interest in Clifford Summers' partial recovery from his stroke when the two uniformed constables of the Metropolitan Police came to take charge of his guest.

Mitchell entered the station foyer weighed down with his collection of plastic bags. They contained a diary, several notebooks and some nine hundred letters, all written in the same small neat hand.

Decker grinned at him. 'Got a new job? Porter?'

Mitchell tried to grin back. Couldn't find it funny. He half ran down the corridor, wrenched open the door of his office and prayed that no one would come in until the chaos inside his head subsided. He was almost afraid, had not ever before felt so out of control of himself.

He dropped into his armchair, felt it trapping him in and jumped up again. He paced the office for a moment, then forced himself to sit on the chair behind the desk and make an attempt to separate the whirling strands of thought and feeling fighting each other in his skull. Concern and anxiety for his wife. Grief for Hannah. Fury with Nazreen but mixed with a curious pity. Contempt for Leonard and a determination that he should suffer. Compassion for young Marie and, to a certain extent, for the feckless mother.

He was stultified by the crimes of Cynthia Summers. Eighteen years of dealing with the whole spectrum of human wickedness and he could still be shocked! Yet, so often, he could see why the perpetrators were driven that particular way. Cynthia would be the only one to suffer for what she had done – apart from her victims, of course. But how much blame attached to her siblings who refused their share of filial duties? How much to the mindless malevolence of one of her victims? How much to Adele Batty's parents who had let her remain undisciplined, unmotivated, without anything to live up to?

Policemen no longer had to fear they were sending the accused to a threat of death. He knew he was not the first to question whether imprisonment for life was worse, at least for some. Maybe, though, Cynthia would be happier in her future life, whether in prison or in hospital. People were more tolerant towards thieves and murderers than they were towards incompetent, insignificant little teachers.

Someone knocked and came in. Someone moved swiftly from the door to the desk. 'Benny! Whatever's wrong? I'll get a doctor.'

He realised the intruder was Jennifer. 'Don't be stupid. I'm not ill.' He realised his teeth were chattering, his hands shaking and his office swinging round him.

'I'll ring Ginny.'

'No!'

'You're right. She's coping with enough already. OK, you'll have to put up with me.' She went back to the door and locked it, then came to him and held him, perfectly chastely, his head against her midriff. Neither spoke for more than a minute. Then he relaxed, and she took her arms away.

'It wasn't all Cynthia's fault, you know.'

His voice shook. Hers was firm. 'No. We women cops know that from the beginning. The better men are hit hard when they realise it. The rest never do.' Without further comment she unlocked the door and left.

Why, Mitchell wondered, on Monday morning, did most of his team believe that there was nothing so tedious as doing today what could easily be put off till tomorrow? If, like himself, they had been raised as next to the youngest in a family of six children, they would have realised very early that tomorrow could not be coped with at all if anything that could be cleared up today had been left undone.

The excitement of the chase – which he enjoyed as much as any of them – was temporarily over and he had sent them off with long faces and a sense of anticlimax. Now, with his desk neat and tidy and Browne's rampant ivies watered, he began on the paperwork he was training himself not to avoid. He was delighted, though, when the superintendent interrupted him.

When Carroll ignored his proffered chair, Mitchell himself stood up, waiting to be given a reason for the visitation. The super usually got straight to the point and Mitchell was becoming uneasy. Had the time come for him to lose his new and temporary status? Was Carroll dissatisfied with his conduct of the cases? He had seemed more than pleased last night. Perhaps someone from on high was insisting that Tom should take official leave and have an official replacement.

The superintendent asked abruptly, 'Do you think perhaps you should have some counselling?'

Mitchell bit back the first reply that sprang to his lips. After a moment, he managed, 'Thank you for that most restorative question.'

Carroll knew when he was losing. 'Then can't you take some time off?'

Mitchell grinned. 'Yes, I will, whilst things are quiet I'll take the week you owe me, unless, of course, things hot up again.'

Carroll nodded and thankfully took his leave. After a minute or two, Mitchell forgave Jennifer for the quiet word she must have had with him.

Mitchell was wondering to what extent his father-in-law would want to be kept in touch with CID events when he received his telephoned summons. Virginia ruled that the visit was a men-only occasion and told the children that their father would be going back to work soon after tea. Mitchell decided this was a reasonable version of the truth.

When Hannah too declined to join them and Browne produced liberal quantities of his home brew, Mitchell felt they were slipping into a new version of an old routine. At his in-laws' home, he and Browne had many times drunk reasonably copiously and discussed fairly heatedly the different stages of a case. This time, their roles were reversed and Mitchell was in charge of the case but not the ale.

Browne filled glasses. 'Let's get on with it. Alex is out with a couple of old school friends he met up with earlier today. We'd better talk all our shop before he comes back.' Mitchell saw that Browne seemed as uneasy in his relations with the young man as Ginny did.

He made no comment on it but began his account as requested. 'It's a first in all sorts of ways – because there's no doubt about a conviction, for a start. She's pleading guilty and her brief's screaming diminished responsibility. All the evidence is already written out in her own hand.'

'A written confession?'

'I suppose so, in a way. The poor woman's out of her skull and yet, in some ways, she's quite sane.'

'She sounds schizophrenic.'

'I seriously think she's suffering from a condition of that nature. She did all this writing up before we found her out.'

'Then you're right. It is a first.'

Mitchell described the scene they had found in Cynthia's room. The walls were quite bare of pictures. No photographs except Rick Robson's framed publicity handout on the bedside table. It was dedicated to Summers in Robinson's own hand but only in recognition of her work in Britain to try to keep him in the public eye.

'We began to get an inkling of what we might have when we opened the wardrobe. On the inside of the doors there was a whole gallery of photographs and clippings. The only things hanging in it were a white wedding dress from Paige's and a sort of see-through dressing-gown thing. Jennifer says Paige's is a fabulously expensive house that dresses "the older bride".

'Cynthia seems to have sat up there and lived in a fantasy in which she was to be married to this singer as soon as they'd solved the problem of not upsetting her father. In her dreams he urged her to put him in a home . . .'

'Her other self speaking.'

'I reckon, yes.'

'And are you saying the man knew absolutely nothing about it?'

'Apart from her running the fan club. She'd met him once in the States, along with other people who'd served him in the same way. He'd bought her an occasional drink. She bought a book especially to write a diary of all the times she'd actually talked to him. Mentions him blowing his nose and what he ate at each meal and so on. For more than three years, she's written him a letter every single day, full of plans for the future. All pure fantasy. She writes about hoping his being a public figure isn't going to turn their wedding into a public spectacle and how they must protect their children from the fans. You find yourself being swept along till you almost believe it yourself.

'She mentions their buying an English home with his money and making it as comfortable as an American one and in one letter she promises to let him choose who will supply her clothes, people who will know how to make her attractive to him. She says she knows he's going to grow out of his taste for all that "razmatazz" and begin to take an interest in serious things.'

'Wow. Hasn't he complained about being bombarded with all this stuff? Had the Post Office stop it?'

'Oh, she didn't post them. Half of her mind understood exactly what she was doing. She kept a daily diary and, in that, she gives a clear-headed description of what she's doing, a sort of case history of herself. She seems to have switched from one to the other as her circumstances and or her feelings led her.'

'Are even the murders in it – this diary?'

Mitchell nodded, both to answer Browne's question and to assent to his glass being refilled. 'From that we know she asked a friend in the hospital pharmacy about fire drills. The hospital is zoned with different alarms for different places. She helped herself to some greens and mingled in with the theatre nurses, helped them evacuate the patient on the table and volunteered, quite openly, to lock the cupboard where the stuff was kept as if it were part of her duties.'

'Tell me about the drug.'

'OK but this is the bit I might get wrong. You'll have to talk to Ledgard. Anaesthetists use it to relax muscles totally. It's given at the same time as the anaesthetic. Cynthia used it on its own so

203

that the girls were conscious but couldn't move. If you get too much your respiratory system shuts down and you die.

'Cynthia had the brilliant idea of giving the proper dose first, as near as she could guess it because it seems to depend on how heavy the patient is. That meant the girls had to be still and listen while she told them that she was going to punish them for their vulgar and cruel behaviour. Then she gave them more and made sure they couldn't offend again. She left Adele on the bus, just got off and abandoned the body. She coaxed Frankie into her car and did the jabbing there, then she dumped her in the park.'

Mitchell saw that Browne had quite forgotten his own troubles and that his mind was entirely on the case. 'Do you think,' he wanted to know, 'that each part of her mind knew about the other?'

Mitchell shrugged. 'I'm not a psychiatrist, am I? You can tell from reading all her stuff that the diary writer knew about the letters, but possibly not the other way round. The diary describes her trip out to choose an engagement ring. She knew what stones he liked. There was one of those yukky magazine articles inside the wardrobe door. You know, an interviewer who asks your favourite colour, holiday place, girl's name and so on. But then, in that night's letter, she thanks him for spending so much money and choosing such a beautiful setting.'

'So, what put a stop to it all and started the killing?'

'Again, you'll need to ask a shrink, but the diary says that when she knew he was seriously attached to someone else the letters didn't give her the same fix. She'd lost the glimmer of hope that, one day, she might be important to him, until she convinced herself that he wasn't to blame. Then she got fixed on the idea of dealing out fair punishments. This is a copy of the key letter.'

He handed the relevant part of it to Browne who studied it carefully.

'Never have I read such filth, and even from Frances.

'I'm sure you understand, Fred, that enough is enough. You would act to protect me if you were here but circumstances make it necessary that I have to defend myself, become a sort of vigilante.

'You mustn't worry about me. I shall keep quite calm and be

quite safe. It's only loud and upsetting confrontations that fluster me. I've found a way of dealing with things that is quite fair. The girls will understand exactly why they've deserved what's happening to them. I'm tempted to put an end to them in a way that will cause them suffering commensurate with that they caused me, but I'm not a vindictive person. I don't want to have my own future happiness and yours spoiled by having needless cruelty on my conscience . . .'

Browne looked up and frowned. 'She's so lacking in confidence in dealing with people in normal situations and then she can be so cold-bloodedly practical?'

'I've thought about that. The drug helped her get the girls on her own level. She was bound by good manners. They had the freedom of always relieving their feelings, whoever it hurt. Besides, she'd been trained to use drugs. She'd probably done hospital work as part of the medical degree she couldn't finish.' Mitchell handed over an envelope file. 'I photocopied this lot,' he remarked casually, 'so you can peruse it all at your leisure. It'll give you an idea of the sea of murk we're paddling in and how much we need you back.'

Tuning in a little early to Radio Cloughton to catch the local news on his way home, Mitchell heard an item that was of considerable interest to him. '. . . local author who has sold the manuscript of his amusing book to the West Yorkshire paperback publisher Micklethwaite. It features a Walter Mitty character, who, instead of imagining himself enjoying heroic adventures, finds wonderful, but equally imaginary ways of disposing of his overbearing wife. In a few minutes we shall be talking to Mr Derek Swindell about *The Millennium Mitty* which will be published early next year and which Micklethwaite confidently expect to become a cult best seller.

'Meanwhile, here is a short passage from an early chapter, recorded by the author.

'"He considered first, as always and with longing, an active method of killing – a hammer, a garotte, a gun, a knife. As always, he rejected them all. He was not a decisive or practical man. If he were he would have no need of these fantasies. Nor was he very imaginative.

'"He mused briefly on the limited nature of his imagination. It failed him whenever he tried to see himself as he would like to be. He could fantasise about attacking Jessica only in a way that, just possibly, if driven far enough, he might actually use. He could see himself setting up a situation only where, at the actual moment of her extinction, he did not need to be present, did not have to watch her die.

'"And then, even if his little reverie were not interrupted, he would find a reason to come out of it before her body was found. He did not need to gloat. It was enough to imagine he had put an end to her inexorable domination of him, to have, if only in his own mind, a respite from the depressing stream of criticism, from the aura of dissatisfaction with which she surrounded them both.

'"There was a limit to the number of ways to murder that fitted his criteria. Poison was beginning to pall. The new idea, when it came to him, took him by surprise. With half his mind on changing down a gear as the road became steeper, the other half remembered the dead light bulb at the head of the cellar steps, and Jessica's annoyance that he had not yet replaced it."'

Mitchell smiled. He doubted that Sue Swindell would be fooled by the change of name, but suspected that the financial reward from her husband's venture would appease her.

'"Inside his head, he had rigged a trip wire before he realised that his subconscious mind had solved his problem. Now he had to find a way to get Jessica to go down the steps. All he could think of was to shout for her from the depths of the house, and that would leave him having to step over her broken body to get out into the light himself. Even in imagination, he knew this was beyond him. In any case, however desperate his cry, Jessica would refuse to venture down the steps in the dark.

'"And, anyway, here he was, back in his own drive, leading to his own garage where, yesterday, she had refused to die of carbon monoxide poisoning."'

Mitchell sighed. Another head case and another method of releasing frustration! He prayed that this one would continue as long as it was needed.

Hannah, sitting alone in the dining-room, clumsily pushed aside the pile of books and pamphlets the social worker had left behind. A quick glance at them had been enough to show their irrelevance to her own circumstances. She could not whip up much interest in a huge research project at Brunel University that would find a cure for her after she had died.

She really didn't care that there had been high profile sufferers from her disease – David Niven, Don Revie, Ian Trethowan, Jacob Javits, Jill Tweedie. She could think of qualities and circumstances she would rather have in common with a director general of the BBC or a US senator than MND.

Nor was she interested in detailed information about the complaint in general, though she would welcome a chance to learn something more about her own situation, something about the progress of Hannah's disease. Time, to the doctors, was measured in years, weeks, days, their prognoses arrived at by studying objective medical tests and statistics. Time to Hannah was personal and social. Was there time for her own family objectives? To see Caitlin start school? To see Alex meet a nice girl who would make him happy? Time to reflect on her past, to reconcile herself, to make her peace?

There was a lot to become reconciled to. She glared at the grab handles that Tom had fixed to the elegant door frame, shuddered at the thought of the stool in the shower, refused to look in the mirror and see herself wearing the easy-on-and-off clothing.

She smiled grimly to herself. The family seemed to think her hearing was disappearing along with her mobility. Of course, they left the room before they talked about her, but still she had heard Benny asking if all the alterations had not been put in tactlessly early and Tom's quieter reply. 'No. The consultant says she'll be past using them before all that long.'

On the other hand, she had heard Ginny haranguing them. 'We want her to need what it's easy for us to give. We've got to give what it's easy for her to take. And she's not going to want to ask us. We'll have to work out what that is for ourselves.'

Hannah gave thanks for her daughter, her husband, her son-in-law and, after some moments, for her son and all her blessings.